Yielding To Unfulfilled Desires Vol 2.

Corey Bryant

Bryant publishing Llc

Contents

Introduction

Why do people choose to bite the forbidden fruit? Maybe because we were told not to. Ignoring all red flags, we bite into the fruits of our Desires; which isn't bad, unless the desires or somewhat forbidden. Like betrayal, stemming from lust, infidelity, and pure disloyalty. Sneaky things or the thrill of the challenge is very enticing! The author, in which would be me, Corey Bryant, created these stories while incarcerated in the Alabama D.o.c [for 27 yrs straight to be exact] from pure imagination and as a form of escape. As well as operating the gift from god in which i discovered in the Belly of the Beast!

Prologue

"The policewomen, and The Convict part 2"

When we made contact, we clashed! "Mmm, come here nigga!" said Ms. Williams, as she stuck her tongue in my mouth and wrapped her right leg around my waist and with her left hand, she was grabbing my stiff dick, placing it where she needed and wanted it! I was slamming her in a corner and jacking her up at the same time! Roughly, ramming this dick deep in her soul. By now she had her mouth wide open, chasing her breath, as if she was a gun shot victim!

Chapter 1

Yielding to unfulfilled desires 2

S tory 1
   "You, me,and We"

Sequel of "Hey lover, Hi friend"

George Benson's voice serenades the room, as I slowly stroke my dick in and out of Beverly, while looking her in the eyes at the same time! When we both felt that Vibe coming from Mary J Blige's song, and what the topic between us was about...we got to it! I sped up a little, it made my Strokes a little harder and deeper. I looked Beverly in her eyes and Tongue kissed her for effect. Beverly is putting her hands down at my pelvic, as to slow or control my thrusts, but she's regularly meeting me halfway! Up and down, side to side , perfect timing! As this moment becomes intense by the second, I feel my muscles, in my whole body Flex up! Beverly threw her legs in my arms, and I immediately turned into a pogo stick! "Yes! Yes Courtney!" moans Beverly, as I fuck her like a pornstar, and right then we both cum! The whole time we are cumming, I'm running my fingers through her hair. Caressing Bev's pretty face, I'm making her look me in my eyes, as I said" I love you!" And what did I do that for!

Chapter 1

(6 months later)

Beverly and I, have been going six months strong, every since that night we fucked, at her book club's annual ball. Everything was cool, for the first three, maybe four months. She and Tisha fell out with each other about me. Tisha made an issue about it off the top! When she put two and two together that night in the parking lot, at the ball, she got on the dumb shit! Blowing my phone up, and Beverly was getting texts and calls back to back from her the next morning. When Beverly did call her back all hell broke loose. "Hello? Tisha?" Why have you been blowing my phone up, acting all strange?" "Acting all strange"!? snapped Tisha."How the fuck I'm acting strange ?!" "By keep fucking texting me ! Asking me crazy questions!" answered Beverly.Now usually, Beverly isn't the type to get in a neck rolling, popping off, ghetto girl match, but if you take it there, she'll go there! "Oh it's crazy, cause I know you were with my man?" accused Tisha. "Yo Maan?!" and who might that be? Said Beverly. Read your text.. Slut! Who do I mention? Slut?!" Screamed Beverly . And on and on from that moment their friendship, God niece/ God Aunt relationship was over! As for me, Tisha was definitely getting on my nerves! I wasn't texting her back or calling her back at first. Till one day, I got tired of her shit, so I called her." Yo.. What's your problem?!" I asked Tisha." You know my problem! Why are you doing me like this?!" asked Tisha. "Tisha.. I ain't your man! Get that in your mind Shawty! I'm not obligated to you or nobody else! I mean.. You know what it was, and what it is.'' I tried not to be harsh with Tisha, I just was brutally honest, and she knows I'm right. "Okay Courtney.. You're right! I caught feelings, it's just.. Beverly? Damn! That's my

God Aunt!" " Shit happens Tisha! What can I say? It was bound to happen, because me and her have always been close." Then I thought to myself , "the ratio of women to men here in Atlanta Georgia and I'm explaining myself to a jump off?" A look.. We had fun, but.. We have to put this on Ice till further notice!" " Nigga, I have no problem sharing, just not with her!" Said "Tisha, let me get back at you on that. Who knows, we might fuck every now and then!" Is what I told her. My success off my book, had me paid, within the six months it's been out. Made me kind of arrogant! So basically I was brushing Tisha off. I was about to lose my job, because I was taking days to go promote my book. I was attending book club parties . Yes, plenty of women! I'm getting out regularly, to see the world, off that one book! Here's what happened: I put the book out, self-published, through IngramSpark, a major book distributor,and wholesaler. They have like 40,000 retailers they distribute to. Paperback, audibles And ebooks. That means my book can be downloaded worldwide, and bought in stores

From there I opened my own Publishing Company. Fuck my job! Small right now, but I'm destined to get major! As for Beverly, like I said earlier the first couple of months shit was hot between us! Don't get me wrong, I'm skilled with women to the point of keeping things hot,it's just that she started becoming controlling and jealous! I don't know if it's the couple of your age difference five years younger than her or was it the fact that she was a headstrong, alpha female? Which is a turn-on to me or could it be my overnight, accidental, stardom is affecting our relationship? It wasn't so much about the money I'm making, it's what comes with the lifestyle! All kinds of spicy, hot ass women, with class and money were at me, like bees on honey! I am very entertaining to attractive women, without even trying hard. I'm 38 years old but I look 28 with an NFL defensive back body . Strikingly handsome , light brown skinned and charismatic. Beverly isn't the only victim of my charm and seduction, but she's an enabler. But in an unconscious way .With the way she had been acting, in the last couple of months, she's making me turn my charm and personal magnetism up, when I'm around beautiful women! A successful up-and-coming author, author of urban romance, gets a lot of Rhythm from women! Book signings, at different book stores, malls, strip malls, beauty salons, Spas, hotel ballrooms. Parties, plenty of women! Professional, some regular, and even some celebrities! So now that I'm Poppin, my attitude towards women, slightly shifted! It's like when a person upgrades their phone, their cars, or whatever. To me it was the same with the women! Don't get me wrong, I didn't look down on them. I still was my same witty, Charming self. But, if you just an ordinary basic Woman, by looks, careers and Swagger.. You get no play with me! I've always had the confidence to pull bad women and the confidence to play on a bigger field. But now I got the money and a small bit of Fame in the writer's world can't tell me shit! "Bev, we need to talk!" "We sure do!" Said Bev With attitude.I sat at the bar, and poured me a glass of Hennessy. We were in my new house out in Buckhead ."You've been acting real.. Distant lately, what's up?" "Well.. I know I told you a long time ago, that at times I will go in my shell, and when I do that I shut everybody out. And I remember telling you that I would never shut you out." Yeah you did that". I said " So what happened? You changed your mind?" I asked. "Well.. Kind of, but.. You don't text me early in the morning like you used to and since your little fame, it seems that you have forgotten about me anyway! Like.. Who inspired you to write? Me! That's who! I should be getting paid half!" Beverly vented out her frustrations, but not without me challenging her. "So it's about the money!?" I asked Beverly. She can't trip because I looked out for her on the strength of our friendship and inspiration. Not to mention how we shop and travel. "Money? No Courtney. I could care less about your money! I got my own!" I downed my glass of Hennessy and stood up." Then what's up?" I asked Beverly, as I casually unbuttoned my shirt, exposing a black polo-tank-top. Beverly's eyes lingered on my chest for a couple of seconds before answering. "I mean.. In the last couple of months, you've been unattentive, unaffectionate. Oh, I barely get the time from you like I used to. Bev, you know what I'm doing. My new career demands my time! Occasionally I get.." " Occasionally you get what?!" Interrupted Beverly." Time to do what? Used to come over to my place, to spend the night or I would be over here! But now you barely come over. You're barely here". "Beverly, you know I've been on the road, hell you used to roll with me!" What did I say that for!? "Yeah, and I wouldn't roll with you again! I'm not the one to be competing for your attention and when I am supposed to have that exclusively!" When the book first jumped off her and the book club, helped with the footwork advertising and marketing aggressively. Setting up book signings, and Beverly somewhat spearheaded the movement, until she saw how the women were all over me! The jealousy and the insecurity kicked in, especially when she heard me Mumble things like "oh shit" before I knew it, when a strikingly beautiful, fine woman approaches me at a function or something. There have been times when that sort of thing happens, it makes Beverly so hot, that she would act all funny with me. Argue a little, and then have some hot makeup sex! When that happens, she tries to out fuck me! Literally. Try to put it on me, so that I wouldn't want any of those women. Her competition was so strong too, so she made it her business to pussy whip me! The problem with that was, I am a dog! Besides, she was more whipped than me, and she was Deep In Love With Me! True, I love Beverly, but my appetite is that of an insatiable, horny guy! Anyway, I'm buzzing off of the Henny and I've been smoking some top Grade weed. Some kush called honey buds or rappers weed! So Beverly's tirade is getting kind of irritating to me,about to blow my high! Yet, the mix of weed and Hennessy got me horny, so let me see is Beverly up for it. I walked off and went and sat on the couch, taking my buttoned down polo shirt off, and throwing it on the love seat."Sit." I said to Beverly, as I patted the couch."Sit?I'm not a dog!" " Well Beverly could you please join me on the couch, so we can talk?" Beverly stood there a couple of seconds, with her arms folded across her breast looking all sexy, with a tight pink AKA sorority t-shirt on and some tight ass Levi's on with some heels on. "What else is there to talk about?" Said Beverly as she reluctantly sat next to me."We don't have to be doing all this baby, you know what it is with me." "What is it with you?!" Said Beverly. "You are my only love." I said to Beverly, as I looked her in her eyes, and slowly twirled a strand of her long curly hair. Ever since she changed her hairstyle to long, I always played with it."I hear what you say Courtney, but I don't know what to believe"! I noticed that her eyes welled up with tears in them . In my mind, I'm just knowing these tears ain't real! Making the wrong move I play it how it goes. "Come here baby." I said as I caught a teardrop, from her left eye with the bend of my right finger." I'm serious Courtney." Said Beverly in a low, sexy tone. I leaned into her, lifted her chin, and planted a slow sensual kiss on Beverly's juicy lips. I was in my Rick James mode, Fire and Desire action! Tasting Beverly teardrop stains off her face. She showed a little resistance at first, but she quickly melted like butter and returned my kisses! At first they were indecisive kisses, but they slowly turned into Hungry kisses.! "ummm."moaned Beverly, signaling her pleasure. I eased back for a second to pull my tank top off. With Beverly's help that shirt was on my glass table . She always was turned on by my body, so she was instantly rubbing all over my arms, which was her favorite and my shoulders and chest. While she was doing that, I was sucking around her neck, till I made it to her Hot Spot, which was right under her throat, where the pulse is. "Courtney!" Moaned Beverly as I slowly Tongue kissed her neck. Beverly was squeezing on my muscles. My biceps and back arms. She was caressing,and squeezing my chest,with a

Lustful urgency. I reached under her shirt and rubbed her stomach as I licked her ear lobes. " Have you eaten your smoothies today?" I asked Beverly , as I rubbed her left titty." Yeah pineapple". Said Beverly . With that I slid my hands between her legs. She hesitated for a moment before opening her thighs to let me rub her coochie through the jeans. I started unfastening Beverly's button on her jeans and she stopped me! "What's up bae ?" I asked Beverly." I didn't come over here for this." Said Beverly ." Come on baby, I want to taste you."Beverly looked in my eyes, and I was putting a puppy dog look on my face! Pleaded with my eyes, I subtly coerced Beverly to yield to an unfulfilled desire! I haven't had sex with Beverly in about a month, so I know she was on fire! Instantly, she was wiggling up out of her tight Levi's on my couch, and I was helping her peel them off! The pink thong she had on, made my dick throb with anticipation. Because when she was pulling them off, I was checking out the way her ass jiggled! By now I came up out of my jeans and put a 9 inch pre cumming dick in Beverly's hand, while I was inserting my middle finger in her Sugar Walls. Using my thumb to play with Beverly's clit, while I gently bit on her neck, had her about to climax already! "I got to taste you boo!" I said, as I felt her body on the verge of melting. I immediately kissed and sucked Beverly bite size titties. In the past whenever I sucked her titties, she would subtly guide me to each tit, by placing her hand on my head. She was putting her hands on my head now! Except she was pushing my head straight down between her legs .. With both hands! She kicked her legs open, one on the floor and the other one on the top of the couch. I kissed her fat pussy lips first. Then I parted them and started licking in the coochie, as I played with her clit! After three or four minutes of devouring Beverly I gave her what she wanted! I had to hurry up and run up in Beverly, because she had been clawing at my shoulders, trying to pull me up to enter her. Almost turning into a wild animal! Once I raised up to enter her. She was about to snatch my dick off, putting it up in her! "Fuck me Courtney!" Moaned Beverly. That's just what I did, fucked Beverly! With no passion. I was feeling some type of way, because of the way Beverly had been acting towards me.I pulled Beverly from the couch, before I fucked it up, and to the floor we went! There, I bent her knees to her elbows and got up on my toes, and stood up in it! Trying hard not to get carpet burns on my knees, they don't feel good! After putting the pound game down for about 5 minutes on the floor, I picked Beverly up, dick still in her and put her up against the wall! She told me that was one of her secret fantasies. "OOOO!"! Moaned Beverly as I was Knocking Pictures Off the Wall with her! Beverly was panting and gasping for air, all of a sudden her thighs tightened around my waist, like some vice grips! I took that as a climax signal, and bang harder! I put my hands flat against the wall, as Beverly wrapped her arms around my neck, squeezing for dear life as if the orgasm she felt coming, was like a free-fall ride at Six Flags! "O Courtney! Oh my God! O! Lord!" moaned Beverly, as I sped it up to climax at the same time as Beverly.. I growled like a dog when I nutted! Almost dropping Beverly because my knees got weak. Beverly juices was running down my leg.We stood there against the wall, hugging and kissing each other for about a minute. Before Beverly Placed her hands on my chest. Squeezing a little and kind of nudged me off of her and brushed past me." What's up Beverly?" Beverly was getting her clothes and putting them on. She looked at me for a couple of seconds before answering. "Oh nothing". Said Beverly and continued to grab her things."You ain't going to chill with me?" Nope." Said Beverly. I walked over to her butt naked." Didn't you enjoy yourself?" She didn't answer. She just kept putting her clothes on ." What's wrong baby?" I asked Bev, as I gently grabbed her arm. She gently pulled her arm from my hand, and walked toward the door. When she got to the door she stopped and looked back." Courtney out of all the things I mentioned earlier, the little things that you used to do, but not do anymore. I thought about it, and I had forgotten, because it's been a minute since I've been with you, but it's one of the most important things. " What's that Beverly ?" "You don't even look me in my eyes anymore, when we.. When we cum together, and afterwards used to tell me you love me." Said Beverly then she turned and walked out the door. Crazy!!

Chapter 2

The next morning 9:30 a.m.

"I love you!" said Beverly. I love you back!" I answered as I leaned in, to kiss her, then a horn blew."Beep, beep, beep! Courtney, Courtney!" I look up and it's not Tisha this time, it's Beverly blowing her horn at us, like she's going crazy! Now I'm going crazy because I just was telling Beverly I love her. Who the fuck is this I'm holding then? I think to myself, as I slowly turn my head to the woman I'm holding, and it's Nakasha! I'm like what the fuck!" Beep!Beep! Courtney! Oh Courtney you don't see me?" I looked up, and it's Beverly,blowing her horn, hollering my name, and hanging out the window,with the pistol pointed at me!" Courtney! I know you see me! Make that your last kiss! I told you not to fuck with me!" Beep, beep, beep! The horn, then the gun went off at the same time." Boom!" Then I woke up! My alarm was going off. I was dreaming! A recurring nightmare. Well, I had that dream a while back, but it was Tisha on the other end with the pistol, instead of Beverly. Now Beverly is busting a gun at me, and now I'm holding a chic I used to be crushing on, since I was in junior high! Nakasha Bradford, was her name. "Damn! What the fuck is going on with me?!" I said to no one in particular. Beverly had walked out on me last night, after we had sex in my living room. So I was in an empty bed. I was propped up on my left elbow Gathering my bearings, once again, trying to figure out a crazy dream! I thought about what my Grandmama had told me about dreams ."Oh, a lot of times, dreams are the opposite of what it looks like or what is taking place! And if it's

some snakes in your dreams, those dreams are warnings of enemies!"
Well, there weren't any snakes involved. It's the females and the role
they're playing is what is getting me! Particularly Beverly! She's playing
the role as a woman scorned! Or a jealous maniac! I guess she's kind
of salty with me, so maybe that's what the dream is about. But where
does Nakasha fit in? I've never been with Nakasha. I haven't seen her in
ages. Nakasha and I have been friends on Facebook since 2010 but we
never communicated. I have sent her a couple of messages years ago,
and she never answered much. The couple of times she did respond,
she wasn't really giving me any rhythm and flow, so I forgot about her.
She's always been an object of my desire. Maybe that's why she's in my
dream like that. Subconscious mind is working! Anyway, I jumped out
of bed to get my day started with Nakasha Bradford on my mind.

1992-flashback

"You and i-i-i, would never stop!" Jodeci's song echoes through the
crowded, and dark gym, serenading the crowd of teenagers, as they
slow dance with each other. The Friday night drop-in, at the rec center,
was always popping. If you were from the ages of 12 to 15 and from the
westside of Atlanta, and your parents were kind of lenient on you, you
were there! Even from other areas, like the South Side, East Side , Etc.
Nakasha Bradford, in particular, was from the southside of Atlanta.
A redbone, with pretty light brown eyes. She had that Halle Berry
hairdo, in which all the pretty girls were rocking. A nice cute smile,
which would make you blush. Especially if you were a little younger
than her .As in my case! I was 13 and Nakasha was 15 looking almost
like a china doll. She would fall up in the rec center on these nights, her
and two of her cousins, looking pretty as hell! All three of them were
slim-fine, pretty, redbones! On this particular night, I had made up
my mind that I was going to ask her to slow dance! Me and my partner
Wenchy, were posted up against the wall, hi off of a nickel bag of good
weed and a six pack of old e! "Hey there they go!" " Who? I asked" I

looked toward the entrance of the gym, and there they were,Nakasha and her two bad cousins, Tay and Angie. All three of them had on plaid mini skirt hookups . Nakasha had on the skirt and top with the different shades of pink and white plaid. Angie's was shades of black, gray, and white . And Tay had on the green plaid and white. Nakasha was leading the pack, heading in our Direction." Here they come my Nigga"! Said Wenchy , who was sweet on Tay. And she liked him also. I was getting butterflies for some reason when they approached." Hey Courtney, hey Wenchy!" Said Nakasha, in her usual bubbly personality way. "Wassup Nakasha!" we said in unison. "What's up Tay, what's up Angie? Look at y'all! All fly and shit! Courtney I like them Jay's!" Said Nakasha, referring to my black 1992 Olympic Air Jordans. The ones with the number nine on the back of them. I was kind of flattered by her compliment. Not that my Jordans were Dusty or something. Shit, my shoes were brand new, plus I had Swagger naturally.But the compliment gave me confidence coming from her pretty ass! "Thanks Nakasha! You don't look so bad yourself!" i said smiling at Nakasha like i seen an elephant fucking a gnat.

"Thanks!"said Nakasha. "You're welcome." I said, still smiling, heart beating like crazy as I anticipate my next move. My next move was supposed to be me asking her for a dance! Nakasha and her cousins were just about to walk off and I built my nerves up to ask Nakasha for a dance." Hey Nakasha, you want to dance?" She stopped in her tracks for a couple of seconds, looked back and smiled at me, and said" nawl, I'll catch you the next time" "! Okay". I answered." Feeling like shit, as her and her cousins prance off into the crowd. My partner Wenchy was laughing. I was smiling but really hurt at the same time. I guess because I had a crush on her and I could tell that she liked me.. At least that's what my mind was telling me. "Man fuck them hoes we will catch some more!" Said Wenchy." " Yea, you right wink,we will" said , affirming my homeboy's statement. Yet my eyes were still on Nakasha

Bradford . She must have felt my vibes, because she looked back and smiled."one day"! I said to myself as I nodded in response to Nakasha's rejection and smile ." One day"!

26 years later..Back to the present

After I got myself together I rolled me a mini cigarillo of some rapper weed , moonrock! That was some potent, high-grade marijuana, that you can let the blunt go out and smoke on it all day! I had plans on writing the sequel or part two of my debut book, once I smoked some of this blunt. No lie, I write better hi! You get Hella Clarity and Imagination gets Keener. I grabbed the blunt, and proceeded to light up! As I sit on my couch smoking and choking, I reminisced on the night before. Beverly and I had some great sex right here on this very couch! And floor and up against the wall! Damn that pussy good! Is what I'm saying to myself. Replaying each scene in my mind,as the potent smoke starts to settle in. The high that it is! Beverly has been illing lately, talking about she is going to just stay to herself. She is going to just start looking out for herself, and all these walls she has put up in her mind. Me being me, I'm thinking she's got another man or her ex is back in her life.. Whatever! Sitting here high as fuck, I grabbed my phone text Beverly.[Hey lil bit!] That's her old college name. I sent another text and response , to a text from this young chick I met in the Club Onyx. Her name is Ayana . Stage name caramel drop! Damn, I missed her last night! I thought to myself as I reread the text.{ Hey boo!! Where are you? Trying to get with you now !} damn!{ Missed you last night! What's up?} Now this stripper wasn't just some woman I was trying to trick off with, because she basically chose me, so to speak. I was in the VIP with two of my cousins, and a couple of Music Industry Executives, when she chose up. I saw her when she first came through. She stood about 5 feet 7 but with the heels on she was about 6 ft 1! Caramel complexion, slim with a fat ass! No stomach, slim waist / nice hips and round athletic thighs which matched her ass! I know it's real! But the top it off she looks just like Rihanna! Eyes and all. Intriguing as hell. What tripped me out though, is how she did a double-take when she looked at our setup." Damn, who is she looking at like that?" I asked." She is ready to get paid cuz! She knows it's money over here! Yo, come here"! Hollered my cousin. Ayanna came over, eyes stayed on me the whole time she was approaching. Maybe she thought I called her but my cousin confirmed that he did when he asked her for a lap dance. With no hesitation, she obliged by getting reverse cowgirl in his lap and commenced grinding off of that song, "Bed"by cash money artist Jacquees." I know you want to love, but I just want to fuck". She grinding to the beat, as I nodded my head to the beat. She and I were eye to eye the whole time. The lyrics and the beat was somewhat magical to the vibe me and this chic shared! Or was it the double shot of Hennessy I had just drunk on top of that OG Kush I have been smoking! I think she is Diggin me! Is what I'm thinking to myself. So immediately after the song went off, I nodded for her to come here. She sashayed over to me and leaned into my ear." My name is Ayanna . What's yours? Courtney!" I said. My number is 404-397-7777.Aight"! That was it just like that! And she walked off. After that incident me and Ayana had talked on the phone and text each other for about a week straight . Up until the last text I missed. So now I'm trying to catch up with this fine young woman. She was 24 but very mature . She said when she saw me she knew she was going to choose me! She was paying her own way through college ,at Moore house. She was trying to be a doctor one day . As I was sitting there thinking about Ayanna, my phone vibrated the glass table had just set it on. I grabbed the phone to see if it was a response to a text, but it was a Facebook notification. I tap the screen to see what was up. It was a picture posted by Nakasha Bradford. I ain't seen her in ages! Let me see how she looks. I said as I went to the notification." Damn! She is still pretty as hell!" I said as I hit the like button and commented," still pretty!" It was strange, because Nakasha was just in my dreams! Coincidental or what?! Anyway, I went through a couple of her photos out of curiosity to see how she was living." Damn! She is still pretty and fine", I said as I continue to scroll through her pics. She must be making a little money I thought to myself, as I looked at a pic of Nakasha posing beside a black Porsche Cayenne truck. She hadn't really aged that much . Still almost at the same slim fine shape

add on a few pounds. You can kind of see the age around her eyes now yet still possess a majestical Beauty about herself. I've always liked her, wanted to do more than just fuck her, I wanted her to be mine! I want to be the only one to see about that coochie! Well, the OBGYN Dr., but other than that only me and her! Unfortunately by us staying in different areas, and as we got older both of our Lives had got kind of hectic! She went off to college in Alabama at Alabama State University in Montgomery and I tried my hand at college for two years at Clark University. I quit that . Dibble and Dabble in the street selling weed and working. Went back to school and got my computer networking degree, work and chase women. Living kind of fast. I ran across her, every now and then. We have rode around and talked a couple of times and each of those times I was on the move trying to go somewhere and set up shop to sell some weed! She was in a relationship with this guy named Chris, who stayed around the street from me. They were together for a long time! They even got married and had a daughter, which I didn't know until later. A notification, interrupting my thoughts and it was Nakasha replying"Thanks Courtney" to my comment." You're welcome"! I responded. Then before I knew it I inboxed her, through Messenger.{ Hey Nakasha you know how long I've been trying to link up with you !?} Then, she responds right back with her number 404-787-6699 damn that was quick! I said out loud. Done fucked around and got happy! I locked her number in, and sent her a text{ what's up} in a few seconds she was calling! Just like that."

Hey Courtney"! "What's up Nakasha?! How have you been doing?!" I Asked Nakasha." I've been doing okay! What about you? Haven't seen you in ages!" I've been doing okay." Said Nakasha,in a somber type of way, and which made me kind of curious." I haven't been living in Atlanta in a long time, I stayed in Montgomery Alabama for about 15 years teaching until I got laid off. Chris and I got separated. I moved back to Atlanta. I've been back about 3 or 4 years." Wow! I didn't know that!" I said. We chatted for about a couple of more minutes, until I saw a call coming in from Ayana. That's the stripper I met at Onyx the Rihanna look-alike! oops got to go!" Well check this out Nakasha, this my mama calling, let me get back at you if it's cool! Oh. Okay no problem, call me back! Said Nakasha." I will!" I said, not giving her time to say bye, I was hitting the answer space! I got younger, tender fish to fry! But I will get back to her!

Chapter 3

Beverly

"Hey, lil bit!" read the text from Courtney. I contemplated texting him back for about the 6th time that I had read the text. I think not! I got to be strong right here. Got to make him sweat! The way he tried to handle me like I'm some type of slut or side piece or something! I don't know what it is, but Courtney is making me second-guess myself. Making me reanalyze my own Theory when it comes to my dealing with men. I kind of slipped and fell in love with Courtney or was it me falling in lust!? Courtney and I have always been good friends, and which kind of made it easier and convenient for us already pretty much knowing one another. But I can't lie, I've always wondered what it would be like to sleep with him. So when our first sexual encounter happen it was like I was having an unfulfilled desire manifest itself! Kind of rocked me! Because I've had thoughts about Courtney at work, while I was at my desk, the bathroom, the break room , then all of a sudden he walks in the breakroom! Talkin about speaking of the devil ! But I don't think I ever had any intentions on making him my man. That just happened! My daddy always told me to be more careful of what you ask for! I had been thinking hard on this subject. The subject of getting back in a relationship. Praying to God, to send me a good man! A man that would love me! Take care of me physically, mentally, and emotionally. My thoughts are being interrupted by this damn phone. It was a Facebook notification. He thinks he's slick ! I said, thinking out loud as I looked at the pic Courtney had just posted on Facebook he was sitting on his leather sofa, arm propped on the back of the sofa, with his shirt off right leg kicked up on the sofa Courtney had this smirk on his face. Like he has this secret joke in his mind, like I fucked somebody on this couch last night! Truthfully, he was looking very inviting, but I had made up my mind that I was going to fall back! I think now, I'm at the point in my life that I want more! I'm 43 years old,1 15yr old Son,. A great career. I'm a single, black professional woman. I have my own house, own cars. I know I look good for my age! I'm 5 ft 2 paper bag brown, smooth skin. I weigh 135 to 140 lb. I'm athletic and built due to my workout and diet. I'm fine! So, I know it's no problem with me finding it man, but will he be what I want and need in my life and more. Courtney could just be that man, but I don't think he's ready for a commitment! Not trying to be a stalker, but out of curiosity I started paying attention to Courtney's likes and comments on his picture. Straight patrolling! I couldn't help it! Courtney isn't a slouch, so I know he's going to get a lot of attention for this pic. As a woman, I can confirm telling a man, "so it's just social media, I don't troll your page!" But at the same time, be doing just that. Patrolling your page, and going through their friends list. Specifically paying attention to the female friends! That's if the female friend is a mutual friend of ours on Facebook, we're going to pay attention to the likes and comments that our men make to those females. Who the female is, and how many times do you like and comment on that particular female's pictures! So now, I'm paying attention to who all is commenting on his pic. I would already be trippin if the woman or women don't look as good as me! Like what the fuck! When he's liking and or commenting on their pic, but this certain chic got special attention from me now! I noticed him replying to some of their comments. Flirting with a couple of younger women. In my mind, A Minor Threat. But this certain female, by the name of Nakasha Bradford, got my special attention. Why does she have my special attention? My female intuition kicked in, and all the warning bells were screaming "major threat major threat!" I went to her page to be nosey. "Hmmm.. She's red and pretty". Actually she got this Majestic Beauty but modest. But she has these light brown eyes, that are not necessarily devious eyes but it's something in those eyes! Anyway, as I continued going through her pics, I noticed that she has a daughter who looks to be about Seventeen or eighteen. Also I see that Nakasha is a Delta. Okay that fits her. I said to myself . Me being AKA I recognize! A couple of photos she's posing in front of a Porsche SUV, so it looks like she may be doing good for herself. Courtneys Style! He knows that I know, when a woman has her eyes on him, even when we were just friends. We would be in the food court, in our building at work or the coffee shop / store there. And when women would come in, I would tell him which women he had been with, or been talkin to, flirted with, or who wanted to get with him! So, I kind of feel like I know his flavor! His likes and dislikes. This woman is definitely his flavor! Even with the modesty, the Majestic Beauty is definitely a plus. The way they went back and forth on his timeline, I automatically assumed that they knew each other! I'll be on the watch! Now I have a message on messenger. Who is this? I say to myself, as I look at the bubble on my phone. "Miguel? .. Oh Miguel Matthews ! My ex, actually my first love at college!"

Chapter 4

Nakasha

"Shy, could you turn that radio down for a minute?" I said as I replaced the phone back to my ear. "Okay.. Okay, I'm going to fix Miss Inez a plate and Mister Joseph one." It was Fourth of July and I was doing what I feel I was put here for, and that is to help people! I organized something with my mom and church members to look out for some Elders, around the way, who may not have had much family or they didn't have much Finance to do something special on the 4th or any holiday! Hell, we didn't have shit to do anyway, but sit on the porch and get drunk! I would do that later, but I just had a root canal, so I don't want to drink on these pills. 'Okay.. Okay mama let me go ahead and get on the ball, because I don't want to be up and down the Highway all night!" "Oh okay girl, go ahead and handle your business!" slurred my mama. She had been drinking all night as we prepared the food. I had been helping her fix some potato salad, right before I talked to Courtney. Speaking of Courtney, it was a surprise to talk to him! I mean it's been so long since I've talked to him or seen him! Besides pictures from Facebook, and I must say, he stlll looks the same! Like he's been in a time machine or something. He's only aged a little, still in good shape, like he works out or something. Fine! Fine and handsome. And I assume he's Rich, considering he writes books now. Oh hell, what do I know? He may just be getting a few royalties off of a book, but nothing major. My curiosity was piqued when he said that he'd been trying to link up with me ! Link up with me how? Oh-oh, he used to like me back in the day. I wonder if he is trying to rehash his Little crush he had on me? Puppy love ! It was cute though. We were friends, with a romantic overtone, but never had sex or just hooked up. "Mama? Are you ready?" Asked my daughter who's standing there with two plastic flip top trays and my car keys in her hand. "Okay then miss busy body, I'm glad you have a lot of energy! I said to my daughter, as I grabbed my purse and headed out the door.

"Damn hold up Shy. I almost left my phone!" I said as I went and got my phone off of the kitchen counter. As I was heading back out the door, I noticed that I had a couple of text messages.. One was from Gerald, my nigga.. Well my nigga when I want one! The next text was from my little cousin Brittany.[Hey chick! What are you up to?] What am I up to? I said to myself as I opened the door to my car. Well my lil crossover Porsche SUV. I texted my little cousin back and told her what I was doing and I left it at that. I really don't feel like being bothered! I love my little cousin Brittany, but right now the only thing I feel like doing is looking out for these old people and going back home. Damn! If I come back home, my other cousins DeAndre, Neil and a couple of more moonshine drinkers will be wanting to sit on my porch and listen to the blues and get drunk. A tradition! As I was about to pull off, I almost forgot to open the other text.. And it was from Courtney![I will call you a little later. If not sooner!] I sat there smiling reading his text and just as I was about to text him back.." Mama!" Moaned my daughter shy. "What shy?!" Whoever that is, sure has your individual undivided attention! You're looking like a high-school girl with a new crush!" Now I'm blushing!" Oh mama I must be telling the truth, cuz you're blushing!" I couldn't hide it being a Redbone!" No I don't have any crush on anybody, and no I'm not blushing!" I said to my daughter as I text Courtney back. [Okay.. I will be out ripping and running the next hour. Hit me up though.] I pulled on off after sending the text. Truth be told, my daughter could be right! I haven't seen or heard from Courtney for ages, so it is something new! I know he's always been fond of me, and I've always been fond of him!" Mama, who is the new guy?"asked Shy." " He isn't a new guy, he's an old friend! We haven't talked in years, and it's kind of a surprise to hear from him." " Okay what did he say to make you blush? Asked Shy. "w

Why you asked?, What are you about to be a reporter or something? With all these questions." "No.. Just wondering. I haven't seen you smile in a while!" " Yes you have shy! I smile all the time! I said. Yeah.. But not that kind of smile!" Said shy." " Oh you trying to be cute or something? What do you mean? What kind of smile is that shy?" " Ma, I'm just saying".. And we went on and on about my smiling because Courtney had texted me. My daughter Shy and I had a good relationship. More like girls . You know this is my home girl / daughter. So I talked to her about a lot of things and I'll be teaching her at the same time! The same way my mama and Grandma used to do me. I pulled Courtney's Facebook page up and went to his photos and handed my daughter the phone. "I'll be back!" I said to my daughter as I grabbed a plate and a soda. I was taking this plate to miss Inez , chitchat for a hot minute, and on to the next stop. When I got back to the truck, Shy was sitting there smiling as she had a blown up picture of Courtney on display." What Shy?!" " The teenage sleuth has solved the big mystery of Mister mystery!" "What are you talking about?" I asked Shy, as I played dumb. "This Negro is fine Mama!" " Watch your mouth! " I'm just telling the truth mama! He swagged out and it looked like he was rich! at least this pic." Courtney had on a black, short sleeve button-down Versace shirt. Which was kind of fitting and he had about three or four buttons on his shirt unbuttoned, exposing his sexy chest through a tank top. A diamond chain,with a diamond Jesus Piece. Not a white Jesus, but a black Jesus with dreads and red eyes! He was laying against the hood of a Rolls-Royce." Okay, you've seen enough, give me my phone"! I said as I playfully snatched my phone out of my daughter's hand." Mama.. He looks way better than Gerald, and he looks like he got money. I saw where he's advertising a couple of books or novels. He's an author?" "Yeah,he already wrote a book." I said, I know where this was going with Shy. Ever since my separation from Chris, her father she's been kind of upset. Especially now that she's at the age to recognize that I've been kind of struggling financially, and yes struggling with relationships with men! So at times, she is on matchmaking time." Remember shy.. Looks aren't everything". "Yeah you're right Mama but money is everything! Know it's not! I said. "Sometimes it is a man who looks good, and has plenty of money, he won't just belong to me. He's my man, her man, and her man! I'm not big on sharing men nor on man hopping!" Okay Mama!" Like I said, me and Courtney go way back as friends. True, we had chemistry".." Have chemistry"! Interrupting Shy calling herself correcting me! I couldn't help but smile at my daughter's intelligence. "OOO mama !! Aayee!you're blushing again! "Anyway.. Okay.. We probably still have chemistry, but I'll have to see how he's coming. And besides, I have a man shy, you know that"! Okay Mama.. Just don't miss the bus!" Okay, now you're stealing my saying"! I said, as I laughed." Take that plate in there to Mr. Joseph before we have some problems." Hahahahaha! Okay mama!" Said Shy and she grabbed the plate, and went to mr. Joseph. . Now I'm sitting back mind running like hell! As I was waiting on my daughter, I was back on Courtney's page looking at his pics. He damn sure looks good! I said to myself thinking out loud. Before I knew it, I was in my message texting his phone back.. [I'm waiting!]

Chapter 5

Courtney

"You're waiting huh?!" I said to myself, as I grabbed my phone, opening Nakasha's text. For some strange reason my dick got harder than Chinese arithmetic! "Damn!" i said .What the fuck my dick getting hard for? It ain't like she said she would come and suck and fuck me Asap! I ain't trippin though, because I've always had the hots for Nakasha and we got chemistry. So that's what it is! I contemplated not texting her right back. Didn't want to seem to Thirsty! Plus I was waiting for this Tender Roni to fall through. The sexy stripper Rihanna look alike! I had got off the phone with Nakasha, earlier acting like it was my mother calling, so I could talk to Ayana. Well, she said it was going to take her a minute to come over, so I might as well go ahead and call Nakasha, while I wait for Ayanna."Hello!" Answered Nakasha." Hey what's up!?" I said. As I was cheesing like a Chester the Cheetah! Smiling like hell." Hey Courtney! So how is your mother doing?! Asked Nakasha ,catching me off guard. Then I remembered she knew my mother through her cousin. "Oh yeah! She is doing okay!" " I thought about Brenda when you and I were talking earlier. I haven't seen her in so long!" " Yeah, she is still the same. Laid-back and easygoing! So what are you up to?" I asked Nakasha, as I took control of the conversation. "I've been taking plates to a couple of old people. The shut-ins and the elderly who may not have a lot of family or can't afford to do much on the 4th of July. Or any holiday for that matter! I'm doing what God put me here for and that's to help people. At least that's what I think, you feel me?" " No doubt!" I said thinking to myself, she still is long-winded. But it's a good thing, in certain situations especially if you're trying to reel the woman in, you let her do most of the talking. She's a real alpha female on top of that! Nevertheless I'll learn a lot in 5 minutes of conversation. At least some of the basics. As she was talkin, I was listening to her background . She told me she was just pulling back up to her house. I heard a few people talking and some blues music blasting." Are you having a party or something?" " No! Just a few of my cousins and Friends sitting on the porch drinking moonshine!" " Are you on it too?" I had to ask her, cause her voice sounded kind of slurred." No! I can't drink.. Not now anyway because I just had a root canal, and I'm on some pain pills." Oh okay." I answered. I hadn't talked to Nakasha in so long, I have forgotten she kind of talks like that naturally. I still was kind of skeptical." So where are you? Are you still in Atlanta?" Asked Nakasha." Yeah." " Well as you may know I was in Montgomery, Alabama for about 15 years teaching special-needs students at Jeff Davis High School. I got laid off at the time when the state was cutting back on teachers.

Ain't that some bullshit?" " Yeah!" I laughed, as Nakasha continued. "Then during that time, me and Chris separated. So then I moved back to Atlanta. You remember where my grandmother used to stay?" " Kind of. On Old Town Road?" I said." Yeah! You remembered! It's right next to my mother's house. But anyway, my daughter and I moved into that house". Oh okay!" I answered.Nakasha was on a roll, so I'm just playing it by ear, being the good listener that I am. "So Courtney, what have you been up to? I heard you are an author now! "Yeah I got a book out! Matter-of-fact it's been out about seven or eight months now. Doing good too!" " That's what's up." " I got another one about to drop in a couple of weeks, maybe a month. Working on a screenplay as we speak"." To a movie?" Asked Nakasha sounding surprised."Yea!" I responded "Damn! You been busy! Are you married?" Asked Nakasha, with no immediate Reserve. I started laughing. "I'm sorry Courtney if I'm being too nosey! I didn't mean nothing by it. We friends! I was just wondering!" Laughing at her own question. "No, I'm just chilling" . I said "You're just chilling, Meaning?" I laughed again before I answered." Meaning.. I have friends! Aint that's what y'all call it?" " Y'all?" countered Nakasha." Oh you mean us women?" " Yeah.. Y'all women! Y'all would say, oh this my homeboy or my little friend and then it will be your boyfriend or your man it's kind of confusing!" I said she laughed at that. "Well I kind of got a Nigga.. When I want one!" She said "See what I'm talkin about!? " But I got you though." I said she laughed at that. "You know when we were young, I used to have a crush on you." " Ooh Courtney! that's so sweet!" " Come on now, don't act like you don't know , or didn't know!" " Well.. I did, but.." But what?" I playfully interrupted she laughed. "But we were cool, and we were friends and then you know I was with Chris, I ain't big on man hopping. And if I'm with a dude I ain't cheating! Oh yeah?!" I asked. From my tone she could tell that I thought she was full of shit with that comment! "Yeah! Courtney!"

you said that like you don't believe me?!" She said.I can count on one hand how many men I have been with in Fulton County!" Right after she said that my doorbell rang! "Ding dong!" I got up and looked at my monitor. Yeah I got cameras around my house ! It was Ayanna!" Yo Nakasha let me get back at you, I got company." Oh.. Okay , get back at me when you get a chance!" Said Nakasha. I! I hung up without even saying bye.

Chapter 6

Oaktown Mike

"Yeah. Yeah.. Okay, but I was thinking more along the lines of Maison margiela, Versace, Ysl.. Yeah I know I just got out, but I got to have my dress code up to par! Shit I'm in Atlanta!" I was on the phone with my little sister Nichole, back in Oakland. She was on some crawl before you walk Theory with me, on the strength that I just got out. I had just done a 20-year bid, in the feds on some conspiracy to distribute crack cocaine and heroin. And on advice from my Uncle Craig, I relocated to Atlanta when I got out from the halfway house. I had got caught up in an indictment of a drug ring and pimping some hoes. Yea, we still believed in working hoes in Oakland at the time I caught my case. I came from a long line of pimps, players, Macs, gangsters, and drug dealers. My pops, my uncle's, and even my granddaddy! My granddaddy rolls with pimps like Fillmore slim and some more of them pimps who were on the HBO special pimps up hoes down! So it's in my DNA to be a player! Getting women was easy for me. It was a natural thing. Oh, ever since I was a jit I knew how to charm women, plus I had the looks which was a major Plus I stood five feet nine weighed in at 205 lb athletic built, due to me being raised in sports. A suntan butter pecan colored Nigga, due to my Dominican heritage. My mother is half Dominican and black, my pops black. Slightly thick eyebrows and good naturally wavy hair which at the time I grew Two long braids. Like most young players I was a loose cannon , especially with my game with the women until my Uncle Craig and his partner vicious red and his bottom Broad Chanel red ,sat me down when I was 16 and sprinkled and seasoned me with the basics of the game! on how to use my natural tools, toward strengthening my game to manipulate and support financial gain !" Purse first and ass last,If you are going to be a pimp!"said Vicious red. Experience taught me the depths and intricacies of the game. Through a female , by the name of Mika. Mika, Was a fast, young bitch just as I was a fast, little young nigga! Her mother had passed away when Mika was kind of young, from an overdose. Her father was in prison, so her and her big brother Ricky had to move in with their aunt Mary. She was gone a lot,so the Streets Raised them. Around the same time I had Witnessed my pops get arrested in the hood, for some armed robberies and attempted murder! So he was gone. My mother, sister, and I stayed with our grandmother. Around the age of 11 we used to go over to their house, to smoke cigarettes, cigars, and weed. She used to pull me in the closet, pull her shirt up and tell me to suck her Little tits! I would Oblige by sucking them . By 13, Me and about two niggaz from my hood, would walk home from school with Mika and two or three of her homegirls. We would go to one of their houses and fuck like some grown folks. Around sixteen, I was peddling rocks, powder, heroin, and weed for my uncle Craig's partner Tony. And at the same time I tried my hand at pimping.. On accident. I had been dealing with girls all of my short life. Mainly because I attracted them to me. I had been dealing with square girls, on some relationship shit. So I didn't really have my feelings together or control to run a street bitch. In other words I had been catching feelings for the square females and took that shit to my first street Runner.. Mika! She had gotten off in the streets pretty deep! Fucking with them old niggaz and old hoes and started snorting cocaine. Mika and I have a slight chemistry, and I got good blow. She gets on the track for me! I'm fresh at trying my hand at pimping, kind of green, even though I had been schooled to the basics. Long story short, my emotions kind of got involved while Mika was turning a trick at her aunt's crib. I was wondering what was taking this bitch so long, so I tipped on the side of the house and grabbed a bucket to stand on. So I can look in the window of her room. I was in luck, because the curtains had a little crack in them and lo and behold the lights in the hallway were on, and I could see them on the bed." What the fuck!" Is what I said before I knew it. Mika and the trick jumped clean up off the bed and I was letting the window up and going through it like a fucking stuntman! A real sucker move! Because I went in there and snatched Mika by the hair and slung her on the bed."Bitch where my money?!" I said "Hold up player! What the fuck you doing ?!" said The trick. Instantly I upped the Big Frame 38 pistol and slapped him in the face. He hit the floor. I grabbed his pants and went in his pocket and grabbed his wallet! Got the money out, threw his wallet and clothes on him."Get the fuck out of here!' I said, as I stuck the $300 bills in my pocket. I kicked him in his naked ass and he ran out of the house."Mike.. What is wrong with you!!" Screamed Mika."What the fuck was taking you so long ?!" The way you were riding that Nigga dick, like you were making love! You don't ride my dick like that!" "Nigga you're tripping! This is what I do!I sell pussy!" Screamed Mika."You my fucking pimp! I was going to give you the money fool! Now you overreacted and ran the trick off. He had more money, I was going to milk the Nigga, for all of it and let you get it!" What do you mean he had more?".. "He had a bank roll out in the car and plus he smoked crack!" Interrupted Mika. I told my Uncle Craig and vicious read about what happened them niggas laughed at me like they saw a chic with eight titties! "Nephew.. Let me sprinkle some more seasoned on you mane!! If you are going to be a pimp , Mack Mane, or a boss player, you have to have the soul of a streetwalker, a heart as cold as a snake! You got the tools nephew, you just got to know how to use them nephew! You can't really give a fuck about the bitch pussy, that's her pussy! Like Pretty Tony said on the movie The Mack: "He won't the honey, all we want is the money! You can't carry your Square girl game, or the way you deal with square bitches into the pimping game! Or vice versa! Straight mind game nephew". Interrupted vicious red "Non-contact sport! The war and the game is not won between the legs but between your ears, said Chanel. "I over E nephew!" Said my Uncle Craig intellect over emotions".

"You got the soul of a streetwalker, but when your heart gets cold as a snake, the world ain't going to be ready for you! I'm going to school you on the Mac game!" Said Craig. Back in those days, my Uncle Craig awakened my awareness of the game. Him, Vicious red, and Chanel red but, my focus got more into the dope game! More than anything. Pimpin and mackin was a sport or a Pastime to me. Hoe money is for show money, but slow money! If the hoe can't make more money than me, it was useless, just depending on her for my come up! In those days, when the dope hit hard a lot of the street Walkers got turned out and geeking! Giving all their money to the dope dealers and a lot of The Pimps went out on crack and heroin! When I got sent to the feds, I met a lot of different kinds of hustlers. A lot of corporate Crooks, and Big Time business owners, Hustlers / players had me looking at things different! Upon my release, my uncle came and picked me up from the halfway house and took me shopping and took me to my family. He was hippin 'me to the changes in the street game. He had gotten old, and was laying low running a clothing store and a strip club. "Relocate to Atlanta nephew! Take your game on the road. If you fuck around in the drug game, get you some of this good California weed and some syrup! and Oh.. And Mac you a square professional bitch or two and live happily ever after. Get a business! But Atlanta is a great City for the whole game! You just gotta step your game up with the hoes. They are pimping on another level now. Fuck the tracks! There Are strip clubs and escort services now. You're probably going to get to tricking off of your dick!" Laughed my uncle laughed," Why do you say that ?!" Because I know you! You loves to fuck! As any real man does.. But remember, you a Mac! It's all about bossing up my nephew! They want the honey, all we want is the money!"

Chapter 7

Beverly

"Miguel oh, I had heard that you had been through a lot but to the extent you are telling me, I would have never known or imagined!" " Yep Beverly, it was rough but God delivered me! Now I have my stuff together, I'm working on my program and making amends to everyone I might've hurt in my past!" "Oh Miguel, that is so sweet and thoughtful of you! But I've forgiven you and moved past that.. Besides, we were young then!" Miguel was my first love in college. Well, he broke my Virgin Hood so really he's my first love.! I was kind of into bad boys when I was in college. Actually, it had always been a fantasy in high school, but my father wasn't having it! Miguel wasn't actually what you would call a full-time Street guy or a thug, but he was a college bad boy from New Jersey. He had caramel skin, naturally wavy hair, stood about 6ft, athletic build. He played football , slanted eyes .. Slanted hazel eyes! It was rumored that Miguel had plenty of women. He was a sophomore, and he had his own car, a Nissan Maxima with rims and loud music. Miguel and I had gone out a couple of times, but I never did give in to his advances, until about the third time! I let Miguel bust my cherry, and I fell deeper in love with him. So deep in love that on the weekends when I was supposed to go home, I will stay in town with him! My best friend Candice, from Gary Indiana didn't like the idea that I have formed a relationship with Miguel. She kept calling him a player and that he wasn't no good and Etc. If we were together and he comes around Candice whole demeanor changes! Come to find out, she had a thing for Miguel and being Miguel, the hoe that everybody said he was, had sex with my best friend Candice! On numerous occasions! That episode killed our friendship,me and Candice. As for Miguel, it was a wrap! He made me very leery of men. I didn't speak to him for a whole year straight! Later, we became friends, but that was it. All the way through college! Well, before he gets expelled. He was involved in a big fight with injuries and when the police came he got caught with drugs. From that point, Miguel was on a long dark Road of drug addiction, rehabs, and jails! We communicated a little.. Off and on, for maybe ten years. I had heard from a friend that Miguel had got caught up in some big trouble! He had got strung out on heroin and he and two more guys got caught up in an armed robbery turned homicide. After doing about 7 years, Miguel's case was overturned due to a technicality in his conviction and he was released from prison.Miguel has been out of prison about three years now, living a clean and sober life . Going to church, living a Christian life. Now he's making amends to everyone he hurt or did any wrongdoing towards. " Beverly, thank you for forgiving me. I just wanted to know if we could keep in contact? I think it will help me a lot to keep in touch with old friends!" "Sure Miguel I don't mind." I said without thinking. "OK Beverly that's what's up! I'll be texting you and sending scriptures periodically or whatever. I'm here if you need an ear. I'm a great listener!" Said Miguel, sounding sincere. "Okay Miguel, thanks.. I will give you a call or text if I need your ear!" I laughed. "No, seriously Beverly. If you need someone to talk to if you're going through something or just want to talk, get in touch with me." softly said Miguel. Sounding like Keith Sweat when he's on his syndicated radio show, Keith Sweat Hotel. Kind of reigniting that old flame! "Okay.. Okay Miguel". I softly answered. "Okay Beverly, you take it easy.. Good night". "Goodnight Miguel." I said as I hit the end on my phone. "Woo!" I said, as I set my phone down on the table, looking at it as it was a foreign object. My mind was actually everywhere. I hadn't talked to Miguel in years! Honestly speaking, I was glad to talk to him to help distract my mind off of what I was going through with Courtney. I guess you can call it a rebound conversation! Kind of like an unfulfilled desire manifested itself in two ways. One :way deep down inside my soul is yearning for a good relationship with a good man. And two .. I've always wondered how me and Miguel would've turned out, if he would have had himself together. Well, it's never too late! Well, I'll have to see, speaking of too late, I wonder if it is too late to text Courtney back. I never did answer his text back, and he never did text me again! I grabbed my phone and texted Courtney simple and dry text..[Hl]

Chapter 8

Courtney

I was digging deep down in Ayanna, when I heard my phone vibrating on my nightstand. Ayanna is the stripper chick I met.The Rihanna look alike! I got her long legs behind her head, looking in those pretty eyes, getting my pound game on! Her sex faces is turning me on, got me about to cum! "Sisss, OOO! OOO Shit! Get this pussy"! Moaned Ayanna.tipping me over the mountain of ecstasy. Splat Splat Splat splat! Our sweaty bodies sounded, as I was pounding harder as I was reaching my climax! "O Courtney! Loudly Moaned Ayanna causing me to blast off, and do some grunting and growling! "Urrgg! Ummph! Shit! Damn baby! You make a nigga want to cuff you!" I said,as I laid between Ayanna's long legs."That will be nice! You stay in this big house by yourself?" " Yeah." I answered, as I kept grinding in Ayanna's young, tight, twat. I'm thinking to myself, why the fuck did I tell her I would cuff her? Because I'm loving this bachelor's single life! Matter of fact, why in the hell do I got the stripper chick at my home? Not that I have anything against strippers, because they're humans and I love them! But I know that some women you can't trust them.Especially young strippers! I've known of guys being set up and robbed by their dealings with strippers! Trying to show out and impress this Rihanna look alike, I invited her to my crib.. Where I lay my head. Fuck it! "So, you mean to tell me that you don't have a woman living with you? Some lucky woman you did cuffed?" Said Ayanna and she was kissing me and subtly tightening her pussy walls around my almost limp dick. " No.. I Haven't found one that is lucky yet." I said. And as if on cue, Ayanna pulled my dick out of her, pulled the condom off, rolled me over on my back and started stroking me." Oh yeah? You haven't found one that is very skillful, not lucky!" Said Ayanna, as she sucked and planted kisses on my chest. Oh yes I have! Very skillful. I said, as I put my left arm behind my head. What's going to make you different? I asked Ayanna , trying to coax her into some action. Her eyes look like a fire lit up in them! With a devious smile on her face, she spit on the head of my hard shaft, and immediately started giving me some slow but aggressive head! " Damn! You ain't nasty girl? I said, as I grabbed a fistful of her hair. She stayed right around the head, yet slowly worked her way down my dick , periodically looking me in the eyes at the same time! I'm smiling at Shawty, cause I know she is trying to lock me in! She is smiling back with her eyes because, now my pulsating tool, has swollen up in her mouth! She makes up for it though when she raises up and licks my dick head like a Blow Pop! Smiles, and acts as if she's going to bite it off, by placing her teeth on it playfully and lowly growl, purr, like a cat and moan and deepthroat all 9 inches of me in one swift motion! She stays down on me for a couple of seconds, making me grab her hair with both hands and slowly grinding her throat like it's a pussy! Her gag reflexes kick in a little, and I can tell she was a pro, because she had great control over her gag reflexes! She raised up to the middle of my rod, and back to the top. Teasing the fuck out of me, by just going a little past the head, but sucking and slurping on me like a popsicle!" Fuck this shit"! I said. Snatching my dick out of her mouth, I made her raise up and straddle me reverse cowgirl! She was grabbing my dick at the same time putting it up in her, like a real porno star! Hands around her waist, I was slamming it up in her, like a camera was on us. She reached back and placed her nails first in my chest and met my thrusts by slamming down on my love wand, like she's possessed by a lust demon? Now I reach up and grab her hair..with both hands! Her pussy is so wet, I'm thinking my dick slipped out, but her coochie is tight, has so much grip and she knows how to expertly work her muscles, that everything is fitting like a glove! I reach around with my right hand, placing my middle finger on her clit. Massaging it, while I still pull her hair with my left hand.! "Uhh,Uhh!" moaned Ayanna." Damn!" I said, as I felt Ayanna's juices overflow. And I found out then that she was a squirter yo! Ayanna was looking back at me, with those Tigres eyes low, full of lust and biting her lips, making me roll her over! Facedown, ass-up, because now I feel this tingling sensation, signaling to me that I was about to explode! Middle finger, still working that clit, left hand still pulling her hair.. For a couple of seconds! Because the nut was building up in me, called for both of my hands to hold tight to her curvy hips and go for the Gusto! My phone is vibrating like hell. I barely pay the phone any attention, because Ayanna and I are both focused on getting off! In a major way! I feel her legs trembling, and at the same time both of us stiffen up, and groan and moan collectively. We collapse on my California king size as we slowly grind and she's milking me for my unborn seeds! My phone starts to vibrate .. Again, continuously. That means somebody's calling. Fuck it, I'm going to answer it! Like the rapper Jeezy said, on him and the dream song I love your girl. Take a phone call while I'm serving you! " Hello.?" I answer, sounding tired, while I'm still slow grinding Ayanna. It was Beverly!.." Hey Courtney! I didn't wake you up did I?" Ask Beverly, sounding suspicious....". I'm just laying back". Ayanna looked back at me, like" what's up?" " Check this out Bev let me get back to you shortly". I said." Oh okay Courtney I was just checking on you.. I see you had texted me earlier, so I figured I would see what was up with you." "Okay.. Let me get back to you. I said to Beverly. I'll call you back in a minute". " Okay" said Beverly, in a somber tone. She's smart! She knows that I'm rushing her off the phone. And by now, she's figured out that I have a woman over here! Oh well. She's been acting all extra anyway. I put my phone back on the nightstand and kissed Ayanna on her earlobe. "You mind me asking who that was?oops my bad, not my place to ask! I apologize." Said Ayanna. "No, you cool. That was a friend." I said. Then to add a little spice and suspense I said",A friend that almost was lucky enough to move in with me, but in your words, wasn't skillful enough! Ayanna looked back at me with a devious smile and winking her eye.

Chapter 9

Nakasha

"Yes Miss Betty, they're kneeling when they play the national anthem at the NFL games. You know right before kick-off, you know how they have someone singing the national anthem?" "Yes". Answered the old white woman. "Yeah.. Most of the black players on different football teams are kneeling, in protest to the Injustice toward black people. You know with all the Press going on about the shootings of unarmed black men, who were shot by white police." " Yes.. I've been hearing the news. Miss Betty was a rich white woman, who was partially blind and kind of sickly. I was being paid to sit with her, make sure she takes her medicine, take her to the doctor appointments, fold laundry, Etc. Sort of like a maid, but not exactly a maid. She paid a girl to walk her dog, someone will come by and do the lawn, wash your cars. She had a couple of grown children and grandchildren, who had moved away a long time ago, who didn't have the time nor patience to see about their mother / grandmother. So, instead of putting her in a nursing home they pay people like me to come and make sure that her daily living is on point. I have been doing this for the last four years, for 7 days a week! At times it felt like modern-day slavery, but at the same time it didn't, because I really got paid good for a maximum of 4 to 5 hours a day of menial work. From 8 a.m. 8 a.m. to 11 a.m. and then I go back at 5 p.m. to 6 p.m. sometimes 7. Wasn't much to it." Wasn't it a quarterback of mixed races who started that stuff?" Where this conversation was heading, because I've already gone through this with her, when this stuff first started, so now I'm about to try and change the direction of the conversation "Miss Betty, what do you think about the opioid crisis?" "The opioid crisis?" Repeated Miss Betty. "Yes". After a slight pause Miss Betty replied." Well.. I think it's like love, if it makes you feel good then it's okay. But if you abuse it, and become dependent on it, physically or mentally, or both God forbid, then you have a problem!" I was nodding my head, as if in full agreement with Miss Betty, because she had a point, but I was wondering what love has to do with it?" Yeah Miss Betty, people are overdosing like crazy in the United States"! It is like Miss Betty was reading my mind. "Just like love Nakasha! Powerful enough to kill you!" I couldn't help but laugh at Miss Betty's comment." You know someone who was killed by love"? I asked Miss Betty, being halfway funny. "Yeah! And in the Name of Love!" Said Miss Betty. I laughed even harder at her comment." It almost killed you Nakasha." said Miss Betty, catching me off guard. Offending me to a certain degree. "Why do you say that Miss Betty?" " Because that's what you told me! In so many words." " I did?" Then it hit me like a ton of bricks. I had told Miss Betty about my separation and divorce from Chris when I first started working for her."Yes you did Nakasha.. I remember!" Then the past, kind of popped up in my head like an old movie. The arguments, the fights, the breakups, the makeups, betrayal . Visits to the marriage counselor, the lawyers, the therapist, the doctor. The Xanax, The anxiety and depression was overwhelming, and at times, it still is! So yes, I would pop a pill here and there to cope..to feel good! "You're right Miss Betty I did tell you about my divorce and separation from my ex! I almost forgot." " Yes indeed Nakasha, you told me all about it ! So you know how I'm equating love to opioid addiction." Miss Betty can be a smart-ass at times but she does make sense." Yes Miss Betty". I said as I was opening a message on my phone. It was from Courtney[hey Nakasha how are you feeling?" Before I knew it I was texting him back fast as Lightning ![Hey! I'm feeling okay! How are you?] "Oh, Nakasha, you didn't tell me about your new friend!" Said Miss Betty. Now how in the world would she know about a new friend." What makes you say that Miss Betty?"!" Because.. You have this little glow going . Along with a smile!" Now, Miss Betty is supposed to be partially legally blind, how could she tell all that? "You're saying the same thing as my daughter! A glow?" You're saying the same thing as my daughter Miss Betty. And plus I smile all the time!" " Yeah you smile.. At times.. A kind of a generic smile"." Generic smile?" I asked surprisingly. "Yea generic.. Meaning you just smiling because it would be the most cordial thing to do at that time. But the smile you just displayed is a warm genuine smile oh, and you can't Fake a Glow!" "Can't fake a glow." I repeated it as I laughed. Courtney was texting me back at the same time. "That's right Nakasha.. You can't fake a glow. I don't know who is texting you outside of your family and friends , but whoever has been texting you lately, like just now, you have a spot for him in your heart! You may have to consider giving him a chance!" Said Miss Betty. I laughed at Miss Betty." Why do you say that Miss Bett ? Because it seems to me that he makes you feel good!" Miss Betty, you are a mess" ! I read Courtney's text. [I'm just cooling! What are you doing for lunch?..] "What am I doing for lunch? How should I answer that?" I was really thinking out loud and Miss Betty thought I was talking to her. "You know how you should answer that Nakasha! I'm reading your body language, so I know how you want to answer that text!" "Body language?!" " Yes body language young lady. You cross your legs and put your left elbow up on that table in front of your face, on your palm. It showed that you were heavily interested in something!" " A mess!" Was my only reply, because she was right! Because, I'm wondering why all of a sudden Courtney wants to have lunch with me? Well.. Maybe it's because he hasn't seen me in a while. "Go to lunch with him Nakasha." said Miss Betty, interrupting my thoughts."How do you know he's not a maniac or something Miss Betty?" " Because I can tell that you know him. I don't know how good you know him, but you know him!" " Okay Miss Betty, I do know him, but we haven't seen or talked to each other in ages! I said, as I proceeded to brief Miss Betty on me and Courtney. Let me see a picture of him. Said Miss Betty. I pulled pics of Courtney up from Facebook and showed them to Miss Betty." He looks handsome Nakasha. Do you remember him being a nice young man?" " Yeah, he was cool, Miss Betty. Well Nakasha what are you waiting for, text that man back and let him know that you would meet him for lunch!" And that's what I was doing no sooner than Miss Betty said it!

Chapter 10

Beverly

As soon as I hung up with Courtney, I was hot as a firecracker. I immediately jumped up and grabbed my keys off of my nightstand and was heading out of my room. " Mom what's up?!" Said my son Anthony, stopping me cold in my tracks. "What's up Anthony?" " Where are you headed?" " What did I tell you about that?" I asked my son, as I proceeded down the stairs."I'm just wondering where you are about to go." "I told you Anthony you're not my daddy." "I know Mama! But I can't be concerned about my mama?!" Now that comment made me stop, Midway on the staircase. It touched me! "Oh, I'm sorry Anthony. I'm just about to run to the store for something I forgot." I lied. My son is a teenager, but he's not slow, and

I think he didn't buy that lie. Because he's kind of squinting his eyes in disbelief. "Okay Mama.. Are you okay?" "Yes I am okay Anthony. Why do you ask me that? " I don't know.. I guess you've been acting kind of extra lately." "Extra?! Watch your mouth young man!" I said, as I proceeded down the stairs. I was truly on a mission." I'll be back shortly Anthony. And don't be sneaking no little nappy head girls in my house while I'm gone! I think that's why you are asking me where I'm going and when I'll be back and all that stuff. Let me find out!" " Let me find out." Repeated, my son, as he laughed. "Bye Mama, and be careful!" That comment stopped me in my tracks as I was heading out the door. I looked back at my son and replied to his comment."I will.. Daddy!" He laughed at that, as I was closing the door. "Be careful" I repeat it to myself, with Courtney on my mind. I was almost in a rage oh, but for what I didn't really know. I could tell he was rushing me off of the phone. And to me, that only meant one thing.. He had a woman at his house! And to make matters worse, he answer the phone in the middle of sex! I'm not sure 100%, with my woman's intuition was telling me I was on point! I could tell by his voice and his breathing! As I was getting into my car, I was texting my cousin Bernice and telling her where I was headed and why I was heading that way! My cousin Bernice and I hadn't been close in years, mostly due to her moving away to California going to college. After graduation she landed a job in Oakland as an advertising or marketing agent . Got engaged and pregnant by a major league baseball player with the Oakland A's, in which was a disappointing fairytale for her, when he dumped her for a white woman! So disappointing, to where it drove her to church and she joined a prison ministry. It was easy for her because we were raised in the church by our families. But after her breakup with the baseball player, she turned to the church Full Throttle wholeheartedly to deal with her depression. Using her activities within the church helped distract her from her hurt. So to become more involved she joined the prison Ministries and started traveling to prisons to hold services with inmates. Long story short she met and fell in love with an inmate at a federal lockup out in California and after hearing his story she decided to somewhat save him or help him get his life back together if he would agree to move to Atlanta. Anyway, me and her were vibing heavily on men. She's somewhat happy, and I'm somewhat mixed up! It's complicated. Anyway, 5 minutes into my drive over to Buckhead, to Courtney's house, my phone is vibing. I checked my phone, and it's my cousin Bernice. Beverly!? See it my cousin when I answer the phone. "Yes?!" " Don't yes me girl! What are you up to?" Asked Bernice ." I told you! You read my text?" I said, as I was almost about to run a red light. "Yes, I read that text and I say you need to calm down and think about what you're doing! And you could be just jumping to conclusions for nothing. And oh yeah, did you say you were pulling back or in your words going in your shell and falling back from Courtney?" " Yeah.. I said that but".. "But what? That would be so young, girlish and ghetto if you go to that man's house and raise hell about a woman at his house or Worse raise hell and you're completely wrong and no one's there! And oh, you'll definitely feel bad if he disses you in the process!" What Bernice was telling me was right, but at that moment I didn't want to hear it. "Girl you just don't know!" Was my only response. "I do know! I know that you're strong and don't want to let go like you Proclaim!" Said Bernice ."And that statement hurt, ouch!" "Ouch nothing Bev! You need to turn that car around and come over to my house and calm down! Besides, Mike has made it to town and I want you to meet him!" Said Bernice. She had calmed me down and had me thinking."Come on Beverly! You done got quiet on me cuz. You know I'm right!" " You're right. I'm coming over, but after I do a drive by his house!" " No! Girl you better not shoot at his house!" Screamed Bernice. I laughed at her ." No I mean, I'm going to just drive by and be a little nosy! I'll be over there in 10 to

15 minutes. I said and hung up on her as she was calling my name. She had called back a couple times, but I didn't answer. My mind was made up about me riding my Courtney's house but she calmed me down from stopping at his house. I was a couple of minutes from Courtney's house, and I started feeling butterflies in my stomach for some reason. I guess I'm nervous about what I might see. My intuition was right! On that road by Courtney's house, I saw a new red Stingray Corvette parked in his driveway, and his bedroom lights were off! I slowed down as I passed by, trying to get a good look at her car. I was a couple of seconds from making the decision of turning around and pulling up in his driveway. But my better judgment took over. This time , I pulled off, mind in a tailspin! It was my fault, by telling Courtney that I was going in my shell and cutting everyone off, including him! Knowing that I didn't mean it was over with, between me and him or did I mean it? Well, he didn't have to rebound that fast! Shit, it seems like he doesn't even care, because he hasn't even put up a fight for our relationship. I'm riding aimlessly, nowhere in particular, just analyzing this situation. My phone snapped me out of my thoughts.I already know this is Bernice. I said to myself as I grabbed my phone. To my surprise, it was Miguel! "Hello?" "Hey Beverly! How are you!?" " Well I'm.. I'm okay!" Said Beverly. "You sure? I mean.. You sound like something is troubling you." "Well.. Kind of. "Tell me about it.. Excuse me! I meant, if you didn't mind, if so".. "No Miguel you're okay.. It's just.. "Wait Beverly. Do you mind if we pray about it first?" " Well.. I'm driving right now Miguel. Okay.. Wait, I'll pull in at the service station. Now normally I wouldn't pull over at a service station to just sit or to just look like I'm just sitting, but due to my mind state at this moment and the area is kind of safe, I'm pulling in to let Miguel pray for me. I pulled into the service station off of Bankhead Drive to a parking space, close to the store, but a little on the side kind of out the way. "Okay Miguel. I said as I put my car in park. "Well

first Beverly, turn your radio down." "oops! I'm sorry Miguel." I had my radio on while listening to Keith Sweat Motel syndicated radio show. The confession hour and the apology line. When people call in mainly women, with their problems, confessions in apologies of infidelity, mostly while he plays slow music. Old and new! Okay, I'm ready Miguel. Okay Beverly.. Lord. And that's what I'm saying at the same time in my mind. Lord!

Chapter 11

Oaktown Mike

"Okay Bernice.. Yeah.. I'm coming over. Give me about an hour.. Okay. Bye.. " This bitch Bernice is off the chain! I don't know if it was a mistake fucking with her, hard as I was fucking with her, now that I'm out! I already had got it understood with her that I would get my own place once I come to the A. Don't get me wrong, she's nice, has a good heart but she kind of scares me. She was a bit of a Holy Roller, when I first met her. I met Bernice while I was doing time out at Taft Federal prison camp.She was in this prison ministry group that was coming to the Chapel at the prison. I wasn't really into the church, I was just going to chill out with the intention to knock me off One of These Fine Church women or to get knocked off! I'm a top Contender so I knew I would get chosen. It was a few dudes there knocking off Church women, and some of them niggaz was straight lames! So, I knew in a matter of time, I would come up. I first noticed Bernice, when they had a Revival about seven years ago. They often came pretty deep, especially on revivals. It might be about 15 to 20 women at those revivals, when this church came, But on the regular, about 7 to 10 women and all of them were looking good and about half of them big boned and the other half fine! In my opinion they are trying to catch! To the unhip, that means she's trying to catch a man. Choosing! The night I knocked Bernice off, she had on this red summer dress with some flower imprint designs, that was loose but was kind of gripping her ass and hips! She's almost power thick! Brown skin, with some juicy lips, and cat eyes. Damn! I need to pull up on her, and put my Mac down! Is what I said to myself when I saw her that night.she had these pretty braids going to the back, with some honey blonde highlights in her hair. From my place, in the back of the church, where I was posted up, I make deliberate and constant eye contact with her. From the time they entered the chapel. While they got up and sang a couple of hymns, I was on her! Trying to work some telekinesis or something of the sort, as was 85% of the inmates in attendance. When they finished singing and were heading back to the pews, I tested my intuition to see if I was right about my feelings of successfully connecting with her mind and it just wasn't some prison psychological mishap going on in my mind. I nodded my head at her, and as she was returning to her seat in the pews on the front row, she smiled and discreetly nodded her head back, As she was sitting down. Affirming my thoughts: she'll go! And it's a go! After a series of long-ass sermons from a couple of preachers, free world and incarcerated ones, it was time for the snacks and fellowshipping. My favorite part! Me and my partner LA Mark fell in line, to get us something to eat, and the whole time we were plotting! "Which one are you stalking Oaktown?" "Nigga, I am a Mac, I don't stalk, I Scout!" I replied. La Mark laughed at that. "What are you an agent or something homie?" asked Mark "No doubt! And not for the lingerie League Nigga! Non-contact sport!" We both laughed at my comment, and grabbed a paper plate, with our pre-written address and info between our fingers, waiting to pass them off to one of the women, if they're ready and willing to fellowship with us.. Or play! Let the games begin! "Pimping follow my lead." I whispered to Mark. "Praise the Lord! Hey, how are you ladies doing today?" "Praise God! Said Bernice and two more women, who were serving food. "How are y'all?" " I'm doing okay.. Let me guess , Georgia Alabama?" I asked Bernice, because she sounded kind of country. Plus she is southern thick. She laughed and looked kind of surprised, before she answered. "Atlanta Georgia." "I should have known that!" I said. "Oh really? How's that?" said Bernice with fake interest, making conversation. "Well.. The obvious!" She blushed at what I said, and I'm thinking to myself, she's ready to play! "The obvious?! Well what's so obvious about me knowing that I'm from Atlanta?" I was looking at her with unyielding eyes, roaming over that sexy body, so I knew she thought I was going to say that fat-ass she got. But I am a finesse player, most definitely! "Your accent and Southern Charm!" "Southern Charm?!"she said with a laugh . I can see the accent, but Southern Charm?" "Yeah.. Southern Charm!" After that comment, she was biting! We sat down and ate and the rest was history. We communicated through letters, phone calls, and until she couldn't take it anymore.. Visits when I got to the halfway house, she was picking me up on passes and now we was fucking on the regular! In our past conversations she was trying me with the no sex before marriage thing, but I never agreed to that! If I would have been on some straight Pimp Shit, I would have agreed and laid it down like that, but I had been bidding two decades masturbating off of naked pics and shit! Plus I want to fuck Bernice badder than a hog needed slop! She forgot all about that Holy law herself, once I was able to leave with her.

7 years later..present

Now that I've touched down in Atlanta, got my own apartment in Midtown, a nice section, got me a new Cadillac . Black on black Ct6 , from one of my uncles Partners here in Atlanta, and now I'm ready to yield to an unfulfilled desire I've always had on the low, and that's the live regular , like a square and have one bottom bitch and just chill. Fuck the streets! My uncle's partner Lonnie from Oakland was there in Atlanta running a jazz lounge in midtown Atlanta had me a job lined up, whenever I was ready to work, through a friend of his at a valet service. At first I was tripping on the fact of a man of my caliber parking cars for people, like a servant! But then I thought of the opportunities, by me being a straight-up opportunist by DNA fuck it I'll do it. I knew a handful of people here in Atlanta from Cali anyway and they showed me around, after Bernice showed me around. I have been chilling with Bernice my first couple of weeks of being here. But my people from Cali who had grown children and they had friends, who had family and friends from the A and any other implants like me, I was catching another vibe now! All the intentions that I had of locking down with Bernice are now being challenged! How? Number one: the ratio of women to men here is like 20 to one. Number two: I am a thoroughbred! A top contender in all areas with attracting and macking women! Number 3: Atlanta is Awakening that old beast in me! Now that I'm free, it seemed like all the shit I said I wasn't going to do, I'm ready to do! What ignited that flame was when I hung out with one of my old school homegirls daughter Ayanna, at her job, which is a strip club! Club Onyx. All the naked young pretty women are one thing, but all that money floating around is another! All these suckers, is what I'm thinking for real. Because the way I came up, we saw this type of behavior as tricking! And these strippers are independent, managing all that paper themselves! No pimp, no Mac and Nigga, no managers.. Well, some of them have managers and depend on their Arrangement which could be Square Biz. But some of them could be players, but it's no surprise to just catch one of them chicks with a moochie Mac! A moochie Mac is more like a Nigga po Pimpin. Lowest in the caste system of broad players! Mooching off of a woman for her earnings for her to take care of him and his Arrested Development activities. Me, when I'm in the field I'm on a whole nother plain.I motivate, and inspire her to live her dreams, and to get a big bag of money.. And share the fruits of her labor with me! What's hers is mine, and I preserve the right to get the bag and flip it and Tumble it and make it grow. And I have her! Whole body, mind, and soul! Since I've been working at the valet service and hanging out at Lonnie's jazz club, I met more interesting people! Top prospects, the women! A lot of badass, Jazzy women have been flirting with me, in a major way! And I've been flirting back! Like this one chick I met, by the name of Nakasha. She's an older pretty Redbone I met at the Jazz Club. Modest but Jazzy. She and one of her friends were having a few drinks when Lonnie and I walked up to their Booth. He's an old player so he's going to talk shit and flirt with the women. In the middle of their flirting Nakasha switched the flirting switch on me! "Oh hey! Don't be rude Lonnie, introduce me to your friend!" "Oh I was about to do that. Mike this is Nakasha, Nakasha this is Mike my nephew from California!" We exchanged pleasantries, and then Nakasha stuck her finger in the Kool-Aid, trying to check my flavor! Or maybe she is just bubbly and down-to-earth? "So what brings you to Atlanta?" Nakasha asked. "Relocating." I said. "Relocating?! Pretty as California is!" said Nakasha. I laughed at that and bluntly told her. "I just got out the pen." "The pen?" asked Nakasha and her friend in unison. "Yeah.. The pen.. So I decided to move Southeast in my quest to restart my life." "Oh!" Slowly Nakasha said . "Great choice of words!" "Oh, leave him alone," Nakasha, said her friend. "Nawl! He is cool. Nakasha waving her friend off. "Anyway this is interesting!" Said Nakasha and proceeded with the questions and led to us exchanging numbers. She was the first female number I had Acquired. And actually we text each other and talk on the phone every now and then. Getting my mojo back! I wasn't really intentionally putting down on Nakasha, trying to mack her, I was just interested in meeting new people. And somewhat playing the field and scouting for a main squeeze.. And some fun, involving sex! Nakasha is kind of aggressive, in ways like taking control of a conversation. Alpha traits. So, I usually just listen, which is a very great weapon in any man's Arsenal. Being a good listener. So I kind of learned a lot about her in no time! Even though I've met a lot of women here already, who could replace Bernice, but as of now I'm kind of digging Nakasha. She might be a top prospect! "Hello!" I said, answering the phone, sounding agitated, because this is Bernice again. "Yeah baby, I'm walking out of the crib now heading your way!" I said as I grabbed my Car keys and texting Nakasha!

Chapter 12

Courtney

After my Rendezvous with Ayanna, that night at my house, I started seeing her on the regular. Beverly has been blowing my phone up the next morning, with texts. She must have driven through here and seen Ayanna's car, because now she's texting me like she's serious about her space and shell. And that if I was seeing someone, to keep on seeing her, and make sure I don't betray her trust like I supposedly did her and yada yada yada! Oh well! I said to myself. {If that's how you feel a little bit} I replied to Beverly in a text. Me knowing her, she's going to be mad at how short that text was. "You won't fight for our relationship," I repeated to myself, mimicking Beverly. Because that is something she has asked me before, and something that she's saying now reading my reply. I was getting myself together and I thought about Nakasha! {Hey Nakasha, how are you feeling?} I was sending her a text as I was brushing my teeth. By the time I was rinsing my mouth out and she was replying! {Hey!} Damn she must be waiting on this text! I said to myself. {Just cooling! What are you doing for lunch?} I replied in that text. I can't trip, because on the low I was glad she hit back that fast. Without even thinking, I asked this woman to lunch! She didn't hit back fast like the first text. Well that would give me time to finish putting my clothes on and text Ayanna. Hope you had a blast last night! Because I did! I said to myself as I was putting my clothes on. That young Tenderoni put it on me last night! Got me wanting to see more of her! Who knows, she might be a keeper, if she got her shit together. You know like good credit, a job, well she's a stripper,

I might have to get her to reconsider that. I see she has her own ride and a condo. We will have to see. I grabbed my other phone, which I use to sell real estate. Yeah, I have invested some money into older homes. I pay some contractors to remodel them and then I resell them for a nice profit. I flip houses! One of my unfulfilled desires is to be an entrepreneur, so I'm working on that fully Focused! Checking my Sellers List, buyers list and leads and which I placed in my database. Damn! I said to myself as I was looking at some of my leads, and I ran across this pretty ass white woman, who is acting as a real estate agent for someone who's trying to sell a house on Zillow. You have to watch people on these sites . So I'm going to look this agent up to see if they're real. After a Google search I found out she was legit! And what was the real purpose and intent for doing that? I'm Thinking With My Dick! I want to make sure this agent is real so I can try to fuck her! Simple as that! I emailed the pretty white agent like I was interested in her house. Which is true and legit, because I am about making this real estate game work for me. But I can, in this business mix business and pleasure. After looking at My leads list, and emailing I smoked a half a blunt of OG Kush and headed out the door to my car, heading to Hardee's, then Planet Fitness to work out. Just as I was getting in the car, I noticed I had two messages. One from Ayanna, and one from Nakasha. Ayanna {yes I had a blast! Should hook up more often!] "Yes! That's what I'm talkin about." I said to the empty BMW feeling a great feeling of accomplishment, about Ayanna's response. [For sure! Let me know when!] I text her back quickly! I should have made her sweat like she did me but fuck it! She knows I'm hooked! I read Nakasha's text. [Sure! We can have lunch.. Where?] Where should I meet Nakasha to dine? I said to myself before pulling out of my driveway. Applebee's ! So I text her back Applebee's off of Old National at 12:30 feeling a sudden Rush of adrenaline mixed with butterflies I sped off, in my BM, like I was in a hurry!

Damn! Why am I feeling like this?! Because I've been liking Naksha! Is what I replied to myself, answering my own question. As if On Cue, that old Jodeci started playing on the radio. "Come and talk to me!" Ain't that a coincidence because that was a hot track back in those days when I was crushing on Nakasha. Actually before then. Reminiscing About back in the days before the Jodeci song, I can remember when Nakasha had her own car. It was a little gray Mustang. She used to come through looking all pretty, and I used to flag her down and she would always stop unless her boyfriend was with her and I would not even think about stopping her then, out of respect. See those were the days before Jodeci, it was more like when Keith Sweat, Al B Sure, and Levert were rocking. "You're naturally mine!" Al B Sure's hit song was echoing through the crowded gym. As I stood there , posted up I should say, watching Nakasha, anticipating stepping to her and telling her how I feel about her! "Beep!! Yo dude, what's up man!? The light is green!" "Damn! My bad!" I said, as I pulled off. I was holding up traffic daydreaming about Nakasha. She knows she got to come on with it now! So, getting my thoughts back on track, it's fuck Hardees, now it's Applebee's to have lunch with Nakasha.

Nakasha

Sitting here with Miss Betty, looking at Golden Girls, bored out of my mind, I grabbed my phone and started scrolling through social media. I was killing time for real, getting myself together mentally, before I got to Applebee's. I don't know why I suddenly feel nervous about having lunch with Courtney. I guess because I have not seen him in so long. Well, he is the one who had the crush on me, so when I'm in his presence I need to remind myself of that! You know, build my confidence up! After scrolling through Instagram and all the rest of the social media I do have, I noticed the time. I had like 15 minutes if the traffic was straight to get to my destination. I reached in my purse and grabbed my Mac Glam. Clear sour apple flavor, and applied some to my juicy lips. Check my eyes, I don't think I need any eyeliner on, that's too much for lunch! After another 30 seconds in the mirror, I exited the bathroom to tell Miss Betty I'm about to go on break and I will see her later. As I was stepping into the den, I had a text message. I was checking it, as I was about to tell Miss Betty by. It was Mike, a guy I just met from California. I guess I had a small smirk on my face because Miss Betty noticed! "That's not the smile!" Said Miss Betty. "No, I guess it's not. This is someone else." "I see." Said Miss Betty. "I can tell, but he's a new friend also!" "Miss Betty, how do you know it's not a female? could be one of my girlfriends or it could be my daughter." I said with my hands on my hip. "Darling, it's all in the Smurks and the body language!" "Okay Miss. Cleo!" I said referring to the psychic back in the days. "Miss Cleo?" Miss Betty asked ."Yeah, the psychic." I said jokingly to Miss Betty. "I'll see you at 5 Miss Betty!" I was heading out of the door, going to my vehicle. I open Mike's text and read it again. [Hey lovely, what are you doing for lunch?] "Damn! Everybody wants to have lunch!" I said as I got in the car, heading to lunch with Courtney !

Beverly

That night Miguel prayed for me over the phone, I felt relieved! So relieved that I stayed on the phone with him, even after walking through Bernice's door, once I got to her house. "Hey chick! I said after Bernice opened the door for me, and I stepped past her laughing at Miguel on the phone. "Wow! Somebody's feeling good suddenly! Thank you, God, for answering my prayers!" Said Bernice as she closed the door and followed me to her kitchen. "My cousin Bernice." I said. I was telling Miguel who I was talking to. "Yeah.. I guess she's been praying for me." I said to Miguel as I was smiling at Bernice, before going into her refrigerator. "Yeah I sure did! She needed it. And who are you talkin to? It better not be".. And I stopped her mid-sentence, by almost putting my smoothie up to her mouth before she said

Courtney's name. Bernice frowned in confusion, as she wondered who I was talking to. I put my finger up to my mouth, telling her to shut up as I frowned back at her! "Oh!" Whispered Bernice, being sarcastic, as she stood there watching me. "Okay Miguel! I sure needed this conversation and prayer. Yes, send me some scriptures or the daily motivation stuff. Okay , talk to you later. Bye!" I said as I ended my conversation with Miguel. "Yes?!" I said to Bernice, being sarcastic. "Yes?!" Repeated Bernice. "Miss lady you got some explaining to do! Who were you talkin to Beverly?" " Why" I asked Bernice as I walked off from her, to go sit on the couch. "Why?! Because a couple of hours ago, you were almost about to wig out, and go to Courtney's crib on some Mad Black Woman stuff. Or should I say Hell hath no fury like a woman scorned"! I laughed as I repeated Bernice's comment. "Yes, a woman scorned!" I laughed. "So, what happened?!" asked Bernice. With an exaggerated sigh, I began feeling Bernice in on what happened. From the time I got off the phone with her, up until the time I walked into her house, and until the time I got off the phone with Miguel. "So.. You didn't flatten any tires nor bust any windows out?" Asked Bernice. I rolled my eyes at her before responding. "No!" "Okay, okay, Beverly! We are past that now? Or should I ask if you're going to work on being over Courtney? Because it should be obvious that he's not that into you anymore." "Damn! You gotta be so mean?" I asked Bernice. "Come on cuz you know me! Ain't no need to sugarcoat it. I'll let you know what it is!" I rolled my eyes at Bernice. But she has always been this way, so I'm not mad at her. I'm putting on the Lil cuz role, even though she's only two years older than me 45 "Why you roll your eyes at me Bev? You know I'm right! I just don't like to see you hurt". "I feel you." I said, as I drank my smoothie up." Now , since we got that out of the way, who is this Miguel fellow?" Said Bernice as she sat down next to me. "My first love ,you don't remember!" Bernice sat there looking at me like she was trying to remember. Then it hit her.

"Oh!" Said Bernice, as she bucked her eyes and put her hand up to her mouth. "I remember you used to call me and talk about him all the time! How did y'all reconnect? Facebook?" "Yes girl! He is into the word heavy now. He had been in a lot of trouble after college. A heap of serious trouble!" "Serious trouble like what Bev?" Asked Bernice. "Let's just say that he and his friends got caught up in a robbery gone wrong! He had got involved with drugs. Selling them, using them!" "Oh. Okay." Said Bernice. So, what are y'all doing? Rekindling an old flame or just being cordial?" "Cordial Bernice, we are not rekindling any Flames!" There was a pregnant pause with that comment, with Bernice looking at me with her mouth twisted up in disbelief. "Now why are you sitting there, looking like you just bit a lemon? What? You don't believe me do you?" "Nope!" Said Bernice. "And why not ?" "Come on Beverly! Your first love?" Said Bernice. "Well technically he's not!" I countered. "Well, he bust your cherry! How about that?!" I had to laugh at Bernice's comment. "Then you're ready to rebound." "I am not!" "Yes you are! You are so ready to get Courtney back! said Bernice. "No, not really. But enough about me, what's up with you and mystery man Mike? I thought he was supposed to be over here. You've been keeping him such a secret!" And it was like on cue or something, her doorbell rang, Interrupting Bernice's rebuttal. She jumped up and went to the door. After looking through the peephole, she turned around and winked her eye at me, with a thumbs up and opened the door. "Hey baby!" said Bernice and she let this guy in, which I assumed to be Mike. She was all over him to the point that I could not even see his face! They Exchanged a sensual but short kiss. Bernice grabbed Mike by the hand and led him over to me, to introduce him. "Beverly, this is my boyfriend Mike, and Mike this is my cousin Beverly." She was showing all 32 teeth. "Hey, how are you doing?!" Said Mike as he smiled and shook my hand. "I'm good?! Nice to meet you." I cordially answered. "Likewise!" Said Mike, with this sneaky / slick smile he got going on. He turned back to Bernice, mesmerizing her to the point she's forgetting I'm here , as she began to slowly plant kisses on Mike's lips and Neck. I coughed to snap them out of their love trance or sex trance. "Oh! my bad cuz. said Bernice and she glanced at me for a moment and was back in Mike's eyes.That is when it occurred to me, to leave and that they wanted to be left alone. "Well.. Bernice, I think I will go home and get some rest." "Girl you don't have to leave!" Said Bernice. "Aww cuz, it's cool. I'm cool, I will be alright." I said . "You sure?" Asked Bernice with no hesitation. So it's obvious I was a third wheel! In other words, I was cock blocking! "Yes Bernice, I am sure." I said as I was grabbing my purse, keys, and phone off of the counter. "It was nice to meet you Mike!" I said as I was walking to the door, with Bernice on my heels. "Girl you know you can sit here and chill for a minute if you want to." Said Bernice. "No cuz, I'm okay. You have a nice time and I will see you tomorrow!" I said as I hugged Bernice. Okay cuz, you be careful.. Call me!" Said Bernice, as I was walking to my car . "Okay! I said as I hopped in my car and cranked it up. My mind was everywhere! One place my mind dwelled the most, was in a dark place of loneliness. That was only for a moment because I had a plan!

Chapter 13

Courtney

Just leaving the gym, I was checking my messages on my iPhone, which is my personal phone, when I was interrupted by a phone call from Nakasha! "Hello?" "Hey." Said Nakasha in her signature laid-back Southern, yet bubbly tone. "Hey, how are you NaKasha?!" "I'm heading to Applebee's now! Where are you?" "I'm just leaving the gym and heading in your direction.. What's up? The gym? Oh-oh, that's right you said you were going to the gym. Well, I didn't want anything, I was just trying to make sure we link up properly. You know I'm a prompt person." Laughed Nakasha. "Yeah, me too! I ain't that late am I?" I said. "No Courtney, I didn't mean it like that!" Laughed Nakasha. "I know. I'm only about 10 minutes away." "Oh.. Okay, we are about the same distance Courtney." "That's what's up!" I said. "Okay.. I will see you when we get there." Said Nakasha. "Okay." i Said as I hit the end button. As I was driving through traffic, my mind was on Nakasha and our near-future rendezvous . I was nervous for some reason! I guess because I have not seen her in a long time. Well, I know I would shake off that little nervousness and handle the situation accordingly. Depending on Nakasha's mind State, we might set up a dinner date or something. Just as I was entertaining that thought my phone rang! I grabbed my phone off the passenger seat, and was looking at the name on the screen , trying to remember who it was. It was a real estate agent, according to my caller ID but I was wondering why she was calling my personal phone! I went ahead and answered the Call. "Hello?" "Hey, is this mr. Courtney Brooks of Brooks real estate investing LLC?" "Yes it is." "Hi, I am Veronica Simpson of Verified real estate agency and I noticed that you made an inquiry about our house I have online for sale at Bent Creek Lane, Lithonia Georgia?" "Yeah. Yeah I did! I laughed" as I said it because it was just dawning on me who this was I was talking to! The fine white girl. The real estate agent! Kylie. That is not her name but that's what I'm calling her because that's who she reminds me of, Kylie Jenner! "So, when do you want to see the house!? When are you available?" My dick started Rising off of the thought of meeting with this agent. Because my intentions and motives are to get her into bed." Well, right now I'm heading to lunch with a client, but.. Can you meet me at the house at 2?" I said knowing what the answer was going to be. "Well, let me check my schedule." Said Kylie. After a couple of seconds, she was making it official. "Okay Mr Courtney. Meet me at 2 p.m. "Okay, deal!" I said. "Okay, I will see you then!" "Okay!" I said as we said our goodbyes hitting the button smiling. Thinking about how I am going to finesse this white girl, while I'm heading to meet Nakasha!

Oaktown Mike

"Oh my God!" Said Bernice as I was pounding her from the back in the shower. I was in straight porno mode! I got so sporty and fly that I rubbed my head to the back, like that nigga Rico in paid in full! Doing the Dougie fresh on that pussy! Just as I was about to nut, I put one leg up like a dog and for what reason I don't know. I guess to help reach inside of me to assist in the mounting nut I am about to bust. In her! "Yes! Jesus Christ! Mike, oh Jesus Christ moaned Bernice. She's boosting my Ego, by calling me Christ! Or at least this is what I'm thinking. Causing me to go at an almost frantic Pace. Bo Hog grind! This is what the country boys say! "Oh shit baby! I moaned as we climaxed together. Causing me to almost fall on her fine ass for being weak at the knees as I was slowly grinding, draining my toolie, getting the rest of the semen out of me. I was caressing Bernice's fat ass and hips and playing in her hair at the same damn time! All this goes with the Macking gang. That's if Mackin is totally your intentions. Right now, at this moment, I'm confused. Meaning my intention wasn't to be putting the game down on Bernice for any kind of financial advantages, nor play with her mind. Just to get ahead,in any kind of way. No! But once I touched down and relocated to Atlanta, I damn near got ghost on her! She's a good girl, but Atlanta with all these women, potential targets for the game, and all the opportunities the city offers is kind of overwhelming for an opportunist like me ! So many bitches where I can be like the rapper Moneybagg Yo song ;"I don't know what to call it!" Mackin and fucking bitches with no discrepancies. "Oh Mike baby! Moaned Bernice as I pulled my limp dick up out of her and jumped around to face me. "You okay baby?" I asked as I caressed that fat ass of hers. "Yes! I am!" Said Bernice , as she placed a wet kiss on my lips. We got out of the shower, dried off, got our self together and we got in the bed. We lay there and kicked it, listening to some old Mint Condition. Old school son You send me Swingin. I used to love that song, so I instantly caught a good vibe at that moment and went into full finesse mode! "You know baby.. I can lay here forever with you." I said, as I caressed the side of Bernice's face and head. She was laying turned in my left armpit, rubbing on my chest , as she looked up into my eyes smiling. "Well Mike.. I can lay here forever too, but".. "But what?" I said, interrupting Bernice. "But.. Somebody got to work! Somebody got to get the money! Laughed Berniece. I was looking at her with a look of surprise on my face. Frowning yet smiling. I was only asking because I know what she is saying. A wet pussy and hard dick do not pay the bills! On some grown folks shit. Romance, without Finance, is a damned nuisance! An old pimp saying, but it fits just right in the Square World also "What? You look surprised that I said that." said Bernice, as she caressed my abdomen as well as my semi hard penis. "Well, not really. I know bills must be paid, and the necessities of life are not free but hey. We might hit the lottery!" I spoke. Bernice laughed hard at that comment. "No baby..something more realistic like a job. Speaking of jobs, how was your job coming along?" "Everything is cool, baby. Except that I got to get used to being almost a servant! I spoke. "Aww baby, you're not a servant and you shouldn't feel like one!" Said Bernice before planting a kiss on my lips. Baby you are a king! Ain't that's what you used to tell me?" "Yeah Bae, I'm just.. "You just what?" interrupted Bernice. "Bae. Just look at the job as a stepping stone. A stepping stone, to some blessing god has been had for you, for a long time. Ain't no telling who you're going to meet! God may put someone right in your path, right there at your job, who can help you! Said Bernice. And she was dead right! That is why I stuck with Bernice, because she is very encouraging and motivating. "You know what Bernice, you're right! All types of people come through there. Rich mutherfuckers!" I said, getting excited. "Right!" Said Bernice. "You just have to be sure of what you want to do. You said you want your own business. Have you figured out exactly what kind of business you wanted to open? What I wanted to say was "yeah, a strip club!" But I knew that would be a straight no no. "Well.. I don't know. Maybe a clothing store or something. What you think!" I asked. Bernice looked at me, as if she was in deep thought. "I don't know Mike. You might not like my ideas!" "Why do you say that baby?" I asked as I ran my fingers through your hair. Well.. "You know you always say that we are country and slick stuff like that." "No baby!" I laughed . I don't mean it like that. I'm just messing with you." "Yeah right!" Said Bernice and she rolled her eyes, smiling at the same time. "For real. I'm just joking." "Okay, what about a lawn service?" Said Bernice. "A who?!" I said in a genuine disdainful tone, before I knew it. "See what I mean?!" Said Bernice. "What?" I asked "Don't be talkin about know what! I knew you wouldn't like my idea. That's country for you Mike. A lawn service". Laughed Bernice. And I was saying to myself, "you're fucking right that's too country for me!" "Well, it ain't Country." I said lying like hell to Bernice. But it's not my style, baby. "That is what I'm saying Mike, your style. You have to find your niche. Bernice was right, but what she didn't know was that I wanted to operate from my niche. Because, I saw a Niche Market here in Atlanta, which would fit my MO .. Modus operandi, which means my most favorable ways of operation. Some people's MO is burglary or robbery Etc. But mine was hustling! Macking women and selling drugs! But I was calling myself, trying to live the Square life. You know, live right and be a law-abiding citizen and oh yes.. Capture and live an unfulfilled desire. The only thing with that is, that's like a coin with me.. It's two-sided!

Chapter 13

Courtney

"What?! Why are you looking at me like that Courtney? Said Nakasha , before putting more salad in her mouth."I don't know. I guess you got me mesmerized. I don't know." She paused in midair with her fork full of Salad , mouth wide open! "You're mesmerized watching me eat?" asked Nakasha. Then slowly put the salad in her mouth, in an enticing way. Looking at me in the eyes, seductively for a brief moment, and then acting as if she's innocent. "What?" I sat there with a smirk on my face, which is my game face. So now it is Gametime! "Nothing." I said as I took a sip from my Sprite. "I don't know.. You got this sneaky look on your face.. What's on your mind boo?" Asked Nakasha. "You think my mind is in the gutter?" I countered. "I don't know. You tell me!" Laughed Nakasha. "Okay, let's finish catching up, before we get too far off track. Stop playing! So who's the lucky lady? Or should I say ladies?" Laughed Nakasha. I laughed right along with Nakasha. "No, I'm a bachelor right now. Who's the lucky man in your life?" "I told you, I have a Nigga when I want one!" "Don't answer a question with a question! I answered your question straight up Nakasha! A bachelor! "So which one of the latest stands a chance of being number one? Neither one! That's what I thought!" Said Nakasha. Not giving me a chance to answer. I sat there and laughed at Nakasha, because she is humorous. At the same time, this flirty Rhythm she is giving me, it's turning me on, so I'm going to put my feet on the gas pedal! Well, just a little. I don't want to come off as thirsty or something. "Well to be honest Nakasha, if you would have acted right back in 92, you would have already been the lucky woman! Nakasha acted as if she was about to choke! Being sarcastic and extra. Nakasha sipped soda and fanned herself at the same time, yet smiling. "Stop it Nakasha!" I said as I returned her smile. "Stop what?" Said Nakasha in a low sexy tone. Oh.. Talkin about you almost making me choke?" I shook my head at that comment. "Yeah! And you Fanning yourself and carrying on and on!" I said, as I subtly leaned forward, so

I could look her deep in those light brown eyes. "Do you feel a little Heat Wave or something?" I asked in a low, Husky, and sex-filled voice, letting her know I'm with it! She laughed at that, and hit me on my arm at the same time. "You are a mess!" I see that gym is doing you some good." Said NaKasha. "She squeezed my right arm all the way down to my fingers. And she caressed those too! She was being very enticing now! I'm too grown to be teased, so I'm about to shoot my shot! Besides, my penis was starting to stir! "Oh yeah? So what are you about to get into after this lunch?" "Well I am supposed to be going back to work.. But I can wait till later, like five." Said Nakasha. Right now my dick was throbbing! I've been wanting to fuck and make love to Nakasha since we were in our adolescents. "Oh yeah?" I asked as I looked at her deep in her pretty brown eyes. "Yes!" Said Nakasha, as she started massaging my left arm. "So can I make a suggestion?' I asked. "Yeah, go ahead." Said Nakasha . "Why don't we go to my place and have a drink and smoke us one. You smoke don't you?" "Yes! Stop playing. Who doesn't smoke?' Laughed Nakasha. "That's what's up!" I said as I stood up and left a tip on the table. Nakasha stood up and grabbed her belongings and out the door we went!

Beverly

"And I will do everything." Johnny Gill's music serenades the crowd at Suites Lounge, downtown Atlanta Georgia. Miguell and I have been sitting here for the last 2 hours, talkin. Yes, I said Miguel! When I said I had a plan, I meant that! After leaving my cousin Bernice's house, I had to call Miguel back. Honestly speaking, oh, I was feeling lonely and left out! Bernice and her man Mike, Oaktown Mike, whatever his name is, were all boo'd up. And here it is: I'm out here, all alone stressing about a man! Huh! I'm not going to continue to beat myself up, throwing a pity party. I'll just get back to where I fit in! I Had to call Miguel back, I had to convince him to catch a plane from Baltimore to Atlanta. And with me paying for his flight, and his suggestion, his own hotel room and finally the damsel-in-distress disguise was a sure bait to lure him to my web! Sure, we both know that it is a great excuse to see each other, but we're both willing to play the game. Live a lie, just to fulfill a desire! "Oh Miguel, I'm saying it again.. I am so sorry to interrupt your night! Especially at such a late hour, and on short notice to come way down here to see about me!" "No, no, Beverly you're perfectly fine!" Said Miguel. Those hazel eyes were sparkling in this dim lit Lounge, full of lust! "I mean.. It's my calling! Not saying that I'm a preacher or a saint, but I obey God's word, God's voice. Meaning when one of his beautiful children is in any kind of distress, it is my duty to extend a helping hand. A word of encouragement, when it is needed. Especially for an old friend." Said Miguel as he touched my hand in a reassuring yet seductive way. "Oh thanks Miguel." I said, as I patted and rubbed his back. "That's so sweet of you." At this point , after all the catching up, reminiscing, and a few drinks, I'm ready to get naughty! Truth and fact is, I know that Miguel is ready to get naughty too and put his Newfound religion to the side! Besides, he's my first love, and I assume we are both single. At least that's what he said. "Beverly, like I told you.. I've always loved you. And I will continue to love you.. No matter what. So, it is my duty to come to your Aid anyway! I know that it is God's will that.. We ended up running into each other again. It's like.. It's something between us, we never achieved. You know what I mean?" Asked Miguel. To be honest, I don't know whether to trust what Miguel is saying, but when I flew him down here, all better judgment was out the window! "Yes Miguel.. I know what you mean." By now my love box is moist,and my clit is throbbing! "I mean like.. When I looked you up on Facebook, it was God working through me to bring the comfort and help you so desperately needed!" "So, you're my angel?" I asked Miguel. "It's possible," laughs Miguel . By now, he had this sexy look in his eyes, which was obviously reflecting what was on his mind and obviously reflecting what was on my mind! And on cue, Miguel, like he was reading my mind said, "Hey if it's no problem Beverly, could we go somewhere quieter?" "I thought you would never ask!" And with that being said Miguel and I stood up from the table and headed towards the exit.

Chapter 13

Courtney

"Hold up boo, What are you doing?!" Moaned Nakasha, as I pinned her thighs to the bed, testing her hamstring flexibility. I have been wanted to fuck Nakasha ever since I was in the eighth grade! Now that the opportunity has presented itself, I'm taking advantage of it by putting in some major work! A high-performance type of sex session is what I'm displaying right now. Something to remember. I'm on my toes dropping my dick down in Nakasha. I was powerdriving and banging, like it's my last time seeing her! "What do you mean what I'm doing?" I casually asked Nakasha. Not breaking a stride, pound game and full effect! Working out in the gym pays off. Nakasha could not answer because she was moaning and carrying on too much. I was measuring her gasps, moans, and body movement, to estimate the time she was about to have an orgasm, so I can do it at the same time! Just fucking awesome! "Boo um.. Oh.... Oh.. Shit! Moaned Nakasha as she tensed up and shook at the same time. I was enjoying every moment because I'm acting a dog as we reached our climax! I almost started singing like Usher ! From the time I stepped into Applebee's and Met Nakasha at our table, I knew I was going to get her in the bed. I just didn't know it was going to be this fast! Like I said earlier, Nakasha and I have always had a great chemistry since we were young. So, the conversation flowed easily and the comfort zone was quite easy to obtain between us. And the attraction was off the meter! A shared attraction that is. When we left Applebees I took her straight to my house out in Buckhead. Not to trick her out of her panties because I could have taken her to a hotel for that. I wanted to flex on her, on

Sly! I want her to see how I am living and what she is missing. Not exactly what she's missing but what she Missed by not giving me the time of day back in the days! Who knows she might be the one! "Damn that was a work out boo!" Said Nakasha. "I ain't no spring chicken no more Courtney, you can't be handling me like that!" That statement caused me to laugh. I guess because of the way she said it and or I know I put it down! My sex game that is. "What are you laughing at?" asked Nakasha as she playfully punched me in my chest. "Nothing." "Yes you are! Hell I can tell you used to fucking them young girls." I laughed even harder. "Damn! Why do you say that?". I asked Nakasha. "Don't play dumb nigga! You know how you were pounding all up and down in me! But I like it though." Said Nakasha , as she rubbed and caressed my stomach down to my manhood. "Okay Nakasha! You're going to start something! Ready for round two?" I asked, as I laid back, giving Nakasha great access to my tool. As she stroked me up and down, making my penis stand at attention. To my surprise, Nakasha went straight to my dick head.. Mouth first! Well, it wasn't really a surprise, because I feel like most women give head. But I guess in my mind, I was looking at the image of a good girl she portrayed in 1992! She was sucking like an amateur at first, but I coaxed the nasty girl out of her once I started caressing the back of her neck and running my fingers through her short hair. The pro in her came out ! "Slurp, slurp, slurp." Nakasha was on my wood like she's eating her favorite popsicle! I felt a tingle, almost like I was about to nut, so I stopped her because in her mouth, I didn't want to cum! Maybe later, but not now. "Hold up baby." I said as I pulled my dick out of Nakasha's mouth and got directly behind her. She tooted that ass up, and I was immediately running up in her! "Oh! Oh my God! Siss, oh my god!" "Are you all right?" "Yeah.. Take it easy baby!" Moaned Nakasha, as I slowed down my stroke to catch an erotic rhythm with Nakasha. Back in the days I wonder how sex with Nakasha would be, and now that I'm here fulfilling that desire, it is all that I figured it would be! Pussy still hot! Wet, and gripping! "Shit Nakasha!" I found myself moaning, before I knew it! Because every stroke her pussy was gripping and snapping on the verge of making me nut! Reaching down and gripping the little handful of Nakasha's natural afro and speeded up the strokes to bring us both to some strong erotic orgasms! Moaning and groaning , as I kept boning and releasing my seeds with such Force, I thought I had flooded the rubber! Or was it Nakasha's River overflowing? I think so, because something was running down my leg! Erotic City in my bedroom like from a sex flick. Neither one of us was aware of the time, till my phone alerted me to a couple of back-to-back notifications. "Put that phone down Courtney!" said Nakasha, as I was checking my phone. "Oh shit, I forgot!" I said, when I saw two reminders from the fine white real estate agent, I was supposed to be meeting at 2 at the house she was trying to sell. And it was 150! I got to go!!

Nakasha

"You got to go?" I asked Courtney, after he put his phone down, to check his text. "Yeah.. I'm sorry, I just forgot I have a meeting with a real estate agent at 2!" "You're late then!"I said, being halfway sarcastic. "So.. I took the rest of my day off for nothing? I mean it wasn't for nothing, because you handled your business." I said. By now Courtney was running to the bathroom, to wash up I assume. He paused for a hot second and looked back at me and blew me a kiss! I smiled at that as I gathered my clothes, because he's going to have to let me wash up also! "Courtney, could you let me in so I can clean myself up?" "Okay, I'm on my way out now, oh, I should have let you go first. Said Courtney as he opened the bathroom door. He was still naked and drying that big, long, and pretty dick of his. I was tempted to give him some more head! But nah I will let him go ahead and handle his business. "What?" Said Courtney. "Oh my bad!" I laughed because he was referring to me hypnotized by his manhood. "You get you some more after this meeting." Said Courtney as he brushed past me kissing me on the jaw and squeezed my ass. "Oh my bad.. Here are the towels and bath cloths." "Thanks!" I said. As I was getting myself together I was thinking about getting with Courtney later on, As He suggests . I did call Miss Betty and let her know that I wasn't coming in at 5 for the little 30 minutes to an hour I do go to work. So, I will see if this is a date later and we finish what we started, after the date? I don't know about the date part. And official date that is, but we are definitely going to pick back up from where we left off! After I got through in the bathroom, Courtney was already dressed and out the door! I grabbed my purse and phone and headed outside to Courtney's car where he was waiting. "We will link up later on.." "Okay Courtney." With that being said he pulled off, and I got into my vehicle. Just as I was about to pull off, I decided to check my phone for any missed calls and text. "Who is this?" I ask myself as I read one of the texts. [Hey lovely, how are you doing?!] "Mike? Oh Mike! The guy I met downtown in the Jazz Lounge." [Hey Mike.] I texted him back before I knew it . Look at me, I ain't shit! Texting another man, and haven't even pulled off from another Nigga house! Oh well they do it too! Anyway Courtney has always liked me and I like him, but I don't know how serious he is about a relationship. The status he's at now, I know he has plenty of bitches. I don't know, I guess I'll have to play it by ear. But then again, Courtney is a good catch! This Nigga done got rich! Or at least that's what it looks like. I don't know, I weigh my options. Really ever since me and Chris separated I've been in a man's mindset! Thinking like a Nigga, but acting like a lady.I wasn't going to get hurt anymore, by a man! I was going to have my cake and eat it too! He would really have to show me that he's loyal and even then I still may play! From the things I've been through with Chris and other men , but especially Chris with cheating, the lies, the drugs.. Drugs he turned me out on! In which I've had a struggle with. Oh well, I'm not going to dwell on it now I'm just going to continue to do me. As I was driving away from Courtney's, Mike had text me again! Now I'm thinking, should I or shouldn't I entertain Mike by continuing texting him? Or what the hell, this indecisive thinking and procrastinating will have a bitch late and possibly missing out on something. Instead of me texting Mike back I called him through the Bluetooth connection to my car. "Hello?" Answered Mike. "Hey Mike, how are you?! This is Nakasha, the one you met at Lonnie's Lounge downtown." "Oh yea!" said Mike. "What's up?!" "Nothing, coming from work." I said lying through my teeth. "What are you up to?" I asked Mike. "I'm just cooling.. Bending corners, High siding through the A! Where are you headed?" Asked Mike in that Oakland, California accent . In which I loved. "Hi siding?!" I asked, sounding lame. "Yeah! High Siding". "You don't know what that means?"! Laughed mike. "No.. I'm slow to California lingo! Where are you from? Oakland right?" I said. "Fa sho!" That's what they call me, Oaktown Mike." "So what does high siding mean? Kind of got an idea." I said being flirtatious. "Hi siding means, I'm riding through looking past people like I'm the shit! You feel me?" "Looking past people huh?" I asked. "Yeah, no doubt, so what are you about to get into?" asked Mike, ignoring my little small talk I was trying to make with him. "Well, I'll probably go home for a minute. What are you up to?" "I'm trying to link up with you ma!" Said Mike. "Right now?" I asked. "Yeah! Right now. Let's go somewhere and have a little lunch." "Aww Mike, that's so sweet but I've already had lunch!" "Damn, I'm a minute late and a dollar short!" Said Mike. "Huh?!" I asked, as I laughed at his reply, noticing the Slickness in Mike's comment. "No, I'm saying if I had just been a little earlier, maybe just maybe, I could be going to lunch with you right now. Or we would have been at lunch.. Ya dig?" Said Mike. "Yes I dig Mike" I said, with a giggle that I couldn't hide. "I tell you what Mike.. Let me go home for a minute, and I'll meet you at Lonnie's a little later on. Is that cool with you?" I asked Mike. "That's cool ma, just hit me up when you're on your way." Said Mike. "Okay Mike, I'll talk to you later. Mike and I exchanged our goodbyes, and now I'm on the way to the house, thinking to myself, "Damn I ain't shit"

Chapter 14

Beverly

"Oh my!" I moaned, as Miguel perform oral sex on me. He had been down between my legs for 5 minutes straight and which seemed like 30 minutes to me! I had cummed about 15 or 16 times! A couple of those times were hard and long, making me run from Miguel, and choke him with my thighs. "P.. Please Miguel, fuck me now!" I growled as I grabbed Miguel by his short curly hair. He ignored my demands, and kept on feasting on me. Licking and sucking my clit and putting his fingers to work at the same damn time! Miguel was great at what he did with his tongue but his finger work was enhancing my orgasms. And I'm thinking to myself, he didn't do this in college, he's supposed to be a man of God, walking the straight and narrow and here he is giving me some A1 head! The preacher man, giving me my sweetest taboo! And to make that statement ironic, as this whole scene is! That song by Sade is serenading this hotel room at the Four Seasons! "Please!" I moaned and whimpered as Miguel finally came up for some air, with my juices shining and coating his lips and Chin. Miguel surprised me, with his tool in his hand, stroking it. It was bigger than I remembered. It didn't matter because I was reaching and Clawing at it, in Desperation to feel it up in me. Miguel, with his freaky ass, allowed me to grab it for a split-second, thinking he would let me put it in but he surprised me. He pulled it back out of my hand and spit on his dick and stroked it and smiled! I was in shock for a couple of seconds. Mouth opened like an Emoji, yet strangely turned on, and before I knew it he was ramming that spit-shined dick up in me! "Oh .. Oh, my God!" I moaned in pain, surprise, and delight, before I knew it. Miguel had planted his left feet in the bed some type of way, in which he had my right leg, almost like in an old wrestler lock in which was called the Ficker-Fo! Or some type of lock. My left leg, almost to the bed. He began to thrust deeply into me, using nothing but the hips and back in a deep circular motion. Making me almost squeal! "Siss, Miguel! Oh lord! Lord yes!" "This is God in the mix baby. Straight from Heaven baby!" Said Miguel. At that moment I had to open my eyes and look at this guy! Because, tonight he has totally surprised me! And when I did look into his eyes, they appeared to be glowing! Oh my God, another surprise. Miguel is a wolf in sheep's clothing! All of that religious talk, and inspirational literature he sends me every morning, does not match his character in bed! Because now, Miguel is in full beast mode, fucking me like a pornstar! "OOh-Ooh-Ummph!I was reaching the ultimate climax, brought on by my college sweetheart, making me fall in love with him, all over again. Shortly after I began to orgasm, Miguel was catching a nut at the same time, which didn't seem to make him break any kind of stride. Miguel pulled his tool out of my pussy and was aggressively rolling me over on my stomach, and entering me from the back. I was thinking to myself this had to be divine intervention from God! "Yes baby!" I screamed, as Miguel began to pound and grind in this pussy. With his hands gripped tight on my hips, Miguel was making up for lost time! Once we both climaxed at the same time, after about my 15th or 20th time climaxing we both collapsed and fell fast asleep. Now that's what I call some great rebound sex! "Fuck you Courtney!" I whisper to myself before I fell asleep.

Courtney

"Yees!" Moaned Kylie, the white girl real estate agent, as I plowed up in her from the back . Yeah I'm already fucking her, just like that! When I arrived at the house to meet with her about buying the house, from our introduction to each other I had a feeling she would go! She had this look in her eyes, as if she wanted to taste me and me

being me, I returned that same look! "Nice to meet you Courtney",
said Veronica. "You don't mind being on a first name basis do you?"
"No!" I answered. "Matter of fact, I was about to ask you the same!"
I said with a laugh, as I looked at her deep in her eyes first, then I kind
of caught my head to the side letting her know that I was scanning
her from head to toe! This white girl was fine like Ice T's wife Coco!
With lust in my eyes and licking my lips, I asked; "So... you're going
to show me the house?" With her hands on her curvy hips, she smiled
and looked me up and down and stopped at the bulge in my pants
with focused eyes, lick their lips and said; "Why sure. She began to
walk slowly through the living room, flexing that fat ass she got. She
had on a tight black skirt, which was gripping her curves perfectly!
She had on a tight red and black flowery , type of almost see-through
shirt , and which showed off her little over Mouth sized titties. "You're
okay?" She asked jokingly. I guess because instead of looking at the
house I was mesmerized at how sexy and fine this white chick was.
"Yeah.. I'm okay.. I was just a little distracted." I said. "I bet you are..
Handsome!" Said Veronica. "Anyway, this house was built in 1985.."
Veronica was just rambling on about the house, and I was fantasizing
about an unfulfilled desire of mine. And that was to meet a fine ass
real estate agent and finesse her with some hot sex and be able to get
all type of real estate leads before they hit the multiple listing service!
"The house has a large basement, which could be converted into a
man cave or whatever. Come on, let's go down here and check it out!"
Said Veronica as she clicked on the lights, and descended down the
stairs. When we got in the basement we slowly walked around and
looked at certain parts of the basement. As we stood there and talked,
she seemed to get closer to me, as she talked and turned, pointing
at certain stuff. I could feel the sexual tension between us, so it was
all on who's going to make the first move. It looks like it's going to
be her! She did it in a Sly manner. "So what do you think?" Asked

Veronica as she turned her back on me and kind of stood close to me to make that fat ass bump me. "Oops! My bad Mr. Courtney". In that instant, my dick was poking through my pants, throbbing visibly to Veronica and I wasn't even trying to hide it. She looked down at it and kind of giggled, putting her right hand up to her mouth. "Oh I'm sorry, did I do that?" "Yeah..you did." I said playing along with her. The sexual attraction between Veronica and I was evident from the moment we met! Like animal attraction or something. She walked up on me grabbing my shirt collars with one hand kissing me, and the other hand she was grabbing my hard and throbbing dick! I politely but yet swiftly pulled up my tool out and placed it dead in her hands! She began to stroke me kind of aggressively while she kissed and sucked on my neck. Quickly I grabbed a fistful of her hair and aimed her head, kind of forcefully to my hard-on, and from there she did what most white girls are famous for, and that is Slob on the knob, giving me some Becky some fire white hot head! While she was on her knees, I had to position my hands on her ears and gripping her hair, pulling that head to meet the thrust of my hips as I mouth fucked her! I'm looking across the back at that Apple Bottom ass of hers getting More turned up, imagining that I was entering from the back. Before I knew it I was kicking my head back inviting the nut I was about to release inside of Veronica's mouth.. Or her face, hair, or somewhere, but it was going to be released! !"Ummph! I was grunting, letting my DNA be swallowed by a sexy ass white woman! She was good at what she did . A true head doctor! It was nothing for her to get me back aroused and that's how we got to this where we are currently positioning now.. Me beating it from the back! "Yes," moaned the white girl agent. I was on the verge of bursting off when she went to getting carried away moaning and hollering ."Yes! Oh, ah! Yes.. Oh my God!" By now I was Full Speed Ahead. Using my manhood, for what it was made for and pulling her hair at the same time! I almost told her to call me a Nigger. But by the time I thought about it, I was emptying a big nut into the condom I had on. After me and Veronica got ourselves together, I discarded my condom into the nearby trash bin. "Okay!.. I guess you can say we've christened the house for whoever!" Laughed Veronica. "Oh, and we have to get rid of the trash. She was referring to the condom. "My bad, it was just convenient at the time. I got it"! I laughed as we walked up the stairs. "Well, you want to finish the tour of the house?" Asked Veronica. "Well.. Yeah that's what I came for!"

Chapter 14

Oak Town Mike

I'm sitting here at Lonnie's Lounge, chopping up game with the old players, while I sip Ciroc and cranberry. I'm kind of waiting on the chic Nakasha to fall through, like she said she would. But truth be told, if she doesn't come I'll just kick back and get chosen! There Are so many fine, sexy, gorgeous, sophisticated, and Jazzy women up here! There's no doubt in my mind that I would not knock one of them off, that's if I want to! No sooner than I said it, two lovely ladies approached our booth. "Hey excuse me, but we were wondering would you like some company? That's if you don't mind? That's if you don't have a lady friend with you do you? I mean are you alone?" Asked the other chick. Before I can say anything my uncle's Partners vicious red spoke up.. "He by himself! You fine ladies have a seat". I looked at him like," Nigga!" "Yeah it's cool, y'all have a seat." I said as I stood up and let one of the females sit down. Then I purposely sat down between the two. Ready to see what's on their mind. One was Cocoa Brown and the other reddish-orange like the inside of a peach! A real Georgia Peach! "So what brings you two ladies beautiful ladies to our booth? I mean, what gives me the honor to be graced by your presence?!" I said. My old school player partner vicious red was in town who was smiling and cheesing like just a cheetah! "Oh.. Nothing really." Said Cocoa Brown. "You caught our attention!" Said the Georgia Peach. "Oh yeah?!" I laughed. "Before this convo goes any further,I'm Mike." I said with an extended hand towards the Georgia Peach who was on my left. "Oh we apologize for being so rude, my name is Tangie, and that's my friend Yvette." "Everything cool Tangie, nice to meet you. And nice to meet you, Yvette.. Oh, this my partner Vicious Red and my partner Lonnie, who is the owner of this Prestige Lounge." "Nice to meet you all?" They both said. "Can I ask you a question?" Said Yvette, talking to Vicious Red. "Yeah baby! You can ask me anything"! said Vicious." Why do they call you vicious red"? asked Yvette. "Let's talk about this over drinks! Do y'all drink?" "Why sure!" said Yvette. We'll both have apple martinis.". Vicious Red ordered the drinks, and I turned my attention to Tangie.. The Georgia Peach. But I just really focused on her face, she strangely reminded me of my girlfriend Bernice.. But much younger. The same juicy lips, complexion, gap teeth, eyes, and body. Except she had those young curves to her hips and ass!" So where are you from?" I asked Tangie. "Atlanta.. Swats." "Swats?" I asked."Yeah.. Southwest Atlanta too strong! But I live in Buckhead. Where are you from?" "I'm from Cali. Oakland to be exact! East side"! We laughed at that. We talked and we hit it off instantly. I found out, Tangie was a registered nurse, and had been a nurse for like 8 years. She was 30 years old, single with no kids.. And like to go both ways! So, I'm like in my mind these hoes ready for a menage! I keep peeping the look Evette keeps giving me and Tangie. Like bitch you're going to share and might I want to try you! "You are so handsome!" Said Yvette as she rubbed my face with her fingertips. "Why thank you!" I said with a smile. Just as I thought! They're right for the picking."You're not so bad yourself." I said with lust in my eyes. "Oh yeah? You think so?" Said Yvette. It was evident that she was into me just as much as Tangie was . And not so into my old school partner! They were old players so they respected it."Yeah! No doubt baby you're finer than cat hair! Both of you!" They started laughing at that comment. After a couple of more drinks, and conversation it was Showtime! "So Mike, where are you heading after you leave here?" Asked Tangie." "It all depends." I said "Depends on what?" Asked Yvette. "Depends on where y'all heading"! I countered with a smirk on my face , as I squeezed Yvette's shoulder. "Well we're heading to my place, which is not far from here." "That's the move then"! I said, as I sat my empty glass on the table and stood up. The ladies stood up along with me and said their goodbyes to my partners and we were on our way. "Y'all hold it down!" I said along with a two-finger salute. Just as we were about to leave my partners , up walks Nakasha!" I guess I'm a minute too late and a date short huh?"! Said Nakasha with sarcasm laced in her voice. Trying to sound like me! " Well Nakasha, I apologize, but I've been here for over 2 hours.. So.. Maybe next time. Okay?" I said as I put my arms around both of my new friends' waistlines, and walked off! Stunting on that old bitch! Oaktown Mike is back!

Nakasha

Now, I'm really feeling pissed off and embarrassed. This nigga leave me standing here, alone, with his arm around two women! Younger women at that! I admit that I was a bit late, but he could have waited. Oh well.. He ain't my man, so I can't be too mad. Now I have to figure out what to do now. Should I go back home or what? I guess I'll call Courtney, to see what's up with him. Now he won't answer! "Excuse me Miss lady, are you alone?" I looked up into the stranger's face, to see what he wanted. It wasn't a stranger. It was Eric! "Hey Eric!" I said as I jumped up and gave him a hug. Eric was a guy I used to sneak around with. He was married, but was liking himself some Nakasha! He was my on and off side piece. Especially when I need a little bill paid or something. He also was good when I needed a little weed or a little sack of powder here and there. Yeah, I play with my nose every now and then behind closed doors. A habit I picked up when I was with Chris! My ex hubby. He sold a lot of it, but he was an avid user.

Me being curious and wanting to be so down with my man, I tried it once or twice and before long I was kind of hooked. But I slowed down years ago. I'll toot here and there, but I switched up to pills. Xanax and Loratabs! That's my drug of choice .. On the low also! I have an image to uphold. Anyway, I'm about to see what Eric is up to!" Hey boo, what are you up to tonight!?" "Shit.. Nothing just hanging out. What are you doing here?" Asked Eric. "You ain't know this was my spot?! This is where I hang! You know it's really cool and laid back". " No doubt!" Said Eric. "But what's up? How long are you going to be here?!" Now Eric was being straight to the point! Must be mad at his wife. But I'm mad too for real! "Say no more Eric, let's go! Oh wait a minute. Buy us a drink before we leave." I said. "Woman, I got liquor and beer in my truck ! Your favorite, that 1,800!" With no hesitation I was grabbing my things. "Let's go! One monkey doesn't stop, no show!"

Beverly

The following morning I woke up to Miguel. Trying to sex me from the back! This guy has an insatiable appetite to be so holy! "Lord Jesus!" Whispered Miguel as he slowly stroked me sideways. "Is it good to you baby?" I asked Miguel as I gripped and squeezed his big dick with the slippery walls of my vagina. "Oh my God, yes!" Said Migue,l as he started pumping harder which brought me to a scream! "Yes Lord Almighty!" Said Miguel as if he was amening my screams! Miguel had his left, middle finger, digging in My twat as he massaged my clit , with his thumb. Now things have gotten very erotic at this moment! Even though we were on our side, I managed to throw my left leg almost behind Miguel's left leg, Almost climbing backwards on him. This move made him put me in the wrestling move the full Nelson! Like the rapper,Lil Baby said. That move is when a person is behind you and puts their arms through your armpits, running their hands up to the back of your neck.. Applying pressure! "Oh Beverly

"! Moaned Miguel as we both climaxed at the same time! "Oh my god"! I said, laying there spent. Now this has gotten very interesting. The whole scenario on how everything has played out between me and Courtney's breakup and me rebounding and reuniting with my college sweetheart Miguel . I really haven't thought about how far things would go with Miguel and I. When I flew him into town, I was mainly acting off of an impulse, to satisfy me being heartbroken, by Courtney and to Yield to an unfulfilled desire of wanting to get with Miguel and fucking his brains out. But fulfilling that desire, I was about to have an earthquake of a rude awakening, in the form of a phone call Miguel received while we were in bed. It was the name he called once he answered the phone. "Hello.. Hey Courtney what's up!?. Yeah man, I text you kind of late last night, once I got settled in. Yeah, I'm in Atlanta right now!" Laughed Miguel. In my mind I'm thinking, oh shit! Courtney? But at the same time how many people named Courtney around Atlanta? "Okay Courtney.. I'm kind of still in bed cuz. Okay. Okay I will meet you there. Okay an hour cuz. Later. That's my cousin Courtney. We haven't seen each other in ages. So I had to text him to let him know I was in town. I owe him an apology For something I did wrong to him! Oh yeah.. My cousin Courtney is an author!" Oh shit! There goes the neighborhood! I thought to myself.

Courtney

After the meeting with the hot white girl real estate agent, I went to the crib and got some rest early! I saw where Nakasha had called me a couple of times, but I will catch up with her later. True, she was a woman that I used to like and wanted as a girlfriend, but I don't know if I wanted that now! I mean the sex was good and things, but I sense some baggage coming along with her. worse.. I sense some skeletons in the closet! I don't know.. Time will tell, but anyway after sleeping all day and part of the night, I noticed a text message from my cousin

Miguel from up north, in Baltimore. I haven't heard from his slimy ass, since he did some bullshit towards me about 12 years ago. It wasn't much or that bad to be holding a grudge against my family. It was just the principle of how he played me! He had been down here for a family gathering that summer. We hung out a little bit. I took him to a couple of strip clubs, introduced him to my girlfriend at the same time and her cousin from Columbus Georgia. Off the top, my then girlfriend, Anithia, seemed as though she was attracted to him! I must admit, cuz, was fly, and very good and persuasive with the women. Even though he was an undercover drug addict, the nigga had swagger and game! To make a long story short, cuz had backdoored me with Anithia and scammed me out of a couple of thousand dollars! I charged it to the game, and just kept on pushing forward , and he went back to Baltimore and went to prison! So this would really be about my second time seeing him since he's been free. Nevertheless I am not holding a grudge against my cousin so I told him to meet me if he can or I will come to him. He sounded like he was laying up somewhere. Knowing my cousin Miguel he was laying up with some female, other than his wife. Well let me get myself together to go get Miguel!

Oaktown Mike

Mane, when I say these two women are the truth in the bed, that's an understatement! Then to go along with that, these chicks are living well. I didn't know that Yvette was a doctor! A nurse and a doctor in the sheets with Mac Mane Mike! Yeah I said it! These two freaks put me dead back in my element! Mackin, playing the game, living the life! I don't know why, but it seemed like, when I got to Yvette's crib, and seeing how big it was, and how good I felt, high and 2/3 drunk in the bed with two fine ass freaky professional women. My senses have sharpened and tuned up! Because really, for me to fulfill a desire to be a one woman In a relationship, and live a square life Was kind of fading away! Don't get me wrong, Bernice is a loyal, good woman! Pretty, thick, and fine as these younger women, But not as financially well off and live as these chicks. They're ripe for the game the way I would like to play it! Bernice is ripe for the game, But not 100% like I would like to play it! Bernice makes a great woman/girlfriend wifey material for me. If I could have my cake and eat it too, I would keep Bernice, these two freaks, and a whole stable of women! "Hmm", I'm saying to myself. Looking like that emoji who's in deep thought. With the game that I've been born and bred with, to go along with the game I've obtained in the federal penitentiary, I might just pull this off, and live the life of a Boss player! "Excuse me. Hello. Is Mike there?" Said Tangie, as she was tapping me on my arm taking me out of my fantasy world. "Oh I'm here baby, just thinking." "Thinking about what?" Yvette was asleep, so it's just me and Tangie up. "Just some future ventures! business ventures that is." " Oh.. Sounds interesting. What kind of business do you want to get into?" "I don't know.. I have a few ideas." I answered . "So, what kind of interest do you have? What are your gifts?" Asked Tangie. Sounding like Bernice with those questions. And strangely reminding me of Bernice. The way she's looking in my face, she's starting to resemble her again! Then her phone rang, just as I was about to tell her about my ideas or sell her a dream! "Hold that thought Mike. This is my cousin Bernice." Said Tangie. When she said Bernice, my mind was running a hundred miles per hour! Was her cousin Bernice, my old lady, my bottom bitch? Oh, for those who don't know, bottom bitch in the pimp, Mac game and street world, bottom bitch means my main chick!" Oh.. Are you on your way over here?" Said Tangie. "Girl,I'm still in bed! Okay.. So you're here now? Well I got to put on some clothes, and plus I have company!" Laughed Tangie. Then the doorbell rang!

To be continued

Frank and Tracy (part 2)

August 2019

"Yes Angela.. Yeah.. I'm leaving Miami now. "Okay. Said Angela. "But it looked like you would have been back home. The game was yesterday! What you went out and partied with college folks after the game? Or you hit a strip club?" "Yeah.. I did go out after the game!" I said, with a little attitude. "Oh, okay.. I mean it ain't no big deal, because.." "We ain't committed." I calmly interrupted . There was a pregnant pause, after I said that. "Hello," I said. "I'm here.. You're right Frank Well you have a nice trip back home." Said Angela forgetting all about the business I was doing here . Angela and I had partnered up, and expanded my sports agency. By her having clout and experience in this arena, I went on ahead and made that move. No lie, she had major clientele, so it was a win-win situation.. On top of us being fuck partners also. Ever since that night In 2017 at that Christmas party when she seduced me in a bathroom stall, we've been messing around off and on. She was trying hard to make me be her man, and I was letting her know that It wasn't an option! I went against the grain, by booing up with Tracy, after I said to myself the relationship thing was over. I ain't going to lie, I kind of fell for Tracy! It hurt me to my heart that she caught me and Angela in that stall. It hurt her even more.I found out she had gone home and fainted! Her blood pressure had risen to a dangerous level. Lucky that her friend Tanita had gone to her place and just so happened Tanita had a key to her house. I think she had called Tanita when she left the party or Tanita just so happened to go to her house. She called 911 for Tracy and it was so coincidental, that Tracy's mother was being rushed to the emergency room at the same time and the same hospital! Tracy's mother was found uncon-scious in a crack house. Tracy was okay, but her mother didn't make it! When her friend Tanita called me with the news, I drove to the hospital as quickly as I could. When I arrived in the ER, It was kind of frantic. When I spotted Tanita, she was on the phone, but looking at me frowning."Yeah.. He just got here." Said Tanita into the phone.

"Yeah, I will call you back girl!" Said Tanita. When I asked Tanita how Tracy was doing, she kind of got an attitude. "She's fine! I'm surprised to see you, since you're the cause for all of this!" " I'm sorry". I said." Yeah, that's the right word for you! Sorry! Anyway, her blood pressure had gone up or something and she fainted. They're moving her to a room tonight. Because they're running some tests on her". "Can she have any visitors right now?" "No! The doctor wants her to rest.. Oh. If I were you, I wouldn't come tomorrow to see her. You'll only make matters worse! And me personally, I don't want you to come, even if she says she wants to see you"! I just stood there and looked at Tanita. I was thinking about what she said about me making matters worse, and I turned around and walked off. The next day, I didn't take heed to Tanita's warning and went to the hospital to see Tracy. I found out what room she was in and went up to see her. When I entered the room it was like the music just stopped or something. It was Tanita and Tawanda visiting Tracy, her best friends. "Oh my God!" I said to myself. " What do you want?"! Asked Tawanda. " I brought these." I said as I handed Tawanda the roses I brought. She looked back at Tracy who had her head down in her hands. "Out! Now!" Said Tanita. "Tracy. I apologize baby." I said as I left the roses on the nearby table and walked out the door. I haven't seen Tracy since! After that day, I vowed to never settle down with a woman again. All that booed up stuff was a no-no! I thought I was ready back then, but I wasn't. Truth is, us men want our cake and eat it too! Temptation comes in and makes us fall weak if we're not ready. So with that being said, I identify with the dog in me. I let most women know off the rip what it is with me! I'm not looking for a relationship, I'm too busy chasing an unfulfilled desire of being a millionaire! And living the jet set life of a rich bachelor. Now to the exact present tense, Angela's instinct was on point! I was out with some young clients from the U! That is the University of Miami. True enough, I went to the game with one of our scouts to check out a star defensive back and an offensive tackle, for Miami. We did our scout notes and got with the prospects after the game, and talked a little bit .Then we hit club Live! It was definitely off the chain, women everywhere! Gorgeous and fine women to be exact. They were wall to wall and I was on the hunt. I was on the hunt for a younger one. Well not that young, but at least 21 years of age and mature. I'm just looking to have a good time tonight and move on! Just as soon as I said it, two fine ass Cuban looking chicks strolled by smiling and looking at me and my scout for my agency up and down, like they were checking us out! I looked at Raphael, my scout, to see his reaction because he was also a Cuban."Yo Raphael, tell those chicks to come over here." I said as I still was looking at them, giving them my pearly whites. A big black bald headed dude like me is probably an object of their desire, and I'm ready to fulfill.. Sexually that is ! Raphael said something in Spanish as we waved them in, they turned right around and came to us."Te invite a una copa"Hello beautiful can I buy you a drink?" Asked Raphael. "Saguaro. "Sure!" Said the shortest of the females. Raphael looked at the other one, and asked her if she wanted a drink also. "Sure." "You speak English?" Asked Raphael. "You do too?" "Yes we do?" Replied the shortest of the two. All of us laughed, and I breathed a sigh of relief. Because I can't speak much Spanish!" Now that we have that out of the way, it's time for me to introduce myself to the tallest Cuban chick." Hey, how are you doing? I'm Frank." I said extending my hand for a friendly handshake. "Hi Frank, nice to meet you. I'm Ariana." "Nice to meet you Ariana! What are you drinking tonight?" "I'll have a Ciroc.. Make 2 double shots of pineapple ciroc." I said, as the bartender approached and we made our orders. I was vibing with Ariana's fine ass pretty quickly. I was turning my magnetism up, by looking deep in her eyes and then admired her beauty and shape with unyielding eyes at the same damn time! Ariana reminded me of this bad chick Played on the movie with Ice Cube and

Kevin Hart. The detective female. I can tell she was a younger woman, but not that young. She was very mature. She was like 28 years old. We got up after a couple of drinks and went to the dance floor. We were out there on the floor grooving off of hot girls summer by Megan the stallion, and Ariana was backing that thing up on me, twerking all classy. Me, I'm not a big dancer but I do know how to groove a little bit. But I was grinding on her, the more she backed up on me! The liquor had me going, and I'm all man though. So it was natural that my dick got semi hard! "Oh! What's that!?" Said Ariana. As she looked back smiling at me. It seems as if she was bumping and grinding harder on me when she felt that boy in my pants! I didn't say anything at first, I just kept on dancing but it wasn't long, I was pulling her up against me whispering in her ears! "Let me know when you're ready to go." She smiled at that. " Where are we going?" Asked Ariana. "To my room. I have a room at the Fountain Blue.. What's up?" I asked as I let my lips brush her ears. "OOO! You are giving me chills! Said Ariana. Well we need to hurry so I can warm you up!" I said, giving her a daring smile, accompanied with a gentle squeeze on her hips. "Let's go!" She said after a couple of seconds of cautionary quietness. "Yes you will be safe baby!" I said, answering the slight fear of the unknown in which she may have been thinking. "Oh I'm good! I'm a big girl." She said that and grabbed me by the hand and guided me across the dance floor to where Raphael and her friend were dirty dancing! She whispered something in her friend's ear and we left. The next 10 minutes we were walking into my hotel room and attacking each other! She didn't waste any time pulling up her thin flowery skirt and dropping her panties and pulling at my pants as I was dropping them. Just as I was about to slide on my rubber, she grabbed my throbbing dick, and started stroking it. "Wow! You have a big one!" Said Ariana as she admired my tool. "I know right. You're going to handle it!?" I asked as I gently Started running my fingers through her hair. She took my hint and dropped to her knees and started slowly sucking the swollen head of my rod. "Yeah baby.. I moaned. as Ariana teases me with her sweet head game. After a while, she eased down the length of my dick, and I had started slow grinding... At first till I saw that she had things under control, I started thrusting in her mouth. Careful not to bring myself to a nut too fast, I pulled out of her mouth, got behind her, as I slid my rubber on I went up in her! Quickly! I was pounding her, in the middle of the floor, then I remembered the bed! I literally walked her to the bed, with my tool still in place.. Up in her twat! Once we got to the bed, she got on her knees at the edge of the bed. My feet were still on the floor, and it gave me great leverage! "Yes papi!" Moaned Ariana. I was on my tiptoes getting to it! "Is it good papi?" "Hell yeah!" I said,as I pulled my dick, out and turned her over, so I can put her in the buck! The long athletic legs she had were very flexible, because I pent them to the bed very easily! She grabbed my dick with both hands and guided me to that spot in her vagina, in which she desired it to be. Almost placing myself in a pushup position, I was dropping my tool down into Arianna, like an oil drill or something! Showing off my skills as an older guy, I got very creative with my stroke game, and was kind of gliding sideways when I was hitting corners in that pussy! Flexing, my almost chiseled back arms, from the pressure of me still holding myself up in a push-up position. You know, giving her something to hold on to! After pounding into Ariana about 10 minutes strong and flipping her into a couple of different positions, I was cumming like a billy goat! Anyway, Ariana and I exchange numbers and promise to keep in touch. I most definitely will keep in contact with her! Once we made it back to The club I immediately went home and dove on my California king size and indulged in some much needed sleep. While drifting off to sleep, I heard a text message notification coming through my phone and a slight vision in my mind with my ex love Tracy on the other end sending the text, as I drifted off to sleep

Chapter 2

Tracy

"Yes Melissa.. I got you! Okay.. See you later baby.. Love you too"!
I said as I hung up the phone with Melissa.. My new bae/counselor.
Yeah, I fell for my counselor. To Top it off She's a woman! I guess you
could say I switched sides. I've never been in to homosexuality, I guess
I'm like a lot of lesbians, who were straight women, but got turned
out.. By circumstances caused by a man! No he didn't turn me out,
but the way he played me, make me say fuck a man! Well at least not in
a relationship. I'll still get with a man, if I'm in need of some penis every
now and then, but on the relationship type of thing, it's strictly clitly!
After the incident around 3 or 4 years ago at the Christmas party, involving my then boyfriend Frank, I made a vow to myself to never ever
give a man my heart again! So that was step one , to me crossing over.
Step 2, was when I started going to counseling and meeting Melissa
who in turn is my counselor! Now my lover. There was no immediate
physical attraction between us. At least not from me. She later revealed
that she was lesbian and that she was attracted to me physically. But
anyway, I had started going one time a week at first. Then I started
going 2 days a week , which turned to three. Melissa was a professional
, so she didn't just come at me sideways off the top. I told her my
problems and she was a great listener. After burying my mother, that's
when I started going to counseling. That was one of the most grueling
experiences a person can endure! So I felt that I actually needed some
counseling to go along with the bullshit that Frank pulled off, it was
very overwhelming! I felt myself getting close to having a nervous
breakdown or something. Anyway, Melissa was there for me, giving
me The emotional support that I so desperately needed. Don't get me
wrong, my friends, well my ride or die chicks, was there for me. Tanita
and Tawanda. But I felt the need for some other kind of emotional
support. I needed to be held, bottom line! Not just physically, but I

need it to be held romantically. Melissa, surprisingly was able to fulfill that desire, just as good as a man could! Maybe better. Like I said, it started when I began counseling sessions with her. She would call or text me outside of the time we do the counseling. She would be just checking on me to see if I'm okay. And she would assure me that after hours counseling would be free! She said as a joke to clear the path to my vulnerable part of my mind. Then she started texting me, good morning and how are you feeling today, all types of messages . And strangely enough, I started feeling tingly when she checked on me, in the mornings. Like she really cared! Like a woman's man should be. She wasn't a butch looking bitch or nothing like that, she just knew the right things to do to get next to a woman ! On a positive note, actually Melissa was a dime piece! Melissa stood about 5 ft 7 weighing about 175 but with a well sculpted body, Naturally built like a track runner. Melissa's three times a week workout keeps her toned up and sexy. Her skin complexion was light skin. Not pale yellow, light skin but brownish red skin. Melissa was very attractive! Unlike me, Melissa wasn't new to homosexuality. She had first experimented with it When she was a junior in college. Drunk and accepted a kiss from her then roommate, who was already turned out. She told me she was like Katy Perry, on her old song. I kissed a girl and I liked it! After that moment, she participated on the low, but still had boyfriends! Talking about having your cake and eating it too! After college, she got a great job being a counselor, and got married to a guy she met her senior year, who in turn was a doctor. His name was Emmanuel. He was a little older than her, probably by 4 or 5 years. Tall, light skinned, with naturally wavy hair, like Rick Fox or someone. A true to life ladies man, from what I heard. They had a son together, who mostly stayed with his father, who was like 17 now. Emmanuel got custody of his son, when he caught Melissa in the bed, with their white next door neighbor, who was a female! To make things more ironic, the female was Emmanuel's secret lover first! Through due diligence and research Melissa had found out that her husband had been sneaking around with their white neighbor. She wasn't the only side piece, but what had Melissa enraged was that it happened right under her nose and it was a white woman! Her neighbor was a widow. Her husband had been a casualty in the war in the Middle East. Anyway what makes Melissa so cold was that she didn't act out or commit to any of the expected behavior of a black woman, in this type of circumstances. Instead she fucked and sucked her too! It was fairly easy, because they visited each other at least two times a week! One of those nights they sat there and engaged in deep sensuall/sexual conversation as they sipped on some cognac and smoked a little exotic marijuana. In which her white soon to be lover provided. After an hour or two of sitting there Google eyeing each other, and making each other hot through conversation and vibing, they finally attacked each other! From that night Forward Melissa made sure that her white neighbor got freaked at least three or four times a week! Outdoing her husband, she made the white lady orgasm multiple times during sex and provided emotional support that her husband would never provide. Melissa's husband's interest was only between The white woman's legs and her mouth! The day Emmanuel caught Melissa and his secret lover in the bed, Melissa was hitting the woman from the back, doggy style with a big black 10-in dildo! When he opened the door, he couldn't believe his eyes! When he was coming up the stairs he heard the music, which wasn't unusual. She always listened to slow music. What was unusual was that he heard a woman moaning and almost squealing with pleasure! He knows his old lady doesn't watch porn . And it didn't sound like her moaning, or was it her? That thought alone made him furious and made him hurry up the stairs at a sprint! Taking three or four stairs at a time. Once he got to the door, he heard H-Town's old song "Some Body rocking knocking the boots," Get extremely loud mixed with the erotic moaning! Emmanuel lost it and busted in the bedroom to find his wife Melissa fucking his side piece and pulling her head back by her hair as if they're some WWE women wrestlers! Instead of him joining in, he reacted like a woman scorned almost! Fast forward to this present time Melissa is divorced, happy and living her best life! Melissa called and was letting me know that she would be working a little late tonight. And that she wanted me to bring her some Taco Bell by her office. I left my office which is in my home to go and get Melissa's Taco Bell. Driving along Perkins Avenue I was caught by a red light. Naturally for a woman, that's the time to check my phone for messages or whatever. Then right before the light changed to green, I noticed out of the corner of my eye, a pretty car pulled up to the next lane. So naturally I glance.. At first. Then, I look.. I actually do a double take. What caught my attention was the car. It was a dark blue Bentley. Then we caught my attention was the driver! This nigga was dark skin, and bald head, which is very common, but this guy resembles my ex-boyfriend Frank So much, that it stalled my takeoff, When the light turned green. My reaction caused him to do a double take! His second look caught me dead on, participating in eye contact with this guy. "What the fuck!" I said before I knew it because this guy just happened to be Frank! Instantly, I put the pedal to the metal, leaving him stunned at the red light. But within a few seconds, he was right beside me , in the right lane.. Smiling and waving! With his Cartier frames on, and showing his pearly whites, I must admit he's looking good.. And very enticing! But my mind immediately went back to that night, at the Christmas party. When I busted in that stall, to find him fucking Angela! Just as I had figured,From the beginning! When they were taking those so-called business trips to Scout football players or whatever. I tried to ignore him as he kept up with me in traffic. At his last attempt at trying to get my attention, I mashed the gas pedal to the floor! Now I'm driving at a speed, which would get me a ticket! Evidently, he wasn't willing to get a ticket, because he slowed down, shaking his head and disbelief. Boy does he have some nerves! Pulling up beside me smiling and waving, as if that disloyal shit he did, was okay or something. I had an urge to run him off the road. But I wouldn't stoop so low. I looked in my rearview mirror, to see how far I had left Frank And I saw him turning off to the Right, maybe heading home or towards that soul food restaurant he likes. "Oh fuck him Tracy!" I said out loud to the inside of my car as tears flowed freely down my face. I was okay till I saw Frank! My mind was going back to the day that we first met and beyond. "Get it together girl!" I said to myself as I wiped away the tears. What had me so upset with him, when I saw him, was that I thought that me and Frank had a future together and that black bastard betrayed me! He cheated on me while I was there. If I would have had a pistol that night, I probably would have shot both of them! Well I'm close to pulling up to Taco Bell And shortly after that, I will be pulling up to Melissa's job, so I'm going to forget about Frank! I ordered Melissa's food and proceeded on my journey to my new Bae. All of a sudden like a thief in the night, Frank invaded the privacy of my thoughts. I'm lying in the bed, on top of the covers of our bed, in a resort. On one of our many trips/ vacations we would take. Frank exits the bathroom naked in his birthday suit! It seemed as if he was shining off of the moonlight which was creeping in a crack in the blinds. As he was approaching the bed, I felt a slight tingle between my thighs, which caused my fingers on my right hand to instinctively move to the tingly sensation between my thighs. Looking at Frank as he approached the bed, I slowly parted my thighs and began to work my fingers! My love box was so moist And hot right now, that I had cummed before Frank even was on the bed good.! I moaned as I kicked my head back! That's when I was jotted out of my reminiscing/dream state by hysterically blown horns and tires screeching, from drivers and traffic! And some moist and wet panties! I had gone so deep into reminiscing about a night with Frank, that I ran a traffic light way after it had turned red! I had to slam on breaks, myself to avoid a terrible wreck. With my fingers under my skirt, middle finger deep in my vagina! "What the fuck!?" I said, as I snapped out of it, and continued on my journey. Whoa, that was too close. I can't believe myself! After seeing Frank, I took my mind back, reminiscing on one of my favorite moments with Frank. Reliving the whole scenario in my head coming to the point of me actually getting myself off, for real! And almost getting myself killed in a car accident, and which I would have been at fault! Let me hurry up and get to Melissa. As I was driving, I was doing a serious evaluation of myself. Because, what just happened, never happened to me before! I had gotten over Frank, a long time ago. He crossed my mind every now and then at first, when we first stopped seeing each other. But, it wasn't long after that, I was being comforted and loved by Melissa and focused on my business ventures." I got it, I got it. I'm over him!" I affirm to myself, as I was pulling in the parking lot to Melissa's office. As I got myself together before I exited my car, I got a friend request from Frank, but it's his sports management page! I had blocked his personal page a while back. And here it is now, he's sending me a friend request in his business name. I sat there for a moment, contemplating on accepting his friend request, but I decided not to at the time. Let me get out of this car, because I'm getting distracted! As I entered Melissa's office, I noticed the smell of her favorite aromatherapy candle. As I approached her desk, she briefly looked over at me and spoke. "Hey baby!" "Hey bae!" I answered as I sat her food on her desk. She was on her computer really intensely. "Just a moment baby". Said Melissa, as she looked from a computer screen to her notepad,in which she was scribbling in at the moment. Then she paused for a moment, looking over her Christian Dior reading glasses at me. "Well damn Ms. Tracy, how was your day?" Asked Melissa. By now I had taken the couch and laid down on it, as if I was in therapy. "Oh my God Melissa! Is it all over my face that something is bothering me? "Yes baby, it is!" Said Melissa as she took off her glasses in full counseling / therapist mode. "Oh my God Melissa! I said. My day was okay.. Until I saw Frank"! Melissa looked at me for a couple of seconds before saying anything. I guess trying to read me to see just how bad I was affected by me saying Frank. "What?" I said , as I was beginning to get agitated by her stare. "Oh nothing.. Just trying to see..".." How bad does it affect me? I said, ending Melissa's sentence for her... "Not really, because like you said earlier, it's written all over your face! I'm just wondering if you're okay! What is you catching an attitude with me? I'm only concerned about your well-being. As you can recall, he did run your blood pressure to a dangerous level when you caught him "Fucking" his co-worker in the bathroom"! Melissa was getting mad, and she didn't have to put emphasis on "Fucking!" "Okay, okay Melissa! I apologize for the attitude. It's just that.." "You haven't seen him in a couple of years, and to see him causes a total recall in your memory. Back to the night. Anger and all, if you allow your mind to go too far." Said Melissa. "Yeah you're right baby." I said as I set up right on the couch. "Tracy, tell me this.. When you saw Frank, did it spark an old flame in you?" I looked up at Melissa as she slowly made her way over to me." No.. Well.. Yes Melissa, I don't know!" I said as I stood up on the verge of being exasperated. "Calm down baby." Softly said Melissa as she walked up to me, putting her hands gently on my face, caressing my ears, running her fingers through my hair as she simultaneously kissed me deep, sweet and long! "Umm!" moaning pleasure as Melissa squeezed my right cheeks on my ass, as she grinds her pussy against mine." Whoa!" I said as we stopped kissing."Thank you baby, I needed that!" You're welcome baby!" said Melissa as she held both of my hands in her hands, and looked me in the eyes at the same time. "I want you to get over him okay?" "Okay." I said as

I fought back tears." Now, let me get to my Taco Bell." Said Melissa as she walked off to grab her food. "Oh by the way Tracy, where did you see Frank?" Asked Melissa. From that point, I told her everything! From the time I saw him at the traffic light, to the almost car crash, I caused and the reason I almost crashed! After I got through telling her My story she looked astounded. Her mouth was wide open! "Close your mouth baby, it's full of food!" I joked. Melissa grabs her soda and wash her food down before talking. "Wow Tracy! Talking about sprung!" "I'm not sprung! It's just.." "It's just when you saw him, you had an automatic recall or should I say the pavlov effect." "Say what?!" I laughed. "Yes.. You had a conditioned response, by a certain stimulus which was Frank! Your coochie got 38 hot when you saw him! Wow he sure does have a stronghold on you"! Said Melissa. I can tell, maybe she was a little pissed about what I told her and was condemning me on sly, but at the same time she was on to something. "Don't go getting all psychological, and clinical on me now!" I said, becoming defensive even though she's right. "No it's true. Do you want me to prove it?" "No! When are you getting off of work?" I asked, smoothly changing the subject. "Now! I'm ready to close shop, so just give me a minute or two." "Okay." I said as I sat back down, and got into my phone. I went straight to Facebook. I looked at Frank's friend request, well the request from his company's page. Off the top, I'm looking at his coworker/lover on the page too. A pic of her and him at their office and at a lot of their client signings and different events. I almost deleted the request and I almost confirmed it too. Then a thought hit me. I'm going to accept it ! A real devious side of me came to life. I have a plan for Frank!

Chapter 3

Frank

"Cuz..I can't believe it!" She smashed out from the red light, like she saw a monster or something!" "Well duh, Mr. I will fuck a thirsty thotted out bitch in a bathroom stall while the love of your life is in the same building!" said my cousin Tasha, and who I got the ticket from to go see this play,where I met my ex-girlfriend Tracy. Tasha has been my comforter/counselor, when it came to women, ever since we were in elementary school. She has always kept it real with me. No sugarcoating. "Frank.. Do you really feel like she has forgiven you? Hell no! Be real with yourself. I mean you were her knight and shining armor then you betrayed her trust. So, when she saw you, she was automatically pissed off. So she didn't want to see you! That's why she smashed out on you! Simple is that." "I understand all that.. But, it just tripped me out I guess. I mean, I can tell she didn't know who I was at first. She was admiring the Bentley. And when she looked up to see who was driving it, it seemed like when she recognized me and she knew that I knew who she was, she put the pedal to the metal!" I laughed. "Hell has no fury like a woman scorned! Just remember that," said Tasha. "I feel you cuz.. You think she's going to accept my friend request?" "A friend request?! Man you trippin! I thought you had made a vow to never lock down again with another woman? Then how y'all split up.. Let me rephrase that, how you fucked up, what do you think? Would you accept your friend request, after you caught her red-handed, getting It in? Getting dicked down? I'll answer it for you.. Hell no!" I couldn't help but laugh at my cousin, because she was putting the hammer to the nail! "You're laughing Frank, but you know I'm telling the truth about the matter." "You're right cuz! I said, as I picked my phone up off of the coffee table to check a notification I had heard. It was a Facebook notification. "Wow!" She accepted my friend request . "Who Tracy?" asked Tasha. "Yeah.. Take a look." I said as I was handing her the phone. "Oh you sent it from your agency page. Wow Frank, how smart can you be? The more I tell you, the dumber you get!" "What do you mean cuz?" "What I mean Frank, don't you and Angela run this company and ain't both of y'all pics on the book?

And there's pics of Angela on there? Probably pics of you and Angela together." "Well.. I didn't think it all the way through before I sent it. I was just excited to see her and acting on impulse. But hell, she just added me!" That's strange Frank.. But then too, maybe she has forgotten over it to a big degree. Then she could have something else up her sleeve! Please use your better judgment cuz." "I will." I said as I picked up my glass of Hennessy and took a sip. "Well Frank I'm about to head on to the house, but remember what I said about using your better judgment Okay?" "Okay, I got you cuz." I said as Tasha went out the door. I was sitting there looking through Tracy's pics. She had deleted all the ones we were on together. But I still looked at her pics and reminisced about old times. Then I snapped out of it . I started remembering the freedom I had regained as a single man, a bachelor! But before I leave her page I got to inbox her. {Hey Tracy, how are you doing? Well if you don't answer me back, I'll understand. I just wanted to apologize.} I sent the text, and that was that. Then my phone rang. It was Angela. "What's up Angela?" "Hey Frank! What are you up to?" "I'm cooling Angela, and you?" "I'm just chilling . What you got going on tonight?" Now Angela is ready to fuck tonight, and I'm not sure if I want to get with her or not. I had some more fish on my hook to fry. I had met this chick named Jamie, I really wanted to get with her bad as a hog needed slop! I had met her at a family gathering with one of my cousins named Anita, and they also had a thick diva type of chick with them named Joyce. I think she and Jamie Were lovers on the low! They work together at the health department here in Tallahassee.She makes good money, tall, about 5 ft 8 in, but with heels on she is about 6 ft or a little over. Dark cocoa brown skin, slim fine. Shit my thoughts are running away with me! Well. Running away from Angela, and running to Jamie! "Well Angela, I was kind of going out tonight with my cousin and her friends. What you got up?" "Well, I kind of want to chill with you tonight.. If it's not a problem." I promised my cousin I would step out with them earlier this week." I said, lying through my teeth. I was ready to Shake Angela now, so I'm not even about to cut any corners with her, because truth be told I'm kind of tired of her. She's a great business partner, pretty and fine as hell, but she is trying to have me to herself. "Well, let me get myself together, so I can be ready when my cousin shows up." Just like that huh Frank?! I mean the way you brush me off, but it's cool, it's cool.. We'll go ahead and have a nice time Frank.. I guess I'll catch you on the rebound!" I laughed at that. "Rebound huh?". "Bye Frank.. Yes, rebound! Bye!" Said Angela as she hung up. Just as soon as she did I was in my cousin Anita's inbox. {What y'all got going on tonight?"} She replied," {Going to a party at Laredos tonight.} {Oh yeah? I know your friends are going too right?} {Yes!} {Okay, I'll be there!} And now it's time for me to get myself together for real and head on out to Laredo's.

Chapter 4

Tracy

"Oh baby! Shit!" I moaned as Melissa worked her tongue between my thighs, pleasing my throbbing clit. It has seen like an eternity that Melissa had been downtown making me cum continuously. My head was kicked back, like a junky getting hit with 30 cc's of heroin in both arms! Pure ecstasy is what I'm feeling at the moment. I know Melissa is putting down her A game because of what happened today. Me seeing Frank and it bothered me! So, in her mind she's going to make me forget about Frank! I understand if that's the case. Then too, if it's not the case then she's an A1 head doctor right now! "Yes, yes, yes Melissa baby!" I moaned in sheer pleasure, as I wrap my thighs around Melissa's head, almost smothering her! She didn't seem to mind or notice the pressure I was applying because all she was doing was gripping me harder and eating me like a ripe Georgia peach! Licking, slurping, and sucking! "Uhh! Ugg!" I was grunting and grabbing Melissa's hair as I was fucking and whining and thrusting harder to

Melissa's face, getting this much needed orgasm out of me. "Whoa!" I said as I laid my head back on the pillar, spent, trying to push Melissa's head away from my tender clit. "Hold up baby! Let me catch my breath." With that being said, Melissa raised from between my thighs, face shiny, especially around her mouth, from my juices and sweat. She kissed me in my mouth! Tongue kisses me down, making me taste myself. Melissa could be nasty when she wants to be. Making me nasty, because I'm all the way for it at this point in this session. Melissa was working her middle finger, in my already near swollen vagina. At least that's how it felt. "Oh my god!" I moaned as Melissa was making me cum back to back. She reached on the nightstand to grab one of our favorite toys. A silver bullet! And in my mind I'm saying, no Melissa! But it seemed as if I couldn't make the word stop or that's enough baby, come out of my mouth. She turned the bullet on and slowly teased my clit and pussy hole. She was rubbing my head and caressing my hair and talking to me, in a very calming and serene way. "You're mine baby. You're going to be great with me. Fuck Frank!" I think she wants to see my reaction to that name and just as expected, I went into a multiple orgasm and almost squirting! That made her grab the 12-in black/dark brown strap on, while I was recovering. Before I knew it, Melissa had removed the silver bullet and semi-rammed the dildor up in my slippery wet vagina! "Oh my Jesus!" I moaned. Melissa was stroking me gently, but yet deep and hard. Melissa's hands slither to the bend of my knees and there I was, in the buck getting pounded and by another female! The whole time, Melissa Was looking me deep into my eyes with a hardened, concentrating, stare,As if she was almost possessed or something. Suddenly, she dropped my legs, and grabbed my hair and ears at the same time and started stroking harder and looking me in the eyes. It became so intense and yet creepy I finally broke out of an erotic stare. My mind all of a sudden was in the bed with Frank, and these type of intense sexual moments! immediately , I threw my legs around

Melissa's neck ! Catching her by surprise, by matching her savage. Picturing that the big 12-in dildo was Frank's penis, plunging down in my vagina. "Ooh!" I moaned/ Hollered as Melissa was gripping my ass. I was shaking and cumming and attempting to pull Melissa's whole body inside of me! I almost slapped the shit out of her! Ask me why.. I really don't know, besides I'm cumming like a river, and I was so pissed at Frank and picturing this was Frank who was responsible for delivering this pain and the pleasure I'm experiencing. I don't know but I'm in outer space or something. After climaxing, I lay there spent, with Melissa laying on top of me, breathing hard. I caught myself still slowly grinding on the fake 12-in strap-on, that's when reality slapped me in the face! This big dilldor is not going to soften up, and this isn't real. The whole lesbian love affair / rebound type of thing is'nt completely what I want! I guess because I saw Frant today for the first time In about 3 or 4 years. Maybe two, it brought back all kinds of feelings! But I'm going to be strong right here, because I still have a plan for Frank! If I let the very vindictive side of me rule, I can follow through with it, get some get back / revenge and have a fulfillment of a desire I so badly want!

Chapter 4

Frank

"Do you want her in the buck like this?!" Said Joyce as she demonstrated on Jamie by grabbing Jamie's right thigh and falling back on the bed almost pinning her knees behind her head! "Flexible too ain't she Frank?" "Stop! Let my legs down!" Protested Jamie. In which she was letting Joyce do it anyway. "Okay now Joyce!" Said Jamie. "That coochie fat ain't it?" Asked Joyce as she petted between Jamie's thighs. I had met up with my cousin Anita and her friends at this party at Baja's Beach club.Upon arrival We immediately got lit ! The alcohol was flowing and the ladies were talking cash shit! "Damn Frank! You still want to try and get a taste of this!" said Joyce as she grabbed a handful of Jamie's ass. "UH-Huh!"I said as I nodded my head, and looking in Jamie's eyes. I'm trying to see if my intuition is on point! I think Joyce is bisexual and a bit jealous of me and Jamie chemistry. Or she wants me to fuck both of them! And which I wouldn't mind doing..tonight! Anyway Joyce was doing the same thing to Jamie at my family gathering. Making my mind play all types of tricks on me! I think the fruit is right for picking tonight. So as the night went on, we were vibing good! We hit the dance floor, and they both were all on me and Joyce was all on Jamie. We left the club together and ended up at Joyce's apartment. From the living room to the bedroom all three of us ended up. "Frank. Do you think you can handle all this?" Asked Joyce, referring to Jamie's, camel toe,between her legs but referring to herself on sly! Joyce is a very thick and bodacious type of chick. Nice double D titties, small waist, very curvaceous with a fat ass! "Huh Frank?" "UH-huh! That dick getting hard now!" said Joyce, as she stood up and slid her thin skirt over her ass! "Hell yeah!" I laughed as I un-buttoned my shirt and approached the two. Joyce's eyes were lighting up, as I peeled my button down Louis V shirt revealing my chiseled frame, under a tank top. Joyce immediately reached out and rubbed my chest. Without hesitation I rubbed that fat ass, which was hiding her thong real well! Jamie rose up as if she wanted to kiss me, but Joyce had beat her to the draw. She was quickly sticking her tongue in my mouth and simultaneously grabbing my dick."Umm!"Moaned Joyce, as she was marveled by the size of my tool. At that moment Jamie was rubbing on my shoulders but reaching for my belt. I helped her out by unfastening my belt and releasing this big black dick into both of their hands! They almost fought for it, but the intensity and passionate lust the moment created, was an instant peace maker, with the help of me instigating the mood, by Guiding Joyce's kisses to Jamie's hungry lips. I urgently started sucking on Jamie's neck as I tugged on her tight pants. She obliged by pulling her pants down with the help of Joyce. By now, my right hand was gripping her left ass cheek, while Joyce was gripping her right ass cheek. Competing With me, Joyce let one of her long fingernails brush up between Jamie's legs to her clit, causing Jamie to almost grunt and get on her tippy toes. Next thing you know cum was running down her caramel thighs. So all along, like I figured I got to go through Joyce, to get to Jamie like I want to! I got behind Joyce, almost forcing her to lay Jamie on the bed and she tooted that ass up for me, busting it open at the same time! I entered her with no remorse! "Ahh!" moaned Joyce with her mouth wide open. I held it there for a couple of seconds, but just slightly moved my waist from side to side. Jamie was grabbing Joyce by her hair making her get to the business of eating her out! As I slowly pulled my throbbing dick out of her halfway, I forcefully went back in, but in an upward hard stroke, letting her know she was about to get fucked! Real good too! I continued my rhythym, but I slowly but surely picked up my speed, almost to a franticPace, looking at Jamie make all kinds of fuck faces! At times, Joyce would stop eating, so she could enjoy this porno style fucking I was putting on her! "Uh, Oh, Oh my god!" moaned Joyce as I was bringing her to multiple orgasms! I really wanted to fuck her too, once I first met her, but Jamie took that attention. But look how the laws of the universe deliver! I have both of them in bed, in the most satisfying way imaginable! I thought I was doing good by not cumming too fast, but it was mounting, in an intense way! "Siss..Hell yeah!"I said Just before busting off. I wasn't about to be finished! I wanted to have sex with sexy ass Jamie! She's the reason for this season right now! I pulled my rod up out of Joyce and went to Joyce's mouth with a shiny dick ready to be sucked. With no hesitation Joyce looked me dead in my eyes and started sucking and slurping all around my penis. She knew what she was doing,because she made my soldier stand at attention, quick like! While she was slurping me down, Jaimie was eating her from the back! Joyce was doing a great job at the same time, looking at me in my eyes periodically. I'm trying to keep my attention off of her friend. It wasn't working well. Because my mind stayed on fucking her good also! Jamie came up for a little air, I was grabbing Jamie her hair, guiding her to me, as Joyce continued to swallow me whole! With lustful eyes Jamie and I were engulfed in a deep compassionate and much anticipated kiss! Tasting Joyce's juices on Jamie's tongue, didn't do but awaken the beast in me! Switching my full attention to Jamie, I pulled out Joyce's mouth, and I entered Jamie, and she laid on back throwing her legs on my shoulders. Ultimate pleasure being shared by the both of us, as we grind and fuck each other as if we have been promising each other we would do this once we met up! No holds barred, Jamie and i was fuckin each other with passion! Joyce tried to join in, but Jamie pushed her back. She wanted all this good loving to herself! "Damn bitch!" Said Joyce who was kind of disappointed in Jamie's decision but at the same time, Joyce was exhausted from our sexscapade, and 2/3 drunk So, she laid to the side and went to sleep just like that! Meanwhile, Jamie and iexperimented in sweaty sex until we both passed out!

Chapter 5

Tracy

"What?! You want me to send Frank a friend request? Or do you want me to send a request to Frank's business page like you did?" "Yes!" I said, answering Melissa's question. "Okay!" Said Melissa, "How is this going to be beneficial to us? I mean.. What's your aim or should I say goal, in doing this?" "Because his girlfriend is your type!" I said. "My type? You mean his business partner Angela? Isn't that her name?" "Yes!" I said as I flicked the icon on our smart TV to the Facebook app and went to Frank's business page. "See." I was pointing to Angela on their business page. "Or you could just send her a friend request to her personal page." Melissa sat there for a moment observing Angela as we trolled her page with a slight smile on her face. "So basically, you want me to take Frank's girlfriend from him?" Laughed Melissa. "No, not like that! What are you trying to tell me? You don't want me anymore." I said to Melissa, jokingly. Girl, find something to do!" laughed Melissa. "I mean. Do him like my ex? Fuck the side chick?" We both laughed at that joke. "Yes!" I said with such enthusiasm that It made Melissa suddenly get quiet! "You're serious Tracy?" "I've never been so serious, probably in my entire life!" "Well.. Here goes nothing!" Said Melissa As she sent Angela and Frank's business page a friend request, and she sent Angela's personal page one. "So.. We are setting a trap for Frank? And if so, why?" asked Melissa. "Well.. Because!" "Because what? You want some type of retribution Tracy?" No Melissa! Well... Hell yeah I do!" 'Remember. The first part of rehabilitating yourself, is to forgive the ones who may have done you wrong." "Melissa I understand where you're coming from, but fuck all that ! I don't need any counseling right now baby! I need you to charm this, this Angela bitch! I need you to see if they're in love, and if that's so, I want you to go in for the kill!" "Okay Tracy, so what if she isn't gay?" Asked Melissa. "Make her gay! Shit, you turned me out!" "No! You turned yourself out Tracy. I just help you identify those homosexual tendencies you had." "Yeah right.. I was seduced." "Okay seduced." Laughed Melissa. At that moment Melissa was receiving a notification that Angela had accepted her friend request. "She didn't even know me and she accepted. Even though that doesn't mean anything." "Well to me it's a start." I said . "Yeah a start... Right!" Melissa said. As she laughed. "Yea Melissa, it's a start because if she bite the hook like I want her to, then it's on!" Melissa was sitting there smiling, as she strolled through Angela's pics. " Hmm Sexy!" said Melissa. As she stopped at a picture of Angela with a skirt on. I was smiling at first So till it dawned on me when that pic was taken. "Funky bitch!" I said before I knew it. Melissa was stunned for a moment. "What?" "I remember when that pic was taken! That was at the Christmas party!"

"Oh!" said Melissa. "Well. She was looking good that night." I looked at Melissa as if I wanted to bite her head off! "Whaat?" said Melissa in her exaggerating tone. "You're with me or not?" I asked, getting a little agitated. "Of course Tracy!" "Okay. We need to find a way to seduce her. Simple as that!" Melissa looked at me with a sparkle in her eyes. "Let's do it!"

Frank

I was sitting back watching the news in my office, when I got a Facebook notification on my phone. I was shocked when I opened the notification. It was from Tracy to my business page! Now I'm looking like the emoji in which he has his hand on his chin as if in deep thought about something. Saying "Humm !?" Of course I accepted it. Off the top, I went scrolling and looked through her photos. I want to see how she is looking these days. She had blocked me from her old pages. "Damn!" I said to myself, as I stopped on one of her pics with some type of khaki color shorts on. Standing to the side, flexing that round booty she got. Tracy had gained a few pounds in all the right places! Tracy was dark brown, Well kind of cocoa brown, with a slim fine physique or should I say slim thick. "Damn Tracy! You are still fine! Finer!" I said out loud as I continued to look through her pics. I noticed on a lot of her pics, she was with this cute light skin chick. "She's fine too!" I said. I never met her the whole time I was with Tracy. Even though I know I haven't met a lot of her friends , as tight as Her and the new woman seem to be,If she's From around here , I would have seen her a lot! Well, it doesn't matter, because I'm glad Tracy thought about me enough to refriend me. Who knows it may lead to something bigger! As I was strolling, I ran up on some pics of her other girlfriends Tawanda and Tanita , and my mind immediately went to her fake ass friend Tanita! They were acting all shitty towards me, that day I came to the hospital. I understood their stance against me at that moment. But I could recall the times when I used to come around Tracy, and they would be all play, play, and flirty, but with Tanita, I had noticed how she would still be flirting with her eyes, way after they would talk their shit! Months and months after Tracy broke up with me, Tanita made her move on me! All of us were friends on Facebook and I think they all unfriended me. I was always pretty active on Instagram, and always encountered all types of people. Women to be specific. Some are real and some are hackers. It's just like any other social media platforms, some be catfished! Fake pages, using a pretty ass woman's picture as a profile pic, and the real one may be ugly and unattractive. Then some on the fake pages, be a person you know, playing childish games. In Tanita's case, That was her! Tanita had started following me on IG under a fake name and a whole fake person! I followed her back, without even thinking at first.. Till she got in my DM . For about a month or so, we just casually message each other. To see if she was fake or not, I video called her unexpectedly. When she wouldn't answer, I threatened to block her! Because now I'm knowing this is a catfish move, and to make matters worse on my end, in my mind I am thinking this may be a homosexual! Jenny was her name. So I told Jenny I thought she was a queer dude, acting like a chick so if she doesn't prove to me that she's a real female, she was getting blocked! So she told me, if I wanted to get with her as well as I said I did, she told me to get a room then better yet, she said that she would get it ! I asked her when? And she said whenever! So we planned it for the following weekend. She claims that she was from Texas and had to catch a flight here in Tallahassee Florida. So I obliged to her idea and agreed to meet up with her. I told her if she isn't who she betrays to be I'm leaving, with no questions asked! And if she's a dude, I have a big pistol with me. This particular weekend, on a Saturday night to be exact, Jenny / Tanita DM me through Instagram telling me to come to the Gate hotel, right outside of Springfield Florida. I was a little skeptical for a moment. But I thought about how pretty this chick was, and was slim-fine! So I went ahead and jumped in my low key whip which was a Chevy Silverado truck and took off to the hotel. I rode around The parking lot, trying to spot a known car or anything that looked funny or out of place. I didn't tell her I was there, I just went in the hotel, got on the elevator and went to the 15th floor, where her room was located. Once I found the room, I hesitated for a moment. Looking almost suspicious myself, I put my ear up against the door to hear anything suspicious! I heard some old school music that sounded like Al.B Sure's, killing me softly! "Hum" , I said to myself. Because Jenny told me she was 29, did she know about Al B Sure!? Then that's kind of dumb on my part, because her parents might've been playing it, so she would have more than likely, liked it. I knocked on the door a couple of times, and with no delay I heard a female voice. "Who is it?" "Frank!" I answered. The door is open, come in. Her voice sounded familiar, but distant. "I'm in the bathroom, I'll be right out." As I walked in the room, I noticed she had the lights turned down a little, but not dark. Automatically, I was clutching on my big block 40 Because these days you never know. Then this is Florida! I even looked up under the bed. I didn't take a seat so I stood there and waited for her to Come out of the bathroom. After about 2 minutes, I became jittery. "Are you okay in there," I asked? Right then, the door opens. Once this so-called Jenny bent the corner, I almost hollered! "What the fuck!" I said as Tanita walked up to me. I was stunned and just knew this was a setup! "Okay Tanita, Enough with y'all childish ass games. Where's Tracy?!" Frank, calm down! This is not a setup!" said Tanita. "Huh?! What do you mean? You're shooting me those messages all the time?! And you're saying not a setup?" "Okay you think that I'm setting you up dressed like this?" Said Tanita. She had on some sexy ass chantilly lace, plunge teddy, with a plunge garter slip. Ask me how I know all of that? Because I bought Tracy a couple of those before! She had a point. "So what's up Tanita? Why play the catfish game?"

"Because, I wasn't sure you would talk to me on that level. All you would have been asking about was Tracy , and that would have been irrelevant to my interior motives." Said Tanita, as she slowly, But in a sexy way, sashayed up to me. She knew I was stunned. "Interior motives?" I asked,Really playing dumb. "Come on Frank! You know what time it is.. When you were with Tracy we shared a chemistry then. I always used to catch you looking at me, Frank." "Looking back at you watching me!" I said in my defense." Oh yeah? So why is your dick getting hard?" Said Tanita, as she leaned back to get a better look at my print. She had her middle finger between her teeth, biting on it, looking sexy as fuck! She almost favored Nia Long, but Tanita was more of a sexy kind of curvy, full-figured woman. "Yeah it is getting hard. I'm letting you know too, if y'all play games, that shit don't count now, because I ain't with Tracy." "What's up then?!" I said as I pulled this 12-inch dick out on her. "Yeah, Let's get this shit cracking!" Said Tanita As she grabbed my dick and stroked it. "Damn Tracy wasn't lying about this big motherfucker." Siss! Umm!" said Tanita   As she gobbled up half of my penis. I wasn't playing with her. I grabbed a fist full of her hair, thrusting slowly in her mouth! I don't know what it is about having secret sex affairs with women you shouldn't be having them with, but it's some type of aphrodisiac. Because right now, I'm so turned on, that my dick got so hard that a cat couldn't scratch it! After I let her treat my dick like a popsicle, I got behind her on the bed and the rest was history! Tanita and i snuck around and fucked for a couple of months, and she started getting kind of crazy and a bit possesive, So I quickly got out of there. Anyway as I'm going through Tracy pics, I built up the nerves to inbox her. [Hey Tracy!] I sent the message, but I wasn't totally Sure she would respond. Me knowing her, she might have me sweat. While I was sitting there looking through emails, I got a call from Angela. "I wonder what's on her mind?" I said to myself as I answered the phone." What's up

Angela?" "Hey Frank! How are you?" "I'm good! What's on your mind?" "I was just doing a little research on this quarterback from University of Alabama, but that ain't why I called you. I called you because I just got a friend request from a chick who is friends with your ex Tracy." "Oh yeah? What's her name?" "Melissa Woods. Her profile says she's a counselor." said Angela. "I'm looking her up now. Wow, this is the same chic on Tracy's page!" I said. "On Tracy's page? I thought y'all weren't friends there anymore?" Said Angela, like she was my old lady. "She sent me a friend request." I answered. "Oh yeah? That's kind of strange! You get a friend request from Tracy and I get one from her friend. Sounds like some messy stuff to me!" Said Angela. And she may be onto something! "You may be right. But what are they going to be messy about?" "It's just messy in nature! They want to be nosy and see what we got going on!" "Kind of harmless." I said, trying to sound modest. "Okay, we will see!" Angela was sounding funny about the whole situation, in which there wasn't anything. After she hung up, I did my own investigation on this Melissa chic. I looked up her Counseling services /business , and it was legit! She had her own business. That's not strange for a woman like Tracy to have friends on the same level as her. Professional / black woman. Now, her sending Angela friend requests may have been coincidental, but it is strange, because I know Tracy told her how I betrayed her, and the way it happened! Well, if she is some type of counselor, she might be Doing some type of study. Oh well, time will tell!

Chapter 6

Tracy

"This nigga done sent me a message!" I said before I knew it. "Of course he sent you a message!" Said Melissa, "What did you think he would do, considering the circumstances?" "Huh? Circumstances?!" I said, as if I was dumbfounded. "Don't play dumb Tracy! You knew that after seeing him in traffic, and you sending him a friend request, would ignite a fire within him! He's thinking that you have forgiven him, for fucking his coworker Angela, at the Christmas party right under your nose! I must add. So.. He's thinking it's on! He feels you might just take him back!"said Melissa. "Okay, okay.. You're right baby, but I do not want him to feel as if he's forgiven." "That's a great way of making him drop his guards." "Okay. Are you going to answer him back?" asked Melissa."Yes.. But not now. Make him sweat a little bit." "Make him sweat a little bit? He's as apprehensive as he's going to be right now! I don't think all of that is necessary." Said Melissa. "And why do you say that?" "Because, he knows you! Yeah, he know he did some fucked up shit, but he knows you enough to not have to be sitting back waiting on yours response.Soon, he's just going to call you! So do you have a strategy up until that point?" "Yes..I do! If he just so happen to call and I'm not ready to talk to him, I just won't answer. And if I answer, I would just be quiet, and let him talk.You know how we do! Play off of his guilt! Then I will play it by ear, and go from there. You can bet, I'm not trying to take him back!" With that being said, Melissa just sat there. What?! I asked Melissa. "Time will tell. That's all I have to say." "Okay. We will see!" I laughed. Now, I don't know if Melissa is being insecure right now, because it's Frank. And she knew how I felt about him, or is she just being concerned about me, wanted me to be cautious? Hell, it was my idea, the whole set up thing. My revenge! "Well Melissa, it's like this.. We're going to stick to our plan! And our plan is for you, to seduce his girlfriend, some kind of way. We need to be putting our heads together on that . And let's not worry about Frank. I will handle him!" "Okay Tracy.. I'm not going to doubt you and your will power towards dealing with Frank, I just want you to be careful." There! Melissa came out with it! She's more concerned about me keeping my guards up on Frank. "Don't worry baby I will." I said, as I went to where Melissa was sitting on the floor, Going through some paperwork. I did something that I really ever do , and that was being the aggressor when it's time to get intimate with her. I reached out with my right hand and gently took my fingers and rubbed the top of her left ear. Smoothing her hair out. I caressed her left jaw, and took my hand and placed it just below her hairline, caressing her neck. Obviously, Melissa was enjoying it! She had her eyes closed, mouth slightly opened, as I began to slowly run my fingers through her hair. "Uh-umm." moaned Melissa. I had my clothes on, but my hot pussy was dead in her face! Immediately I unbuttoned and unzipped my jeans and in a slightly hurried fashion, I pulled my jeans down to my knees, and guided Melissa's face directly to my slippery slit between my legs. being the professional pussy eater that she is, she started tongue kissing my swollen lips, and sucking my throbbing clit.. With no hands! It felt awkward because normally I'm on my back, when she's eating me out, but now, I'm standing up like I'm a dude, getting some head! By no means, am I a butch bitch. We're just regular lesbians, although Melissa is the aggressor mostly but she isn't Butch! I'm just in a super freaky mode right now. I guess my plans for Frank and Angela had me hot! Truth be told, I was picturing Melissa as Frank eating me, as I stood over him! I guess I feel empowered, if I make him bow down, and suck my clit! But with no feelings attached. "Damn baby! What are you trying to do? You don't have a dick. Why you're trying to fuck my mouth?" Said Melissa, as she looked up at me with my juices and cum shining around her mouth. I guess I had zoned out, while I was imagining she was Frank giving me head! So I was being a dog with it! "My bad baby!" I said, as I continued rubbing her head. She stood right up and kissed me like she's missing me! This wasn't the first time I had tasted my own juices, coming from Melissa's mouth, but at the same time , this act was very intense.. And nasty! Not nasty to my taste buds, but the very act itself was a porno moment! "Whoa! Let's catch our breath baby!" I said, it seems as if Melissa was in a zone. Because her response wasn't in words, nothing but actions!

She started running her fingers through my hair, subtly guiding me to my knees. With no hesitation, I blessed her nonverbal requests , as she was dropping the booty short she had on, to her ankles. When I got to my steamy destination, it was hot and sticky. Melissa gently grabs a fist full of my hair, pulls my head back so she can look me in my eyes. "Now baby, I want you to pretend that this pussy is Frank's dick, while I pretend or imagine that you are Angela eating this pussy! Just like you just imagined, I was Frank eating your pussy, and then your plan to get that revenge you want so badly will manifest!" Said Melissa as she slammed my face into her pussy! "Let's manifest baby!"

Chapter 7

Angela

After hanging the phone up, from my call to Frank, I was sitting there going through this chic's, Melissa's Facebook page.That's something normal, I guess when you get a friend request from someone you don't know, especially if that person is a friend of someone who doesn't like you, maybe your competition. And some strange way a potential composition. In this case,it's potential opposition. The reason I'm feeling this way is because she's friends with Tracy! Not just Facebook friends, but real friends! They are in a lot of pics together and some of the pics are somewhat intimate or should I say, it seems as if their besties are lovers! I'm going to call it like I see it. Like my grandfather used to say a shovel is a shovel and a spade is a spade! So to me, like I told Frank I think it's messy shit going on! Before I go too far, and make too many pre-judgmental assumptions. Let me think about it. "Hmm,some messy shit!" I said out loud, because if they're close as they look, Tracy told her about when she caught me red-handed with Frank! In the bathroom stall at that! How slutty of me. But I basically took Frank from Miss Tracy, so I know she knows who I am! This Melissa girl. But if she wants to be nosy, messy, or whatever her motives are, I'm going to entertain it! With that thought, I accepted her friend request and immediately got in her inbox. " Hello?" I said with my text, to really get it poppin. If she inboxes me back, then I'm going to pick her head. The shit really got me curious! Frank, he doesn't really think much of the whole ordeal. All he's probably thinking about is Tracy. Thinking she's ready to take him back! Hmph! We will see about that. Well, Frank and I haven't really been on good terms. We haven't had sex in a minute. We rarely talk unless it's business. That's cool though, because Frank is not the only fish in the sea! To have sex with him, and to take him from that want to be, bougie chick, Tracy, was me fulfilling an unfulfilled desire. I didn't mind helping him when he came to the sports agency where we used to work. I didn't mind helping him with his dream of opening and owning a sports agency. Hell, it was my dream too! To own a sports agency. So with my clout, experience, reputation, and clientele and some money.. Well, mostly his money, we made it happen! I helped him or should I say we fulfilled a desire, which was much needed. The money is rolling in, our clientele building, so we are basically in a good position. So, back to my relationship with Frank! He's very cool and all, but he's been handling me, like I'm one of his young side pieces. So, me being the Boss Bitch / cougar I am, I should snatch me up a young side piece NFL football player. Yes, one of our clients and a young female sports trainer! Yes, I go both ways.Mostly, I love men. But I can't lie.. An attractive female, especially when I'm feeling super freaky, will do the job. I don't know, it seems like the orgasm will be 100 times more intense, when I get a woman. That part of me was first exposed when I was a senior in high school. I had started hanging, with one of my home girl's cousins, who was a little older than us. She was like a junior in college, and me being a little fast ass, I like to go on campus with her, over at Florida A&M. I attended a lot of parties and kickbacks with her. I knew she went both ways, but I didn't have a problem with it, she was schooling me to the college lifestyle and the streets! But mostly the college lifestyle. Long story short, I kind of turned myself out, into the lesbian world. I was already curious, and Alicia, my home girl's cousin, was a very attractive girl, and on the low, I was very attracted to her. It was obvious that she was attracted to me. She looked, but never touched or said anything out of the way, to me. One night, we attended a wild party, which was an off campus party. We got drunk and headed to her apartment. I don't know what happened, but once we entered the apartment inside on the couch. Within 10 seconds Alicia and I were attacking each other! Sexual attacks attacking each other that is. And the rest was history. I was still heavily into men but, when the chance permitted itself I was crossing that line and getting with some women! Fast forward to the present, I'm sitting here, thinking about some wild sex tonight, with my young chic and then I get a messenger notification. "Damn! About time." I said as I was hoping for this Melissa chic inbox. [Hey, how are you?] Read the text. [I'm fine and you?] I replied. [I'm great! Thanks for asking.] Damn! She is on it! I mean she's responding back so fast! Let me get to the nitty gritty of this conversation. "So.. How am I so highly honored to receive a friend request from you?" Getting to the point and getting in her shit at the same time, but in a nice professional way. [You look kind of familiar, and to be honest you're a very attractive woman!] "Damn!" I said, out loud before I knew it. "She just came right out with it! How does she know if I get down like that or not!?" I said to no one in particular because I was in my office with the door closed. Now should I take the offensive approach or should I just thank her for the compliment? [Bold statement to make to a total stranger! But I'll accept the compliment. Thank you!] Well, I checked her and accepted her compliment at the same time! [Well.. I apologize if I offended you.] I could tell that she is ready to dialogue to the fullest. She was texting back so fast! [Oh before I go too far, I am a lesbian , but I still like men. Lol. But I don't want to think I'm making a pass at you!] Wow this chic is tripping! I said [How are you not making a pass at me? Lol!] [Because I didn't ask you out, nor did I say anything sexually to you. But I do find you intriguing.] Just like that! This Melissa chick is sly and aggressive! Interesting, because she doesn't look like she's a butch bitch. And she finds me intriguing. Lord, I have heard it all! I am kind of speechless at the moment. So I take a moment to respond. As I'm sitting here contemplating on what to say, she initiated the move. [Hello?] Said Melissa in her text. I'm sitting here thinking, if I respond in the wrong way, it may send the wrong signal. If I don't just straight up tell her to get the fuck out of my inbox, That would be a slight clue that I might just be a little interested in her sneaky indecent proposal! My mind is telling me to straight dis this freak, but my body and the freak in me is telling me to respond in a straight up, let's get it poppin way! Along with the tingling and moistness in my panties! Fuck it, i'm following the tingling and the hardness of my clit! She can be catfishing me. Well, I'm about to see. [Hey Miss Melissa, let's cut through the chase. Let's meet at Starbucks tomorrow. Pick a time!] there! I said as I pressed the send button. "You want to get entertained? Let's do it Miss Melissa. With your fine ass!" I said to the computer screen.

Tracy

"Oh - my - God! You made the shit look easy! I told you bitch!" I said As I gave Melissa a high five. "I mean.. I wasn't even looking for her to respond like that! At least not this quick." Said Melissa. "But what did I tell you? I told you if she's not gay, you can turn her out!" I said to Melissa. "Tracy.. It's clear that this woman is gay! I mean, she goes both ways, no doubt about it but once she didn't correct my advances towards her and stick to it, bam! That was a no-brainer then. She wasn't used to a woman that doesn't look butch being the aggressor. You know what I mean?" "Right! And she didn't ask you anything about me. Because I know she's done been all through your page and photos!" "Oh no doubt about it, so we got to see where her brain is at the moment." Said Melissa. Now, my brain is telling me that this bitch Angela, is curious about Melissa. I know she's going to ask Melissa about me. But we are going to play past all of her curiosity, some kind of way. She wants to meet Melissa tomorrow at Starbucks. I wonder what's her motive? "Melissa baby, what is Angela's interior motive for wanting to meet you tomorrow?" "Well... She's curious, because obviously she knows you and I are friends, but her motive is purely deceit, and action! She's one of those women that love a challenge and heavy competition! So all of that supports her actions and therefore her ulterior motives!" Said Melissa, in straight evaluation mode. When I thought about her evaluation of Angela and the whole situation, I totally agreed with her. "Baby you're right! Everything you said about her and her ulterior motives is dead right! Very accurate of you!" "Why thank you! Now let's put our heads together, to see how we are going to skin this cat!" I said, giving Melissa another high five.

Frank

"You got a message from.. Tracy's friend huh?" I was talking to Angela in my office. She was filling me in on her communication with the female who I saw in Tracy's pics. "Yeah.. In fact, we inboxed each other to the point of setting up a small coffee date!" Laughs Angela." A date?" I asked in surprise. So you're saying she's gay?" I want Angela to confirm my instincts. "I guess.. Or it may be the fact that I look so good, that a bitch will turn gay to try to get with me! You feel me?!" Said Angela, as she was turning around posing and flexing. I mean, with this all white see-through leather skirt. I must say, the skirt is catching every curve she may have in her lower body. "Ummph!"I said before I knew it. "Oh, you're liking what you see?" said Angela. I laid back and started smiling. "You haven't had it in a minute. It's even tighter than before." said Angela, as she was looking down admiring herself. "We will see! But how did you find out she was gay?" I said, to change the subject. Because truth be told, I'm ready to have a long fuck session with Angela. Now! "Well.. Long story short, when I asked her what's up, why did she contact me , she said she found me attractive and we went from there! I set up a meeting for lunch or coffee today. I was sitting there, with my finger on my chin and deep thoughts. I was feeling a little jealous, because of the female and got my Tracy! I guess what happened between Angela and I drove her to women! "Hello!" said Angela, snapping her fingers in my face. "Oh my bad! My mind had drifted off." I said. "I bet it did! What are you thinking about? That sexy ass counselor bitch, eating and licking Tracy to sleep!" Laughed Angela, she strutted off to the door. "I'll see you later.. I have a coffee date, so don't wait up for me!" I just smiled at Angela, and she went out the door. I was most definitely picturing Melissa and Tracy getting it on! I was feeling some type of way for real It first. But now, my mind is straight in the gutter! Because now the playing field has changed. My competition is a woman, and she has possession so to speak of my woman! Well my ex-woman, but still my pride kind of hurts. I guess it's an ego thing though. So now that hurt has turned to getting even! I really don't have any reason to get even, but these gutter thoughts got me formulating a plan! My plan is to disrupt their peace. Not a domestic violence type of way, but put this big dick in the picture amongst nothing but pussy, I think if I play it like it goes, I can have my cake and eat it too! If Tracy won't accept me back, I'll just wiggle my way in through Angela And fuck her lover Melissa! Have a threesome with her and Angela. Matter of fact the resentment I'm feeling towards Tracy for letting a woman take my place, got me wanting to take Melissa from her and have Angela also! "Damn!" I said to myself . Because I'm thinking kind of petty right here. Or am I? I mean, I know I'm wrong for thinking like this, because I'm the reason for Tracy leaving me, when I played Adam and bit the forbidden fruit, what Angela offered me. Yes! She was Eve in the situation! And the serpent was us, yielding to our unfulfilled desires!

Oh well, I just have to come up with the strategy to get in where I fit in!

Chapter 8

Tracy

I'm sitting in my office, trying to concentrate on my work, but it seems at the moment, my mind is everywhere. Why? Because Melissa has been on her little coffee date with Angela, for the last 3 hours! Damn, is Melissa already between that hot, bitch, thighs? Well, I wouldn't count it out. I have sent two or three text messages. Oh well, I guess I'll just wait on her. While I was waiting for Melissa I decided I would stroll through my messages from Facebook. I'm so used to people sending attachments and off-brand men, all in my inbox, that I barely pay any attention to them. I forgot Frank had inbox me, and I have contemplated long and hard on answering him back! Well, Melissa and I came up with our little scheme on him and Angela, I might as well play it like it goes! I was procrastinating on replying to Frank, because I wasn't sure that my emotions was ready! Well, I'm ready now.. I think! [Hey Frank, how are you?] There it is! I responded to Frank, so it's time for me to participate all the way! Frank is probably right now in his office, looking at his phone or computer, smiling. I know his hope has risen, thinking I want him back. That is so far from the truth! While I sat there thinking about Frank's reaction to my message, he was responding. [I can't complain Tracy.. I'm so glad you responded! Lol.] [I bet you are.] I text back. Frank.. [Look.. On a serious note, I apologize.] There he goes! Opening up old wounds. He's smart enough to know not to do that! But at the same time, he's probably so excited, he didn't really know which route to take. So I'm going to play it cool and not go off on him. Even though my emotions are almost raging! But I got to control my emotions and play the game how it's supposed to be played! [I forgive you Frank.. I haven't forgotten, but I do forgive you!] Now that he thinks that he's forgiven, he's about to ask me out! I'll bet $100 against a bucket of shit. Frank.[.Whew! Thanks Tracy.. Can I take you out to dinner or something?] "Wow! This fool is all gas no breaks" I said! "I think not Buster! I said out loud being silly. Me.. [Homey, I am so over you, so pump your brakes! I mean we are cool, I can be cool, but no dates!] I had to be harsh with Frank in that text message. I am nipping it in the bud, like the old folks say. Shut it down before he gets it started. Frank.. [My bad Tracy! I didn't mean any harm.] Me.. [You're straight.] So now, Frank Mind is wondering. The exact thing, in which I wanted to happen. For him to be confused! Take him to the top, and then let him drop! I'm going to continue and lead him on, by being friendly In time he makes any kind of advancements towards me, I'm shutting him down! After that last message, Frank hasn't hit back yet, but Melissa has! [Melissa .. What's up boo?! Everything seems to be going as planned!] me.. [You seduced her already and you're somewhere bumping pussy and eating Angela's whole inside out!] Melissa..[No silly! we're still sitting here talking. She's going to the restroom now. But she's very ready and willing to go the distance!] Me.. [That's what's up! Go the distance?] Melissa.. [Yes! The distance. Very soon! Like real soon, the weekend soon!] Wow! Melissa works very fast! I can barely wait for her to come home, so she can give me every detail! Me.. [Okay.. You need to hurry up and come home! Lol]. I inboxed Melissa, now here's a message from Frank. Frank..[Well, whenever time permits, can I at least talk to you? On some real life friendly conversation type of thing?] Haha! He wants to talk! I think I will play with him.. well. We will see. And with that, I got off of messenger. That's when Melissa came through the door smiling. "Tracy, this plan is about to go down! I swear!" Said Melissa. Melissa was so excited, when she came in the house, she dropped her purse on the coffee table Hard as hell! "Hey don't break that table!" I said, as Melissa sat down next to me on the couch." Look. I got her! What I found out, she has been gay! I mean she liked men, but she dibble and dabbled with females also! So it wasn't hard to get her, she was just super curious...as to.." "Why did you choose her and your friends with me!" I said, interrupting and finishing Melissa's statement. "Well.. Yes! There you have it. But she's a daring ass bitch!" I said to Melissa."What did she say about me?" "I'm getting to that part! Pipe down Miss Tracy! Basically, she wanted to know what was our involvement, you and I. I told her we were friends with benefits. She covered her mouth, as if she had heard something bad, but it doesn't deter her for wanting to hook up with me. Matter of fact, it seem like it made her hot or something ! Willing to get with me. So willing, she is ready this weekend!" Said Melissa. Now, my mind is wondering like a mother fucker. I wonder what she has against me! She wants to disrupt my life, by fucking everybody I fuck! Let me calm down because it was my plan from the beginning. "Okay, that sounds great". Everything is going smoothly. I love it when a plan comes together.

Chapter 9

Frank

"Say what!" I said before I knew it. I was on the phone with Angela, and she was filling me in on her meeting with Melissa, who is a friend of my ex-girl Tracy. "You mean to tell me you all have a date or something?" "Why do you sound surprised, Frank? Underestimated my skills?" Said Angela being cocky. I had learned a couple of years ago that Angela went both ways. She likes men and women! Let me rephrase that. She likes women, but loves men! "No Angela, I didn't underestimate your skills. I just didn't know what was up with this Melissa chick. So, you're saying she's gay right?" "Yes Frank. She is gay, and yes I do believe that your dear Tracy is her lover! No cap!" Said Angela. She knew that she was striking a nerve, by insinuating that Melissa and Tracy are lovers. As a man , we are naturally going to be offended, our ego suffers a temporary shattering, if a female takes our own woman. Well, in my case, Melissa didn't necessarily take my woman. But it still kind of fucks with me and my ego! "Hello - hello! Cat must got your tongue? Oh.. But we know it's not Tracy's cat!" Laughed Angela. "Yeah, I am here! Like I said, I was just thinking." "No, you're discombobulated! Never would you ever believe that sweet Tracy was into girls!" No, no, Angela. Well. I am surprised! All of that uppity shit was a facade!" I said. "She can be uppity and be gay at the same time. Everybody isn't wide open like that. Or have you ever blamed yourself?" asked Angela and that struck a nerve in which made me jump! "Blame myself? For her going gay? Well for a moment, I did! No lie. I did that! I was thinking back, when she caught me with your conniving ass, that had such a bad effect on her mind, that she said to hell with all men!" "Wait a minute.. You called me, conniving Frank ?!" Said Angela. "Yes I did Angela, but let's not waste time debating about that little bit right now." "Umph!..Excuse me then! Conniving.. But anyway, I have a date with Melissa, unofficially this weekend, and I'm going to relax and see what the night brings!." said Angela I was sitting there picturing the two involved in uninhibited sex, my dick was Getting bone hard! "Frank, are you there?" "Oh my bad! I was sitting here... In a daze".. "fantasizing about me and Melissa. Getting freaky!" Interrupted Angela. "I can't invite you now, maybe next time! "Haha, very funny Angela. I couldn't do that because, I don't think you're ready for that kind of action!" "Oh really? I'm ready. Are you ready? I mean..Ah-Ha!I take that back! You are ready!" Said Angela, as she was having an ah-ha moment. "You want me to lock in with Melissa, So you can get some revenge on your sweet little Tracy! Am I right?!" "No you're totally wrong Angela!" I said, "But you know what? Now there's a light bulb going off in my head!" "No, I'm Totally right! I think.. Do you want me to get Melissa to do a threesome with you, and we film it!?" "Hell no! We can't get caught up in anything like that. Remember we are sports agents, not porn stars." Angela found all of this to be funny, but the wheels in my head are turning like crazy. I got to play reverse psychology best as I can with Angela, to uphold a certain image, but the only problem with that is Angela have made me fall weak before and it fucked up my perfect fairytale relationship I had with Tracy! Look Frank.. I'm going to go out with Melissa or whatever, but you know me, I'm trying to push it to the limit! And taste this little chic! Who knows, I might persuade her to get Tracy lil sexy ass in the bed with us! I'll holla back!" Said Angela and hung up on me. Angela was dead serious, but was saying it as a joke. In all actuality, Angela's twisted thinking has become my own reasoning at this point. Even though Tracy is not my girl anymore, I do feel some kind of way about her and Melissa. So hell yeah, I'm with Angela! I grabbed my phone and called her. Yes, right. I said Angela. Hey Angela! I'm with you on what you were talking about, but let's work on Melissa first. "Let's work on Melissa first?!" Repeated Angela. "Oh, what brings on the change of heart? Revenge? Or is it just that your male ego is more fragile than you pretend?" "Angela.. I pictured me, fucking you and that little pretty sexy ass Melissa to sleep!

Chapter 10

The weekend

Tracy

"So, where are you and Miss Hot panties meeting up?" "Well, first we are meeting up at the lounge at Market Square, to have a few drinks, then I guess we will let the night take over!" Said Melissa, somewhat being sarcastic. "Whoa! What's up with the hostility?!" I asked. "There isn't any hostility Tracy. Why are you picking a fight? Remember, this whole thing was your idea! So that was not the time to be jumping in your feelings, thinking I'm in my feelings, when all the time that's you lashing out ! Displaying your inner jealousy!" I sat there with my mouth wide open, in Mock surprise. Not just in what Tracy has said, but the mere fact that she was correct. But I'm under control! "Come on Melissa now. It's not the time to be clinical either! Come here!" I said, being more the dominant lover, than usual. In which kind of surprised Melissa, I must confess she was looking rather tasty at this moment. She had on a tight khaki color semi short skirt on, with a sexy pink strapless blouse on. "Are you deaf? Come here." I said with my right hand on my hip. Melissa knew when I meant business, when I wanted her to submit to that submissive side of her. She approached me with caution in her step. Aggressively I ran my left hand through her hair, impassionately tonguing her down! After 20 to 30 seconds of mesmerizing Melissa top I quickly dropped to my knees, pulled her skirt up, panties to the side, and started passionately tongue kissing her throbbing spur tongue! "St-stop Tracy!" Moaned Melissa. She was rubbing my head with both hands And she's slowly grinding her hips against my face. Melissa wrapped her right leg around my head, as she fell against the wall. I could tell when she was close to having an orgasm, so within seconds of her reaching her climax, I suddenly stopped licking and I rose up and kissed her hungrily! Making her taste all over her juices and pre-cum. Melissa gasped at my spontaneous move, and I ran my middle finger up into her throbbing and wet love canal. Bringing her to that ultimate nut she was chasing! "Oh! Oh my God baby!" Moaned Melissa, as she slid down the wall. "Tracy baby, what are you trying to do? Make me miss my date with Angela?" "No. I'm getting you warmed up for that slut! Now go get her!" After Melissa got herself together, she headed out the door. She stopped and looked back at me.. "Tracy? Don't stay up and wait on me." Laughed Melissa. "Because I might bring her home and I don't want any bullshit to jump off!" "Don't worry Melissa.. Matter of fact tell her I forgive her." With that statement, Melissa winked her eyes and walked out of the door.

Angela

"Hey Melissa! How are you love?!" "I'm good, just getting in the car." Said Melissa, sounding out of breath. "Are you okay? You sound tired and out of breath already! Are you nervous?" I asked Melissa. "No! Laughed Melissa. "No, I'm kind of in a rush and.. You know how that is." "Yeah.. "You good, because I'm just getting in the car myself ! You know how us girls are! Last minute adjustments, have us running late! Well, I'm not going to hold you up, I'll meet you at the spot." "Okay." I'm cheesing like Chester the cheater, about the whole situation. These little pissy hoes think they're slick. I know this is some type of setup! If it's not, I'm down for the fun .. And the sex. If it is a setup, a dangerous one, threatening my life, I have a 9 mm. If it's some kind of get back at Frank type of setup, I'm with it! Only thing is, I'm going to win all the way around the board! I just play it by ear. Who knows, Frank might just get a chance to get in there on a threesome. Or a foursome!

The Rendezvous

Melissa

Angela and I have been here at the lounge now, for about an hour. Conversation is flowing. We have a great vibe going. Not to mention the drinks are flowing pretty consistently. We started out drinking mixed drinks after a couple of those, we started taking shots of patron silver! I saw this glow in Angela's eyes, like she was ready to get freaky. And no lie, my pussy was throbbing as if it was matching my heartbeat! "So what's on your mind?" asked Angela. "What's on my mind? Take a wild guess!" I said being flirty. "Hmmm...curiosity.. You're curious about leaving this bar with me!" said Angela, in a slow, sexy way. "Leaving this bar with you?" I asked Angela. "Yeah! Leaving this bar with me." "Yes and no." I said. I had to play a little bit. "Yes and no? You're being quite evasive. Don't make me chase you." Said Angela , sounding like Prince on When Doves Cry. I laughed at that. "I know the yes part, you're leaving the bar with me, but what's the no part?" I'm waiting for a moment before answering Angela. I took a sip from my drink, in a teasing manner, before answering her. "Well, the no part. I was wondering what flavor you had!" Angela laughed at that. "Hmm,You feel all freaky like me then! What do you think about blowing this place right now?" Angela was hotter than a prostitute who would fuck on credit! "Cool.. But where are we going?" I asked. "Well.. We can go to your place, but that would be a no-no!" "Umm..I don't think it would be, if Tracy's there".. "No, no.. Let's go to my place! We have to make sure Ms Tracy would be comfortable with me coming around. I know she hates my guts!" "Okay let's go. I said. Truth be told, Tracy does hate her guts, but at the same time, she probably could go around Tracy and it wouldn't be any problems. But I'll cross that bridge when I get to it.

Angela

No lie, my pussy is moist and clit throbbing! Thinking about what's about to go down. Melissa has no idea what's in store for her! No kind of physical harm, but my goal is to turn her ass all the way out! Get her entangled in my web! They want to play with me, I'm going to seduce her ass in a way she might not have ever experienced! "What's the secret joke?" Asked Melissa, snapping me out of erotic city. "Oh my bad! I was just thinking about something, which made me smile. I was smiling to myself, huh?" "Very much so!" Said Melissa." What were you thinking about?" Asked Melissa. I had to follow Melissa to her house, to pick her up, and now we were heading to my house. While I was trailing her, I was texting Frank, to see if he could come over in about 45 minutes and if so, I will leave the door unlocked. So I had something to Smile about. "Oh I was thinking about.. Sexing you! Like that old Jodeci song? Freaking you!" I said. Actually I sang it to her. "Wow! You're so wild!" Said Melissa. I looked at her and winked my right eye at her. In a few more minutes we were pulling up to my house. "Well.. We are here!" I said, as I turned my car off. Just as we were getting out of my Range Rover, I received a text. It was from Frank! Finally. Because I've been waiting to see, was he coming over. Well sneaking over and playing the surprise game, or whatever. [Okay.. I will be there.. Dick in my hand!] [Okay..] I texted Frank back and headed inside my house. "Ta-Da!I said as I clicked on my lights, in my living room. "This is nice!" Said Melissa. "Thanks, come on, let me give you a tour!" I said as I kicked my heels off and showed Melissa around. As we entered my bedroom, she was in awe of my interior design. Pink and white themed all over, but what captured her attention was my strategically placed mirrors. I had them on the ceilings on the side of the bed, on the walls. Every area, where I could look at myself in action! "I like your mirrors!" said Melissa. "Do you like them good enough to see Yourself in a triple X showdown?" I asked, as I approached Melissa. Surprisingly, Melissa kicked her shoes off and took her glasses off and met me halfway. Immediately, we were tongue locked, tasting each other's liqour we had drunk earlier. Both of us were slightly intoxicated. Not just with alcohol, but with pure lust and desire, which caused us to basically attack each other! Sloppy, hard, wet kisses, met with the moans of urgency mixed with the old school Teddy Pendergrass, "Come on and go with me." Mood enhanced to a severe level, that I literally tore The cute shoulderless blouse off of Melissa. "I'll buy another one!" I whispered As Melissa and I fell on my king size serta, I quickly came out of my blouse and sports bra , as Melissa was tugging at my skirt. We both got naked and from there, I was the aggressor ! I might be pretty and fine, and all the way feminine, but in the bed, I am a beast! Especially with a sexy woman. I got on top of her and continued kissing her. We were bumping our pussies together very passionately and hard. As if I had a dick and she was thrusting and throwing it back like I had a 9-in dick in her or she was wishing I had a whole 12-inch dick! As I was kissing and biting her ears, I had eased a strong ass X pill to the side of the pillar she was on. When we first attacked each other I already had pulled it out, without her noticing! From her neck, her shoulders

, to her juicy tits, I was working my tongue! My middle finger brushed her throbbing spur tongue, causing her to gasp. "You okay?" I asked, as I ran my finger an inch or two up in her wet pussy, which was tight. "Uh, umm, ooh,oh-my god!"Moaned Melissa as I rose up, and gave her a very deep tongue kiss, as I was grabbing the ex pill. I drugged my tongue down her abdomen and from there, I dove head first into that fat, tight, cunt of Melissa's. I expertly locked my lips around her spur tongue and twirled my tongue. "Angela, a-a Angela, oh, oh!" Melissa was at a total loss of words almost, which is the perfect moment, to pop this bean dead up in her asshole! "OOO!"Moaned Melissa, as I popped that ex pill up in her butt. I know for a fact, she is about to be climbing the walls here, in the next minute or less. It's going to be in her bloodstream quicker, causing the effects to be multiplied, and a quicker high. She thinks she is hot as fuck now. By then Frank should be sliding through the door. I pent Melissa's knees to the mattress, and started licking her like a lollipop! She was nutting and shaking back to back . I know the pill is about to take effect very soon. At that moment, I heard a message notification on my phone. I hope it's Frank! I had to use some ingenuity, to check my phone, without her noticing and keep her attention on what's going on in this bed! As I was sucking Melissa juicy, and tight coochie, I started to play with her spur tongue. This really got her going! Luckily, my phone was in arm's reach, so I swiftly slid it over to me. Never breaking a stride, I checked my text, and it was Frank.[Am i on time, because I'm in your living room!] Frank was right on time. I hit him with the thumbs up. "Fuck me!" Moaned Melissa as she wrapped her thighs around my head. That pill had kicked in . She was thrusting her pussy so hard in my face, I had to come up for some air! By now Frank had entered the room. When I looked at Frank, he had this look in his eyes, which I had never seen before, coming from his eyes. And I love the way he played his role! "What the fuck!" said Frank, startling

Melissa. "Oh my god!" said Melissa. "Calm down baby, everything is cool." I said to calm Melissa down. "Wow! Frank, I didn't know you were coming." I laughed. "Umm.. This is Melissa, Melissa this is Frank. Such an awkward position you caught me in baby, but you're welcome to join us." "Wait.. That's Tracy's ex!". "And?" said Frank, as he pulled his already hard, 12-inch dick out. "Tracy is not my girl anymore. Besides, I came here for you. And she can join if she wants to!" Said Frank, as he smoothly got butt naked. "Oh my" said Melissa, as she stared at Frank's throbbing dick. "What you oh my ing for? You want to join us?" I asked, as I grabbed Frank's dick, as if it was a microphone! "Ummm!" I moaned, when I took the swollen head of Frank's shaft into my mouth.I was cutting my eyes at Melissa the whole time, as I was performing. She was in a slight daze, as if she hadn't witnessed this type of action before. I looked up at Frank, and he was looking at Melissa with pure lust in his eyes. She was returning a lustful gaze at Frank and his big tool. Which was getting spit shined by me. That ex pill had done to kick in real good, and Melissa was showing it! "Siss ooo! Tracy said you had a big dick! A big black shiny dick!" Moaned Melissa. She had laid beside us and started masturbating. "I see you want this big dick!" Said Frank, as he pulled his dick out of my mouth and slid between Melissa's thighs. "Oh my God! Lord your dick too big! Hold up." i said.Ipulled Frank's throbbing tool out of Melissa's hot pussy and spit on it! Yeah I got good and nasty and started sucking on it !He was surely lubed up pretty good now. I stopped giving him head and dove into Melissa's hot twat head first! She was squealing and moaning with ecstasy. In Beast Mode Frank grabbed me by my hair, moved me out of the way, and plunged into Melissa! Causing her to gasp for air. Frank waited only a second or two for her to catch her breath and he started stroking! In a hard, but yet slow matter, he was easing his whole 12-inch dick in her! To my surprise, Melissa was kicking her legs in the buck holding them all the way back to her ears herself. "Whoa!" I said. Talking about wanting Frank's dick! She's been yearning for this moment, it seems to me! A successful manifestation on her part. Rather deliberately or by default, she's fulfilled a much fantasized desire!

Tracy

My instincts had told me to get Melissa's phone and put a GPS on it. I mean, so I can know where she's at. Especially at a moment like this! I'm not big on stalking, but this situation is a special situation. My curiosity has taken over And now I'm heading in the direction of the address Melissa is at.

Pulling up in the neighborhood where the GPS led me, I am kind of impressed. I guess this is where Angela lives. She does make good money with her and Frank sports agency. Speaking of Frank, this car in the driveway looks just like his! I immediately opened my dashboard to grab my little purple and chrome 9mm. Why did I grab it? I don't know! It was by Impulse.. I guess. I put my Gun in my fanny pack, and got out of the car. I don't know why I'm here, but I'm here. I was standing there at the door, wanting to ring the doorbell. She had the kind that's hooked up to a surveillance camera and all. So, before I knew it, I twisted the door knob. To my surprise, it was unlocked. "Wow!" I said as I entered Angela's house. Not only was I in awe of Angela's interior design of her home, but I was in awe of myself! Committing an unauthorized entry to a residence is a crime! Oh well, I don't think anyone saw me, and her alarm isn't going off. I slowly, and cautiously walked around Angela's living room, making my way to the stairs. I slowly Tipped up the stairwell and stopped at the top. The first thing that caught my ears was a woman moaning hard and loud! "Ummph,ooo,oh,whoa!" What the fuck! I said, before I knew it. Whoever that was moaning and hollering like that, is busting nuts back to back! She was almost drowning the music out. That was playing "Freaking You, by Jodeci." The chorus part of that song was hypnotizing at this moment. It was like the Pied Piper was calling, because I was following the harmony of the sex noise and music right up to the bedroom door! Where the noise was coming from.. And it was cracked open! I braced myself for what I might witness. "Sisss Yea!" Said Angela, as Melissa gave her head. And I couldn't believe my eyes when I saw the cause of the moans and hollering.. It was Frank! My ex-boyfriend! Dicking my lover Melissa down! He was fucking Melissa from the back delivering the pain and pleasure, in which was intertwined, In those moans and screams. The sleazy bitch Angela, was propped up, on one knee, while her right foot was planted in the bed. She was fucking Melissa's face, while Frank was pounding her from the back! These motherfuckers set this shit up the whole time! While I thought I was getting my revenge! I can't take it anymore, I'm going in! Instinctively I grabbed my pistol out of my fanny pack and stepped in the room. They didn't even seem to notice me at first. It was Frank who noticed first. "Oh shit!" Said Frank. Then Angela "Oh hell nawl! How the fuck.." said Angela, but she couldn't finish your sentence, because the gunshot cut her off!

To be continued.

The officer and the convict..part 2

2020

"Damn!" I said to myself for the thousandth time. I was back in the slammer, but this time in the fucking Feds! I'm grateful to be alive though.. Thanks to Maria! That fateful night in 2017, in Montgomery Alabama. At the Renaissance Hotel. Officer Andrea Studderman,shot me in the leg, and my right shoulder. Attempted to make me shoot her with a throwaway pistol that she had. Stood over me with tears running down her face, about to take me out! But thank God that Maria was coming in The room, a minute and a half behind Andrea. Firing her weapon, in the ceiling of the hotel room, distracting Andrea, long enough for me to knock the pistol out of her hands. A stupid move by Andrea, was that she didn't have her body cam on! On the other hand, Maria had hers, so that helped me out a lot! But Maria was so amazing and on point, that she caught everything, from the time that Andrea was spitting in Kalisha's face, up until the time she was About to kill me or frame me or both. It was on a body cam. I still ended up getting some time from the conspiracy to distribute cocaine etc. I received a sentence of 10 years in which I have on appeal and is looking very promising for me! The government made a few mistakes, and my attorney is capitalizing on it! Meanwhile, the three years plus I have been incarcerated , I've been to a couple of joints. From Montgomery, to Atlanta, from Atlanta to Talladega. But only for a moment. It was in my file that I was involved with some Montgomery police women . So the federal bureau of prisons, somehow found out I was close to Montgomery, Alabama and had me transferred to three rivers Texas federal correctional institute! A fucking blessing in disguise for an optimistic person like me! Like the old people say, what the devil meant to be bad for you, God saw fit for you to be blessed! Or however it goes. Anyway, Maria was still rolling with me on the low. Her name was not implicated in the drug conspiracy. She had played Andrea to the left on that part, early in our relationship. Maria had a family in Texas who were really cool and connected. Just so happened, one of her cousins had a female friend who worked at that prison as a correctional officer! "Oh my!" Is what I said when she first told me. Me being who I am, a straight opportunist, the wheels started spinning in my head! This prison shit, I was hip to, so I had already peeped the hustle game. Then what made my situation sweet, thus far, was that Maria's cousin's friend was a captain. A female captain, and a Mexican chick Who looks like the boss chick on Queen of the South. Camellia. "Oh my God!" I said when I saw her. Instant attraction! I know it's not that prison mind talking. This old chic looks good, in her work uniform, In which convicts call monkey suits. I know she looks good in civilian clothes..

Or naked! I had been there about 2 or 3 weeks before I saw her. I think she had been on vacation or whatever. But as soon as she got back, she called me to her office in the morning. "Hello Mr Tory, Have a seat. I'm Captain Diaz." I sat down across from her sexy ass, and was checking her out the whole time. She was looking at the computer monitor, as if she was reading something,but I knew she was short peeping me. A psychological tactic used in interviewing especially government and law officials. They analyze your movements, body language. By being a highly self-monitored person,I knew just how to play it. I sat there very calmly. I would look at her, and lick my lips, like LL Cool J while she looked at the computer monitor. Bite my bottom lip, while looking at her, as if I didn't know she was already looking at me, through her peripheral vision. In the pen, we call that short peeping! I was almost lost in the vibe, in which I'm slowly creating by admiring her beauty! I was so lost that I grabbed my throbbing dick and said, "Umph" Before I knew it. That's when she looked directly at me, from the corner of her eyes! "Excuse me?" Said Captain Diaz. So I cleared my throat, as if that is Why I made the lustful noise. "Oh I was just clearing my throat." I said with a nervous laugh. I'm kind of playing it green, like I'm almost a lame, but at the same time, I'm so laced with the game, that when the opportunity presents itself, I can't help but seize the moment! So here I am, halfway, looking Captain Diaz dead in her eyes, giving off the energy of a man who knows when a woman is sneaky and freaky. Then a dead give away, is how she stays looking out of the corner of her eyes. Looking at my dick print, and back to my eyes. "Oh, she will go!" I said to myself. She started smiling, and she looked back at the computer monitor. "Okay Mr Tory.. I'm sitting here reading about you. Very interesting! And oh. My cousin's friend told me to look out for you.. Etc." As she looked up from the monitor. "I don't even have to ask. I have the rundown on you. You're a stand-up guy. Which is a good thing. I tell you what. You're going to work for me. I looked up with a frown at first. "No.. Not my snitch.. The whole prison knows, I despise rats! I want you to be my runner, you know. Run errands for me, clean my office, etc. Are you cool with that?" "Yes ma'am!" I answer. "I mean. That's the only way I can look out for you. That's the only way you can be close to me or should I say, close enough for me to look out for you. You understand?" "Yes I do! When do you want me to start?" I said, try to suppress my excitement. "Well.. Report to this offset 8:00 a.m. and we will go from there. Okay?" "Okay Miss Diaz." I said as I got up from my chair. "I'll see you in the morning." "Okay Tory. I'll see you then.. Oh..And it's nice to meet you!" Said Captain Diaz. "Nice to meet you too." I got kind of sexy when I said that and walked down the hall, singing to myself, in my Bobby Valentino voice. "Wee-wee-wee-wee!"

Chapter 2

A meeting of the minds

That day, after leaving the captain's office, all I did was strategize, visualize, fantasize about how I wanted this morning to unfold in my favor! I had did all the mental work, that I know of to try to manifest the outcome in which I wanted to happen! I guess you can say I've been reading a lot of positive thinking books! The last time I had done a bid, I wasn't really good or should I say very skilled for that playing all the way up under a female correctional officer. But hell, I did better Than that. I knocked off a real police woman! So, I'm equipped with all the tools, especially if I'm around her a lot and a space where it is mostly just the two of us.. Alone! "Let's get this shit cracking!" I said to myself, as I entered Captain Diaz's office. I have enough common sense in the game, to know not to spoil a blessing. Meaning I'm not going to let my dick think for me, when I probably can get her to help me more by not trying to fuck her. Besides, she's an officer. "Hey Captain Diaz, how are you doing this morning?" "Good morning Tory.. How are you?" "I'm good cap. ... First off Tory, you don't have to be so formal, with Captain Diaz and all that. Just call me Miss Diaz." With that statement, I smiled. "Now have a seat, Tory. Okay... Miss Diaz." "Now.. Before I put you to work, and before I get too busy, let's have a meeting of the minds! Let's get to know each other." I laughed a little before responding. "What's funny Tory?" "No disrespect, but you kind of caught me off guard, because you said something I read before." "George Jackson.The letters of George Jackson to be exact! Impressive huh? You didn't think a Mexican woman would have such good material?" "Well not really, but I suppose that since you're working in a penitentiary, you might just run up on that type of literature." She laughed at that statement. "You're absolutely right!" Said Miss Diaz. Miss Diaz and I sat there and talked for a couple of hours, getting to know each other. Lunch time came around , and I didn't even have to go to the chow hall! Miss Diaz fed me lunch. Some chicken burritos, and tacos. Now that was a great gesture coming from Ms Diaz, on my first day. Like my mama told me, back in 89 when I got my first pair of Jordans.. "You're cooking with Crisco now ain't you?" Well, I'm cooking with Crisco now!

3 days later

Working with Miss Diaz old sexy ass, is coming along just fine. In the last 3 days, she has been feeding me like clock work! Which was a great benefit to a person who's currently locked up, but my eyes were on money and pussy! It was in my nature,to hustle Wherever I go, and to fuck me some women. Over the last few days, Miss Diaz and I have been in some tight areas. Like big walk in closets, tight aisles between shelves, and the sly way rub game, was in full effect! Like one day, we were in the basement of the prison, in this closet looking through boxes for coats. Now, of course my dick is almost throbbing! Just because I'm in a secluded area with a sexy ass woman, Due to my current incarceration. On top of that, I've noticed her pants have gotten tighter by the day! Anyway, Ms Diaz was at the end of this aisle, Trying to grab a box from the top shelf,which she could barely reach. She was all on her tiptoes, and at that moment, I noticed that Ms.Diaz had a nice upside down Valentine ass! Time to make a move, is what I'm thinking, as I instinctively step up to help her. Besides, I'm taller than her and I'm the man right here. "Let me help you get that." I said as I tried to come from her right side to assist her. Now, the shelf is damn near 6 and 1/2, 7 ft high. And I'm not that tall, I'm like 5'8 and she's a little shorter than me, So we're kind of struggling to grab the box. In that tight corner, we have no other choice but to bump up against each other, as we both almost have the box on our fingertips. The box kind of tumbled, almost falling on our heads, and of course I caught it. And in that moment Ms. Diaz was acting like she was catching it, and falling ass first, against my already rock hard and throbbing dick! Already in an awkward position, I fell back against another shelf which was only about 3 ft away, but bolted in the wall, so it didn't budge, And I couldn't either. I almost nutted, when I felt all of Ms Diaz firm but soft ass against my rod! On top of that, I instinctively had my left arm around her waist, to catch her from falling. There's no doubt in my mind that she doesn't feel my dick and how it's stretched out through these prison khakis. Stressed out enough to make a woman jump like; "Oh shit!" But not Miss Diaz. She's laying into it. "My bad!" I said, acting kind of green , as I took my arm from around her waist . She just looked back at me, Dead in my eyes, then down to my dick. "What do you mean you're bad? About putting your arm around my waist or that?" She said as she pointed at my dick and smiled. I looked deep in her eyes and with a crooked, "yeah bitch" smile and said nothing. The heat was there, and untamed lust between the both of us, was about to manifest in a raw form! We were instinctively about to lean into each other, until I pulled my dick on her. "Wow!" Whispered Miss Diaz,"Dejame tenerte" She whispered in Spanish, As she grabbed it and started tongue kissing me. "Huh?"

I asked, because I didn't know what she said. But I know it's good how she is stroking my dick! "Let me have it" is what I said! And at that moment I was pulling her head down, So I can see what that head is like! Miss Diaz, had a little age on her, like 54, so she wasn't a spring chicken. As we say in the south. So, she was a vet! Very skilled at sucking dick. So skilled that she brought me to an ultimate nut in no time. She didn't raise up off of my cumming dick. She swallowed it, and continued licking my love pole, making that motherfucker back rock hard! I pulled my dick out of her mouth, turned her around and she already was pulling her pants down. "Damn!" I said as I admired Ms Diaz Derriere. She was fine like a black woman! Little waist, with nice curves and ass kind of fat! I didn't hesitate to run up in Miss Diaz from the back. "Oh my!" Said Miss Diaz. I didn't have much dick in her, and she was already busting off!! "Oh my! Oh my! Oh Dios mio". "Oh my God!" "Shh!" Just trying to get her to calm down, even though we were in the basement. That day there, I made my mark with Miss Diaz. I fucked her real good, and from that point on, it was on and popping!

Chapter 3

After that day, in the basement with Miss Diaz, everything was up! Meaning, I had a lot of favor in terms of making things happen, which was beneficial to me and my pockets! At first, Miss Diaz was on the lookout for me. The food and cigarettes. True, in the Feds cigarettes are big money, because they're not smoking facilities. But, I really Want to get that major big money! Dope games are popping in all prisons, so my mind was in that space. I could do stuff like getting disciplinaries disapproved, when it comes across the captain's desk, and get paid a little something. But, that's misdemeanor money. I need to get my hands on some narcotics at this facility. The heroin is leading the pack in terms of major money making. You had a few cocaine users, weed smokers, synthetic weed smokers, peel poppers, and meth heads!

My mind was telling me to get some dog food. That Heroin! I knew some Nigerian Niggaz, in there who had major money moving that dog food. But I don't know if Ms. Diaz is willing to bring that kind of pack in! Well, it was time to see if she would. There wasn't much doubt in my mind that she wouldn't do it, it's just how much she would tote, and how often. That morning i was in deep thought, listening to the Steve Harvey morning show on the radio. A routine of mine, ever since I had done time in the state pen. My meditation time. Anyway I was visualizing how my conversation with Miss Diaz would transpire. I'm picturing her saying yes, to my proposal of sorts. I had to show her where she would be safe and get paid at the same time! Making her check from the government. Schemed out You might say. But at this point, it's all about survival G! After getting me a workout in, a shower, and a good joint of that zaza, I was ready for the day to kick off. Not to mention, I was feeling very very elated about the progress in my post conviction proceedings. I had just received some legal mail, from my lawyer and the federal courts, about me getting an evidentiary hearing granted! So, that was another reason, I was ready to step my hustle game up to get this penitentiary money up, turn it to real money! Just in case if the courts grant my appeal soon, then I will be getting my freedom! Therefore, I got to be ready. The courts haven't given me a date for my other hearing yet, so I have a nice little time to build a foundation! Anyway, I made my way to Captain Diaz's office, to start cleaning up early. To my surprise, Sergeant Williams was in the Captain's office.. Early! "Oh! Sergeant Williams Excuse me , you kind of scared me. I wasn't expecting nobody to be here this early. How are you doing?!" "I'm fine Tory, how are you?" "I'm good!" I said, in a very bubbly and cordial tone. What I really wanted to say was: "you're fucking right you're fine Sergeant Williams!" This chocolate almost black angel, was the absolute fucking truth. She stood about 5. ft 5. or 5. ft 6 in. with a short hairdo . Plain Jane, but cute on her head. She had a body like she's played softball and volleyball all of her life! Kind of athletic, so she has small and little under mouth size titties, small waist, and a round basketball shaped ass! She was in the top three of the finest females at that facility. She had nice hips and walked on her toes. Every male, who wasn't gay, including the guards, wanted to fuck Ms Williams! "What brings you in so early Ms Williams." "Your show is being nosy!" Said Miss Williams, in her normal sassy, but playful way. She always acted as if she didn't really like me, but at the same time, I found out a long time ago, in some cases, what they hate was love turned inside out. That is with women! Our first couple of encounters occurred in the captain's office. Well, they kind of shared a space within the same office, but her desk is in the front, whereas Miss Diaz desk is in an office within that office. Sergeant Williams, basically was Miss Diaz secretary, in a uniform and stripes! Anyway Ms Williams, would be a fake mean to me. You know, like trying to put a hard facade up, but can hardly look me in my eyes long without blushing. Yeah, I make a chocolate female blush! Sometimes, I catch her watching me and when I catch her, she rolls her eyes with a smile on her face. I'll be thinking she knows about me and Miss Diaz, and it's showing her jealousy . Or maybe Miss Diaz was telling her, how I put the dick down, and she wanted her some! Anyway, I'm trying to stick to the script, which is me going ahead and cleaning up early, so when Miss Diaz comes, I can have enough time to talk to her about getting me some dog food up in their prison! Before I continue cleaning up, I must address Ms Williams concerning her comment about me being nosy. "My bad Sergeant Williams, I wasn't trying to get in your business." "Yeah right!" Said Sergeant Williams. "You're there now!" I laughed at that. "I'm there now?" "Yes you are Tory. All in my business." I was emptying all the little trash cans in the office, so when I got to her desk, she was acting like she was so into the computer that she didn't know that I needed to get her trash can. At least that's how she was acting. "Excuse me. Can I get your trash can?" She looked up at me rolling her eyes, twisting her lips up, and smacking her lips. She pushed away from the desk and leaned back in her chair, insinuating that I get her little trash can myself. Instead of her grabbing it for me. I didn't trip in any kind of way, but I did take a quick glance at that fat monkey between her thighs! In which she was positioned to be seen. Like a player, I just kept doing what I was doing and didn't pay her much attention. I did her like that a lot, because she thought that she was hot shit! I felt her eyes on me the whole time, I just kept doing my job. "You think you're slick!" Said Sergeant Williams. By now, I'm putting a bag in the trash can, and she is still sitting there, but now her feet are propped up on both sides of the chair, kind of busting her thighs open. Now, my prison mind is telling me she's doing this for me, but I'm still not paying much attention. As though it seems. Then all of a sudden, I stopped working and stood there.. Almost between her legs. "What do you mean by that?" Looking her dead in her eyes, and dick semi hard. She looked down at my print, and back in my eyes. "You know what I mean? You do it all the time, but try not to act like you do. Especially around Miss Diaz! She got your ass scared to even look at a black woman!" "What the fuck!" I said before I knew it and started laughing. I knew it! Her ratchet ass couldn't take it anymore. Sergeant Williams, is straight from the projects, out of the third ward in Texas. Houston that is. Got family members who were locked up and on top of that, Shorty is an ex stripper. I found all of this info About her from the captain. I wanted to tell her no :"Miss Williams, I'm not scared to look at a black woman, I'm just reversing the game on you! But I didn't. "Captain, don't have me scared to look at a black woman. You make me scared to look at one!" With that comment, she cocked her head to the side. "I have you scared? Nigga get the fuck out of here with that reverse psychology you're trying to run on me!" Whispered Miss Williams. My mind was like a laughing emoji.

"Damn there goes the neighborhood!" I said to sergeant Williams. As I laughed. "Yeah, I told you that you thought you were slick! There ain't no way, that I got you scared, Miss Diaz has you scared and you know why!" Perfect example of when jealousy peeps its ugly face In your picture, photo bombing! I looked at her and was surprised at first. Then I quickly fixed my face. "I don't know what you're talking about Sergeant Williams!" "Oh yes you do! Tory. I'm straight from the hood and I peep game! Just know that." Said Sergeant Williams, as she got up from her desk, and strutted past me with a little extra stank to her walk! Making me actually feign for her! But one thing I have found out, she is ready! I will swindle a bitch out of her pussy by toying with her feelings! Her feelings of secluded lusts, lusts in which she is hiding, or at least she thinks she is. Those are the thoughts I'm having about sergeant Williams. It's going to happen and real soon!

Chapter 4

Later on, Miss Diaz had come in and I was already through cleaning up. I was sitting there reading My legal mail, when she came in. Smelling all good, like some kind of Victoria's Secret perfume. "Hey Tory, how are you doing this morning?" "I'm good Miss Diaz, how are you?" "I'm okay Tory.. Kind of tired!" I was still into my legal mail, real heavy, at least I pretended to be! With me halfway responding to Miss Diaz, when she said that she was tired, that got her attention and made her stop doing what she was doing, in midair. "Tory are you okay? Seems like that mail you're reading really has your attention." "Oh, my bad Ms Diaz, I was so into my legal mail." I almost called her by her first name, which is Carla. I've been on a first name basis with Miss Diaz, When we are alone. But I rarely did unless I was whispering in her ear, trying to fuck her, or in the actual act of fucking her! "Siss ooo Carla baby!"Shit like that. "So what do you have some good news?" Miss Diaz asked. "Well, I have an evidentiary hearing coming up." I said. "What's that?" Miss Diaz was very curious, especially when it came to me. I briefly explained to her What an evidentiary hearing was. "Wow, So you might be getting out soon!" "Great possibility!" I said. "It all depends on my greedy lawyer! I had an almost sad puppy look in my eyes. I got quiet for a moment. For effect, acting like I didn't want to look her in the eyes. I'm getting very dramatic right here! Straight soap opera style. "Hey you okay?" Said Miss Diaz out of concern. She had to walk from around her desk like she wanted to console me or something. I looked up at her with a somber smile on my face. "Yeah, I'm okay. It's just frustrating because this motherfucker wants more money! Shit!" Captain was closing her office door by now. "So.. What you don't have the money? What about your family?" "Man, they're broker than a joke!" I said . Even though my lawyer was paid, I was setting the stage to see just how much sympathy she had for me. I really need her to empathize with me. See things from my eyes!" Damn! So what do you think he's going to do, if you don't have the money?" The greedy son of a bitch is probably going to get off of my case, and leave me out to dry!" "Wow, that's fucked up! Tory oh my God! What are you going to do? I mean if I had the money, I would give it to you! I want you out! So we can be together for real!" Now here is where the plot thickens! "I know! That's all been on my mind Carla!" I said, as I stood up and embraced her! "Fuck..I got to come up with a plan! We were in her office with the door closed, so I could kind of get raw! I was standing there caressing her back, like she needed consoling. "We are going to make it happen, I just need your help!" I said. "What is it baby?" Miss Diaz asked. "I need something to hustle with and I'm not talking about cigarettes, I have them." She looked at me and started shaking her head, like no! "I don't think I can do that. I know you're talking drugs and I can't knock you, but I can't bring it in! I can, but I can't. I mean, I can get whatever you want, on that tip, because my nephews are connected. You would have to figure out a way to bring it in." Now my wheels were turning in my head. I didn't want to go through any of the inmates. I would, but I needed my own mule to make sure my endeavors were successful! I let go of my embrace. I had her caressing her in. "What's the matter?" asked Miss Diaz. I was slowly pacing around her office now. "What's the matter? I'm trying to figure out who I could get to tote for me!" Then a light bulb went off in my head! I was thinking about asking her about Sergeant Williams or should I play all the way up under Sergeant Williams? It takes time. I think I'll get Miss Diaz to ask her. "How close are you to Sergeant Williams?" She kind of flinched on that question. But with a sparkle in her eyes she was smiling. "Well.. Can you trust her? You're smiling like you two are very close." Captain Diaz laughed at that statement and went to her desk and sat down. "So how much do you need?" Asked Captain Diaz. "Oh, let me rephrase that question. What do you need and how much?" "I need some heroin. That's what's making a lot of money here." She paused in the middle of looking at her computer, and looked at me with a frown on her face. "I would have to think about that a little bit. I mean my nephews sell drugs, and I could get it. But I don't know if Sergeant Williams is willing to take that chance." I was thinking like hell, but I was careful not to speak so fast. "She owes me some favors, so it shouldn't be much of a factor. Besides.. I think she likes you! Or should I say she wants to fuck you anyway! With that being said, it shouldn't take much to convince her, but she's going to want something. Other than that big dick you got!" I smiled at that and unconsciously grabbed my seat and my heart too. "Look at you ! That got you excited?" Said Ms Diaz. "Yeah.. To Be honest! Because the way you're talking, you've already told her about you and I!" I said. In which I was praying she did. I already figured that out, from the way Miss. Williams acted towards me earlier. "Don't worry, she's trustworthy." Said Miss Diaz. "So you told her?" "Yes I did." "Okay. No problem, but do you think she's jealous? I mean, jealous of the whole situation with you being Mexican and me black." "Look, don't worry about her! I got it." Interrupted Ms Diaz. "Okay." I said and left it at that. "I will talk to my nephew later, and I will let you know something tomorrow." "Bet!" After I got that business taken care of, I went and ran some errands for Miss. Diaz, and went on about my day, with big money on my mind!

Chapter 5

The next day, like clockwork sergeant Williams was there real early. Now, my mind is doing all kinds of marathon thinking. Like "Okay Tory, take it at a pace!" Meaning I'm going to play Miss. Williams by ear, and and don't come off to thirsty, because you know that she wants to have sex with you!" That's how I'm talking to myself in my mind. Ever since Miss. Diaz told me that sergeant Williams want to have sex with me, out of nowhere my dick just stands in attention! Time I think about her. So I was dealing with controlling myself to the fullest in her presence. "Good morning Miss. Williams!" I said as she was settling at her desk. "Good morning. Mr Tory!" Sarcastically said Miss Williams, with her lips all twisted with a smile though. I paused from doing my little chores, for a second. "Are you doing okay today?" I asked. Being very cordial as usual. "I am doing excellent!" said Miss. Williams, leaning back in her chair for me to grab her trash can. Busting them thighs open, flexing that fat monkey between her legs, as she does every other day. But today was different. I let it be known that I was looking! I stopped right between her legs, as I was grabbing her trash can. This kind of surprised her since I never really looked this bold. And my dick was poking through those prison khakis! Like Pinocchio's nose, when he's lying! She was cocking her head to the side, mouth opened in surprise. "And so how are you doing today?" said Miss.Williams as she stared below my waist and back to my eyes. "I'm doing good, Miss Williams."I said, in a low, sexy tone. As I lick my lips. "What's up?" I asked as if I was saying enough playing, "let's do this damn thing!."Umm...I have something for you, and I can't do it right here." Said Ms Williams.Putting emphasis on doing it. "So you need to calm that down!" She was referring to my rod in my pants. "Okay." I said, as I kind of made my soldier lay down by grabbing and pushing it down. Looking deep in her eyes the whole time. So much sexual tension between us, that both of us are breathing uneasy, and I'm beginning to sweat around my lips and eyebrows! I'm ready to get her down in this basement, and stroke her lights out! I wish I could play some music right now. It would be some old school Prince. "Do me baby!" "Come on, let's go to the basement." Said Sergeant Williams. "Let's go!" I couldn't wait till I got her chocolate ass down in the spot. We both were walking kind of fast, in an urgent matter, to the point, people in the hallway, we're looking at us. She was in front of me, leading the way. "Hey Sarge, is everything okay?" asked one of the correctional officers, who was working the hallway. "Yeah everything okay. Trying to go get something for the captain before she gets here!" She shook the guard very swiftly, and We proceeded on our way to the basement. Once we got down there, and made sure no one was in there, we literally attacked each other! She grabbed me in my collars, like she was about to jack me up and I was grabbing her right leg, and jacking her up, in a dark corner of the basement. Shrouded by tall shelves. "Wait before we go too far!" whispered Ms Williams. She was pushing me back, as she was un-fastening her pants, and for a minute, I was following suit. "No, hold on for a minute, on that." Said Ms Williams as she reached in her pants, and I assume she had a pack up her pussy! "Miss Diaz!" I said to myself. "Here! Y'all motherfuckers are going to pay me!" "I got you!" I said as I stuck the pack down in a box full of blankets. I will get that shortly. I was stepping out of my khakis, as she was doing the same. When we made contact, we clashed! "Mmm, come here nigga! said Miss Williams, as she stuck her tongue in my mouth and wrapped her right leg around my waist and with her left hand, she was grabbing my stiff dick. Placing it where she needed it and wanted it! I was slamming her, in a corner , and jacking her up at the same time! Roughly, ramming this dick deep up in her soul. By now, she had her mouth wide open, chasing her breath, as if she was a gunshot victim! "You okay?" "Yeah.. Yeah.. Oh..shit!" I pulled out and bent her over. I wanted to be fucking her from the back when I nut! Thinking about the times when she has turned her nose up at me. Acting all stank, when all the time, she wanted me to beat her back out! Like I'm doing now! "Siis, OOO fuck!What did I do to you?" Moaned Sergeant Williams, as I fucked her like a mad Russian! "Being you!" I said with a growl in my voice, as I came to a climax. "What the fuck!" Whispered Sgt. Williams. She had to get herself together, because I really laid it down!

Chapter 6

6 months later

Everything was going just as planned. I was still working for Captain Diaz. Cleaning her office, running little errands. Etc. Still fucking her, whenever I wasn't fucking Ms Williams. Come to find out Captain Diaz had been told Sergeant Williams, about our affair. Telling her how I was fucking her in the basement. What made Sergeant curious about me, more than she already was, Captain went into details about my case. And how big my tool was and how good I was at using it! So, basically she was already walking into her fantasy of having sex with me, by showing me that fake, dislike, but yet giving me rhythm! I just speeded the process up by getting Captain Diaz to have Sergeant Williams bring that dog food / heroin up in the federal prison. Speaking of drugs, everything was going like Clockwork. I had stacked up about $250,000! Yep from behind bars. See, the thing is, in the pen, a person can sell drugs, way higher than it would sell on the streets! Miss Diaz gave me the first ounce and from there it was on! I had the money on Green Dot cards, PayPal, cash app, Venmo, etc. Then, to top it all off, I had an evidentiary hearing, and I was granted a new trial! That had transpired about three months ago. And now I was waiting on my lawyer to tell me that the government wanted to accept a plea to a lower offense! Fuck the new trial! They can have the conviction. Just let me go! Everything was looking good on my end. The only thing now for me to do is figure out where I am going to start my life over, once I'm free! Miss Diaz wants me to move down here in Texas . But I'm not all the way sure just yet. I had to weigh my options. I don't know if I should just move in with Ms Diaz, off the top. Jumping in a relationship that fast, and don't really know the person, could prove to end fucked up! Especially considering how I ended up back in the can! Since I've been almost killed by a crazy bitch, I would have to get to know Ms Diaz a little better. Before moving in with her. Even though, she's giving me the option of just being fuck friends and living in separate places, but I know how that can be said but not really meant! She lives in San Antonio, and I think I could live in San Antonio so that is a plus. Big city, plenty of money there, and plenty of pretty women! Not to mention all the cocaine and the rest of the drugs there! My opportunist / hustler mentality tells me to make that move!

3 Days later

To my delight, I had legal mail that night at the mail call. Two envelopes. One from my attorney, and another one from the Federal court of the middle district. I waited until I got to myself, before opening the mail. I'm kind of nervous, because they had made a decision about my evidentiary hearing. So, this mail is going to tell it all! Either they gave me a reversal of my conviction, or denied it! Damn! We haven't even had a new trial! "Fuck it, whatever, whatever." I said to no one in particular. My cell partner was gone. "Congrats Mr Tory your case was resolved, just as we expected, and based on the main issues, so for a lesser included offense, I negotiated a plea agreement for a 40 month sentence,to run retroactive in which will free you A. S. A. P! "Yeah! Okay!" I hollered like Lil -John. I started reading the rest of the mail. "Tory, by the time you read this, the following day we are going to have a zoom call with you, one of the officials, and the judge and I. A video hearing will take place and you will be free to go home!" I immediately jumped up and went to my hiding spot, and grabbed my cell phone, which I use strictly for business! I texted Miss Diaz and told her first. She screamed. "Thank God! Wow you must be excited?!" "Yes I am!" I said. "I'll make sure that the hearing happens in my office. Do you have a way of leaving there? Oh I know they will take you to the bus station, but.. Where are you going? Are you going home to your family or..." "Hold it Carla.. Hold up. I whispered. Referring to Miss Diaz calling her by her real name. "I've decided to stay in San Antonio! But.. I want my own place." She laughed at that. "As you wish Tory.. Well, I'll have one of my nephews, to have someone to pick you up. It would look suspicious, if I take you home!" "Okay. That's cool. Look, let me get off of this phone. I will see you tomorrow." I hung up the phone and made a few more calls, to my family, which was in Alabama and Atlanta And I told Maria, who had made it to a federal agent now, in the Gulf Coast area, In Mobile Alabama. She was curious about where I was going to move. "I'm going to chill out this way for a moment, in San Antonio." "Okay Tory, that's great! I'm coming to see you ASAP!" "Whoa.. Give me a couple of days to get things sorted out. Oh.. Okay." said Maria Sounding disappointed, and curious. Now I'm getting kind of paranoid about her feelings. I mean she wasn't my woman exclusively, but she did save my life, and her testimony helped me out. So, I got to keep it real with her. "Check this out Maria.. I'm going to keep it 100 with you .." "You are going to spend time with my friend's cousin, who works at the prison.. Which is fine with me." Interrupted Maria. "Okay you're right! But we still can link up. I said. "Oh yeah.. Just be real with me Tory. Well .. Call me and let me know something. You need some clothes, just give me an address or whatever!" "Okay Maria, that's what's up. Let me put this phone up and I will talk to you later." "Okay, Tory and congratulations." "Thanks." Now that I have hollered at a few people I wanted to know that I was about to touch down, I put my phone up and made a few rounds in the camp. Too solidify some things with some guys, then I'm laying back waiting on the next day!

Chapter 7

Go free day

Now it's time for me to make my debut! I've only slept about 3 hours all night, so I was up and ready by the time Captain got there. Sergeant Williams was there early. We sat in her office and talked about all types of shit! "So you're staying down here in San Antonio?" Asked Sgt. Williams. "Yes!" I answered. She was glowing like a lightning bug! "That's what's up! We will be able to have our way with you!" Said Sergeant Williams, looking all freaky and aggressive. "Nawl, I ain't into no dominatrix shit now!" I had to let her know that off the rip! "No, silly!" Laughed Miss Williams. "I mean, we both can have our cake and eat it too! Get that dick when we want to!" "Oh my God! You're a dick demon!" I said joking with Ms Williams. "I will be able to get that pussy like I want to. In bed, stretching your fine ass out! I will be able to train you now!" "Train who? I ain't no fucking dog nigga! Said Sergeant Williams, as she slowly approached me. "No, I mean like your physical fitness trainer baby!" Putting on that smile which I find to be very effective with women. "Yeah right, Mac Daddy!" At that moment the captain was signaling for me to come into her office. When I got into her office, I could see my attorney, looking at me through Miss Diaz's computer screen. "Hey Tory, how are you doing? Are you ready to get this show on the road?" said my attorney. "Yes .. Let's go with it!" The hearing only took about 5 minutes, and we were through. "Well Tory, got all your stuff together?" Miss Diaz asked. "Yeah, I only have legal work that I'm taking home with me. Let's go with it!" I said, as I jumped up from my seat. "My nephew's friend is already out there, waiting on you! I left them with an outfit for you. Oh. And I reserved a room for you downtown San Antonio at the Omni LA mansion Del Rio! I booked it for a week, for you.. Or should I say us?" Said Miss Diaz. The strange thing about that statement was, when she said us she did some body language move with her head and eyes, like she was suggesting us meaning sergeant Williams too! A mother fucking threesome! "I'm down with that!" I said showing all 32 teeth. I was released from the federal prison shortly after that conversation. It's on and popping! **

Ms.Diaz or now we can call her by her first name Carla, nephews, friend was very cool. A young Mexican man, with a fade haircut with three or four braids at the top. Driving a white Ferrari, he was flexing hard! His name was Felipe. Felipe took me downtown San Antonio to my hotel, where I met Carla's nephew Ricardo, in the lobby. "Hola my friend. You are Tory right?" "Yeah that's me!" I said, as we shook hands. "I heard a lot about you." Said Ricardo. "Oh yeah?! Of course, I've heard a lot about you! I used to work for your aunt!" "You used to pop that Punta!" Said Ricardo. And he and his homeboy laughed at that. "Just joking my friend! It's none of my business. But I do know, you were making a nice bit of money off of that dog food from in there behind the walls, and that says a lot. You are a top hustler! A businessman!" Said Ricardo. Gassing me up, but then he's telling the truth. "Yeah, I did that! And since I'm out, I would like to continue doing business with you. If that's no problem." "Why Sure! Are you living in San Antonio?" Asked Ricardo. "Yeah for a minute. But look, I want to go to my room and make a few calls and settle in a little bit. Then we can get together, a little later on and talk more in depth." "That's a bet Tory! But don't settle in too much, I'm coming back to get you in the next hour or two! Take you shopping and go out for a couple of drinks! Get some girls! Oh.. Maybe you can't get the girls tonight. Auntie is going to want to spend the night with you! Maybe some other time on the girls!" Laughed Ricardo. I pulled my phone out, the same one I had in the pen! "What's your number? And I will call you when I'm ready." Ricardo gave me his number . We bumped fists and I hit the elevator and to my room I went

Chapter 8

As promised, Ricardo picked me up in a couple of hours of me checking into my room. He took me out on the town. I had a nice time hitting a few bars, and strip clubs. Introduced me to some fine ass mixed black and Mexican chicks! Got me a phone number, right quick from a chick named Jessica! Ricardo wasn't tripping. It wasn't long though, Carla, Ricardo's auntie aka Miss Diaz, was calling me! "What's up baby! You are having a nice time!" "Yes, I am Carla. "Are you ready for me?" I asked. "No.. The question is are you ready for me! I meant us?!" Laughed Carla. "Us?" I was bewildered by the US part! "Yeah us!" said Carla." Well I guess I am! I'm heading back to my room now!" "Okay Tory, we are on our way. What's the room number?" "Room 1415." "Gotcha!" Said Carla. Sounding totally different from when she's at work at the prison. Once arriving at the hotel, Ricardo and I made a pact! That we would get to the money, in a major way! I hurried to the elevator so I can get to my room and chill and hype myself up for Carla and whoever us is! I was sitting in my hotel room, anticipating Carla's arrival.. And whoever else she had with her! I believe I know who it is. Just as I was thinking about them there was a knock at my room door! I got up and looked out the peephole, and it was Carla turning around and posing with her nice workout body! She had on a red, Linen looking summer dress, with a split up the side! That dress was gripping her hips and ass! Making it poke out! I hurried up and opened the door. " Wow!" I said as I admired Carla's Shapely ass. "Wow, that's all you see is my ass!" Said Carla as she hugged me. But what really took the cake, when Ms Williams, who's real name is Patricia, Bent the Corner looking all sexy with some six inch heels on with a tight leather pants suit hook up. Like it was clear up her right leg, I guess with some sheer material. Straps crossing her stomach, showing off her almost six pack! The top was made almost like a wife beater type of style but with a bra-like hookup , covering her mouth size tits and her back was out! "Damn! Miss Williams, I meant Patricia, my bad!" I said as I hugged her and twirled her around admiring her extra fine ass! "So y'all all dressed up where we going?!" "I know my nephew took you out for a moment, but It's our turn now! You're not drunk are you?" asked Carla. "No. I'm buzzing. I've been drinking a little! But I have been smoking za-za!" They both laughed at that, and Patricia pulled a little Pack with some purple runts in it. "Get the fuck out of here! I didn't know you smoked!" They looked at each other and laughed. Tory, it's a lot you didn't know!" Said Patricia. "So are you ready?" Asked Carla. "Yes. Let's go!" I said, and we exited the room and headed out

Chapter 9

They took me to a place called the Jet Setter. We sat down and had a few drinks. We had smoked a blunt of purple runts on the way there, so I was feeling really good and horny! So was Carla and Patricia. We got up and danced a little. I was intrigued by how they were dancing on each other. I mean there's nothing strange nowadays and witnessing something like that, but not with two federal corrections officers. One is a captain at the age of 55. And a sergeant at the age of 40. I don't know! It could just be me, but the way they're dancing on each other is kind of sensual! Make me wonder, if they gay or not! I know one thing, this Ciroc and cranberry juice got me hoping they were gay! We might get into some XXX throwdown type of moves. We partied into the wee-wee hours, like three in the morning! I made sure I didn't overdo it, to the point that I wouldn't be able to function or perform in the bed! Once we left the club, we went straight to the hotel, to my room and kicked back. The ladies kicked off their heels and I kicked off my shoes. "Well Tory, tell me how it feels?" Asked Carla. "How does it feel to be free? It feels great!" I answered. Nawl nigga, you know what she means!" Interrupt Patricia and she sat back on her elbows, on the bed, promoting that fat pussy through those tight leather pants she had on! My whole face, reflecting lust, and savage sex! "Oh yeah? So what does she mean? I don't know." I said as I lay back on my elbows on the bed. We're all sitting on one king size bed, so it's about to get nasty! "What I mean is, how does it feel to finesse your way out of prison, before your go home date.. "Blessings from the court!" I interrupted. "Let her finish!" Said Patricia, as she poked my leg with her feet and love lick! Anyway, before you finessed the courts, you finessed two federal female employees!" "Correctional officers, I might add." Said Patricia. Nudging me with their feet again. Another love lick!! "Finessed?" I jokingly asked, as I nudged Patricia's leg with my feet. Love lick! By now, she's smiling like crazy. Women who have rank in that shit! Then you manage to fuck not one, but two women of rank!" I'm sitting there, with my mouth wide open, in fake surprise. And had us trafficking drugs!" chimed in Patricia. "Not for free!" I said. And that was no joke. They were getting paid well by me. Money and dick! "And now you're free, in a pretty five-star hotel, with the same women you have finessed to your advantage!" Carla was really Putting on. But I enjoyed it! "They warned us about men like you in training." Said Patricia. We laughed at that, but I'm about to tell them How much I appreciate their help. "Look all jokes aside, I think y'all for y'alls help. It is nothing I won't do for either one of you! "Oh, how sweet of you!" Said Carla, and she crawled over to me, leaning in, giving me a kiss and another one, and another one! Each kiss, was getting more sensual and hot! I'm already on go, like a dog running behind a female dog and heat. Dick half way out of the hairs! Then the liqour, is putting me all the way in porno mode! Out of the corner of my eye, I see Patricia is peeling herself out of her sexy leather pants,

Off the top, that made me start to unbuckle and unbutton my pants, to release this nine - 10-inch dragon, from his dungeon. In the form of boxer drawers and jeans! Standing tall saluting and throbbing, ready for combat! "Yeah, give me that!" Whisper Carla, as she grabbed my dick, slowly stroking it in a slow circular motion. By now I was taking off my shirt and sliding out of my jeans and boxes at the same damn time! To my surprise, Patricia was naked and sliding up under Carla's dress from the back, while Carla was leaning over me planting kisses all the way down my chest, and finally my penis! She kissed the head of it, like she missed it or something! She quickly started tongue kissing my My tomato head, occupied with a moan, induced by Patricia's own tongue kissing ritual from the back of Carla. I was living my best life right here, grabbing a fistfull of Carlas silky hair, biting my bottom lip, meeting Carla's wet mouth, with slow thrusts. She was looking me dead in my eyes, almost causing me to lose control! But I refuse to bust off that fast, without fucking first. Carla must have read my mind, because she was nudging Patricia off of her, from the back and crawling on top of me! Holding my dick at the same time, as if she was taking her claim. "Oh shit!" moaned Carla, once she eased About a third of the way down my pole. I wasn't even about to spare the rod! I gripped her by her ass, and basically slammed her down on this dick! She made a hissing noise, with her mouth, like when you accidentally scald yourself with some hot water! "Oh my.. Maria madre de Jesus!" "Mary the mother of Jesus." Was what she was saying in Spanish. I was lifting her up and throwing dick up at her at the same time! She was almost, fucking me around coming with that talk she was talking! I was looking in her eyes, watching her sexual expressions! In the hood we call it fuck faces! We were exchanging fuck faces, like the song Scarface made. See, I know when a woman is on top, she's somewhere in control of How a nigga hit the G-spot, but this technique that I'm putting down, is making her lose that vantage point of control and I can tell! Going off of her body language, I applied pressure! Careful not to injure my tool, I snatched Carla down on me! My full length is up in her. And I held her there! She was grunting like she was possessed or something! She had her nails in my chest about to drop blood! I had done fucked all past and through her G-spot. Thrusting and elevating my hips, upward as if I was cumming, in which I wasn't . I was making Carla's love come down! Dripping all down my nuts and the inside of my thighs. She had her head back, mouth open, eyes closed, basking in ecstasy as if she's on some ecstasy! No, but just this dick! Making her feel like she took an ecstasy pill. I looked over at Patricia, who was laid back engaging in some masturbation. She rose up and started tongue kissing Carla. I was watching that fat ass she has, and kind of lifted Carla off of my dick, so I can get to Patricia! I got directly behind her, and on cue, Carla laid back guiding Patricia to her swollen love box! Patricia was eating pussy! "This was truly an omg moment for me. Considering the circumstances in which surround us. With no hesitation, I took advantage of the arch and face down, ass up position and went straight to applying pressure! Upon entrance, I looked down at Patricia's pink shining pussy. She was a very dark skin woman, that turned me on to the max! My sudden plunge into Patricia's shallow pussy interrupted the head game she was giving Carla, causing her to let out a deep gasp and moan! Carla grabbed Patricia with both hands, gripping her hair! She had spread her legs, as wide as they could spread, and was rotating her hips. Extra hard! As if she was having a mind-blowing orgasm. The whole time, biting her lips and looking me in the eyes , as I continuously pound Patricia from the back! Working with her. That night we fucked ourselves straight to sleep! I am the truth!

Chapter 10

6 months later

"Yeah.. I'm in Birmingham Alabama right now." I said, I was on the phone with Carla. Everything had taken off pretty fast for me, within the 6 months I had been free. I stayed down in San Antonio making it do what it do! I stayed at the hotel for about a month straight, before I got my own place. Sure, Carla was willing to let me live with her till I get on my feet, but just like the last time I got out of prison, I got my own place. I got an apartment out in Huebner oaks. Luxury apartments. I was driving rentals for a minute, then I went on ahead and got me a black Mercedes S550 Benz! I made a lot of money in the federal pen and my operation is still popping! With the help of Carla and Patricia. Well mainly Patricia. Out of all the people! She had about two more mules working with her now! They would work together and get it to my partner Fredo out of Birmingham Alabama. That was the main reason I was in Birmingham Alabama, handling some business with Fredo's sister, Katina. I had met Katina over the phone, when I first got locked back up. Fredo and I were roommates in Atlanta and ended up roommates in Texas. Katina was what you would call a down ass bitch! A bad bitch, a real hot girl / dope chick. Katina stood about 5'6 or 5'7 Redbone, with real cat eyes! She had long pretty hair that almost reached her shoulders. Juicy lips, with a sexy gap in her teeth. Nice round titties, small waist, curvy hips, and a fat ass! So naturally I'm trying to get off of the phone with Carla ! "Okay baby, handle your business and be careful." Said Carla. "Okay, I will call you back." I said and hung up without saying bye before I knew it! Now it's time to call Katina. We have a little business to take care of, and after that, we're going to hang out a little bit! See, from our dealings through her brother, when I was locked up, Katina had come up! She was already hustling pretty good. Selling cocaine, a variety of pills, syrup, and through her brother and I, heroin! Now she was doing big things and I was her plug. Courtesy of Carla's nephew Ricardo! He set me straight as fuck! He knew I was a bonafide hustler, from all that money I was sending him from the feds. So once I got out and off the top spending a hundred K with him, he blessed me down! I didn't know he had dope like that! For the 100K he sold me a brick of heroin and two keys of cocaine, but he fronted me the same as what I had bought! These Mexicans products were so pure and fire, That people bought them quickly.! A few people OD'd on the heroin. When that happens, not only do the laws get curious but users are running to it, like ants on candy! With the help of Katina and her brother in the Feds, I was moving that shit almost just as fast as I got it! So now, the game has escalated! Meaning I was getting more product, and Katina was getting more product from me. My phone was ringing, I knew it was Katina, but I'm about to play a little bit. "Yo!" "Yo? That's how you answer the phone for a queen nigga?!" Said Katina. "Who is this?" I said, as if I didn't recognize her voice. "Nigga? Bruh?! Really?" Said Katina on the other end. "Oh my bad! What's up baby?!" Sounding surprised, I added iron to the fire! "Then you're trying to play it off! Nigga you ain't never forgetting my voice! Stop playing!" I laughed at Katina. "Okay baby my bad. Where are you?" "At yo hotel, on my way up." "That's what's up!" I said, as my dick began to stir in my polo boxers! Katina had that kind of effect on me! Since I've been out, Katina and I have done business face to face about three times. Any other time, it was through the mail. And which was about five times. But out of the three times we met face to face, we fucked like some mad Russians! And I couldn't wait to fuck her tonight! But business first. I had her a couple of bricks of cocaine and heroin up here for her! I was at the Marriott International in Homewood, so I was somewhat ducked off. On the 5th floor waiting on this fine ass dope chick! I had been there for about an hour chilling, so she's finally here and I'm ready! "Hey what's up!" I said, as Katina sashayed her way in. I locked the door and walked over to Katina and attempted to hug her and she stopped me with her freshly done nails planted in my chest!

"Hold it Mr! Now how are you going to sit there and not recognize my voice?!! Nigga, this voice was music to your ears, not long ago. In your time of darkness, I was the light guiding you to the end of the tunnel nigga! Like that lady on Poltergeist! "Come to the light Carol ann! Said Katina, in her silly mode. Pronouncing the word "light" like a redneck! Lite! "Yeah, and when you want to see that cobra head in your time of horniness, who dick was in that camera lite?"! I said, pronouncing light, like a redneck was saying. Light. "Oh that's bullshit nigga! I was helping your freaky ass get off! Because a bad bitch like me can get a dick whenever!" said Katina, as she leaned in for a kiss, but suddenly stopped! "What's up?" I asked. "You know what time it is!" Said Katina pointing down below my waist. She was referring to me, displaying my tool, so she can admire it! I don't know, but I think she fell in love with admiring my dick when I was locked up! I didn't trip, I just obliged by giving her what she wanted, and up the dick on her. "Here it is!" I said, as I slowly stroked it looking deep in her eyes! She was looking at it, smiling. "Uh-umm!"pretty ass dick! Said Katina, as she leaned in and gave me a kiss and grabbed and stroked me at the same time. I was gripping her ass and massaging it, sticking my tongue down her throat! We were hot for each other, when I first met her over a video call! She came up out of those red bottom 6-in heels she had on. I took off my shirt, revealing a somewhat workout body, and she proceeded to suck on my chest and nipples. Making me put her head on down to her favorite friend.. My throbbing dick! "This big red mother fucker!" Said Katina, smiling just as she was slurping that head up! "Ooh - wee!" I moaned. "Don't make me nut quick, I got to fuck you"! That statement made her go on down the pole, about midway. I had some music playing down low In the background, that Usher, "Bad Habits." Boy that had me thinking about myself, as I was getting me some dope bitch head! Priceless! "Oh my God!" I moaned, as I was thinking of how I was messing up my love life. Thinking I'd be having the right one to do right by, and then here comes another one, who makes me run head first into traffic of infidelity! But then, what the Fuck am I thinking! I'm fucking two friends, in which work together, and we gets money together! So fuck it! Katina was working on me, with that head game she got! I stopped her though, because I truly enjoy fucking Katina like I'm mad at her! I didn't give her time to take off her short Chanel skirt, I bent her over, pulled her thong down, and straight got to it!

Chapter 11

After Katina and I fucked for about an hour, we handled business. I showered while she went and put her product up. And to shower and to get herself together. We were going out! She said she was taking me to this classy club called Paper Doll for a moment, then we're heading to a place called the Roof! One of her girlfriends was having a party and she wanted to show her plug / out of town lover off! I told her to be careful about that. "For two reasons. number one the wrong motherfucker knows that I'm the plug, and now we got to watch for police shit or robbers! Number two your girlfriends might get jealous, and just want a piece of me anyway!" Not knowing that I was speaking the truth into existence! "Humph!"Well, as for me showing my plug off, that was just me talking bullshit! Seriously! Number two, I ain't worried about my girlfriend wanting a piece of you, that's cool. As long as you don't bite the bait"! Said Katina. I laughed at that. "Bite the bait huh?" "Yeah, don't bite the bait nigga. Unless I want to share! Ya dig?!" Said Katina. "Yeah I dig." I was smiling like crazy at What Katina said. The boss bitch!

We hit the first spot, the Paper Doll, it was okay. A lot of jazzy chicks were there. Dressed to impress. But I ain't going to lie, Katina and I were shining! I had on a short sleeve, button down Chanel. Black with the brown C's on them, shirt. With some black Chanel slacks , and black and brown Chanel slippers! Katina, with her fine ass, had a brown and black Chanel dress on. With the thin straps at the shoulders, and splits up the side, revealing sexy legs and thighs! And gripping around her hips and ass! Of course she was rocking some 6-in heels by Chanel. We were Shanaynay to the floor! We sat in that club for about an hour, and then we headed on out to the club called the Roof! Now this spot was off the chain! And you're talking about a lot of bad chics, wall to wall. We made our way through the crowd, upon the roof, to her girlfriends section. "Katina! Hey girl!" "Hey Monique!" Said Katina, as they hug and exchange pleasantries. "Who is this handsome man you got with you?!" Said Melanie. One of Katina's friends. "Oh yeah! Sure is handsome and Shanay- nay to the flo!" Chimed in another chic. She was Coco Brown skin, with the short sexy hairdo, stood about 5 ft 4 with a body like that chic Alexis Sky. She was the birthday girl. She had the money pinned on her! I had said "Got damn!" before I knew it. "Aight nigga! Talking about some got damn! I told you don't bite the bait!" Joked Katina. I just replied with a smile. "Before y'all thirsty bitches attack my friend, can I at least introduce y'all!?" said Katina. "Well come on with it!" Said the birthday girl and she gave me the come fuck me eyes! I was ready to walk into her vision, and fulfill that desire she has! "Tory, this is my friend / sis, the birthday girl, Joyce Marie!" "Joyce, this is my friend Tory!" "Nice to meet you Mr Tory! "Nice to meet you Joyce!" "Oh this nigga sound like Barry White or somebody!" Joke Joyce Marie. Katina rolled her eyes, but she was smiling. "Anyway, Monique, this is Tory!" She introduced me to a few more of her friends, after that we went to drinking, And hit the dance floor! These Birmingham women was live as fuck. I later found out that a couple of these females were on! What I mean by that, they were some hustlers / dope chicks! They had a fly little crew, with Joyce Maria being a lieutenant in Katinas' circle! So shorty Pretty much knows what time it is with me! That's probably why she's continuously flirting with me, openly and on the low. I don't think Katina is with sharing no nigga with her friends. She's already said, but I can tell how she looks at Joyce when she catches her flirting with me like "really?" I'm in here playing naive to the situation, because Katina really likes me and has expressed some feelings to me a while back. I thought she was bullshitting, but being around some more boss chicks, which is showing that they are willing.. She showed that she wasn't bullshitting! Giving me them cat eyes, but without a smile occupied with them. "Okay!" I said to no one In particular. Katina, like she caught on instantly, whispered in my ear "let's go." "Okay." "Hey y'all, I had a nice time, but we are about to go!" Said Katina. "Oh so soon?" Asked Joyce Marie, being sarcastic." "Yes so soon.. I'm sorry but we gotta get up early in the morning." said Katina, as we stood, prepared to exit the building. I'm steadily playing games with facial expressions toward Joyce Marie. One expression is saying, "Oh well!" And the other one is saying, "We shall meet again!" And her expression was "Okay.. And you're fucking right!" Not paying attention to my phone call 10 missed calls from Carla! "Damn!"

Chapter 12

Meanwhile in San-Antonio

"I don't know what the fuck you tripping on Carla! You know this nigga ain't shit from the get-go!" said Patricia. Patricia was speaking on Tory, in a typical{ I don't want you to have him, because I want him to myself} way! Carla had been suspicious about Tory's trips, and told Patricia what was on her mind! A couple of times. After her message wasn't answered she started calling him back and back. "He must be having a nice time, he won't answer the phone!" Patricia knew that Mexican women can be very jealous, so she put irons on the fire so to speak. "I mean.. All the shit we have done for him.. Well what we are doing for him! We've been read his file. He uses women! Especially law enforcement women!" "Patricia chillout! I'm trying to think." Said Carla, as she was pacing back and forth, with her phone in her hand. "Think!? Oh you're ready to give him the benefit of the doubt huh?" Yea Patricia! He's moving products there in Alabama! And according to my nephew, he's doing good! So yes, I have to give him the benefit of the doubt. I'm just wondering why he won't answer his phone!" "Humph! Go figure!" Said Patricia who was now on her phone, Slyway texting Tory! [Hey handsome, be glad when you bring your sexy ass back! Then she came behind that text with .. Oh yeah.. Your boss lady is blowing up, about you. getting curious about you.] "Look.. You might as well just stop pacing and get your mind right!" Said Patricia, as she stood up putting her hands on her hips. In full Black Woman Power mode. "Look, this is your first time fucking with a black man and baby".. "No it's not my first time having a relationship with a black man! What are you talking about?" Interrupted Carla. "No.. The black dudes I know you dealt with wasn't that nigga like Tory, I promise you. You only messed around with correctional officers. Not a convict / street nigga/playboy/dope boy! Big difference Carla! I'm from the hood boo boo! And I've had".. "Plenty of hood dudes!" Interrupted Carla. "Experience!" Said Patricia. By now Carla and Patricia were almost face to face. "So much experience that you want to rain on my parade. And for what? Do you want him? Asked Carla. In such a calm way, that is eerie, but sexy! "What do you mean? Both of us fucks him, you cuffs him!" Said Patricia, Just as calmly as Carla's statement was. "No bitch, I cuff you!" Said Carla and the two crashed into each other..lips first! Patricia pulled away for a second. "Bitch don't try to boss up now, because you think I won't Tory! Carla was pulling Patricia back to her aggressively! Reaching under Patricia's skirt and running her middle finger up in her wetness.! "OOOH!" moaned Patricia."You know I've been bossed up over you! You can never take what's mine!!" "OOO!" moaned Patricia, as Carla kissed and eased her to her Versace sofa. It wasn't much of a secret, between the two, who was the alpha female. Carla and Patricia had been lovers, on the low, for about 5 years now. They never shared a man, all the both of them have had men while they were undercover lovers. So now that a big dick was added to the equation, causing a wave in normal waters! The reason being, Carla has caught feelings for Tory, being curious about having a fling or a relationship with an inmate While at the time being a correction officer. The captain at that! Fulfilling a fantasy, in which she's been having for the past 20 years she's been working in prisons .Curiosity killed the cat! In her case, curiosity killed the cat between her legs! Carla reached under the sofa pillows and pulled out a big black 12-in diador. A strap on at that! She figured if she fucked Patricia or should I say grudge fuck Patricia that would take her mind off of Tory. Patricia's mind too! She played around Patricia's clit with the head of the fake dick, just before ramming it up in her! "Ahh!" Gasped Patricia, as she throws her head back, enjoying the pain and the pleasure the toy is inflicting. Carla is mounting her As if she was a man! Holding Patricia down and slamming that fake dick in her! Sweating likeThey're working out, Carla exerting a lot of pent up stressful sexual energy and frustration! She's biting down on her own teeth as if she's about to start growling! You would think she's popping ex pills or something. How she's zoned out on Patricia! She was bringing Patricia to multiple orgasm by the seconds. They found themselves in a sweaty, cummy, aftermath when it was all over. After Patricia caught her breath, she made a statement in which had Stunned Carla.. "Ain't nothing like the real thing boo boo!"

Chapter 13

After partying damn near all night, I slept kind of late. Katina and I had left the club and went back to the room and fucked and sucked on each other like some honeymooners! After getting myself together, I was checking my phone! I had plenty of missed calls from Carla and some texts from Patricia, during the same time! That was rather strange. After reading Patricia's text messages, I felt like she was being funny and rather messy! I need to get a move on shortly, but first I'm going to call Carla and answer Patricia's text messages. I was kind of glad that Katina was still asleep, because she somewhat displayed her jealousy at the club. I didn't need the extra drama at the moment! I walked out on the balcony to talk to Carla. "Hey baby what's up?!" I asked Carla, when she answered the phone. "Oh nothing." Said Carla, sounding all sleepy and dry. "Yeah.. You must have had a long night or something? Are you still asleep?" I asked Carla, trying to push the conversation on. "Humph!"sarcastically laughed Carla. I hate when she does that shit! "Yeah you can say that. I guess you had a long night yourself?" "Oh here we go with this shit!" I said before I knew it. "Here we go with what shit? I just said you had a long night yourself!" "Yeah, yeah, yeah being sarcastic! I see you call me about 10 times. I couldn't hear it, I was in the club." I said. She tried to be all sarcastic and I've been tired of that shit anyway. One of the main reasons I didn't move in with her! "Yes! I called you about 10 times! How you didn't know that I might have had an emergency? Then I might have been calling you to check on you and your well-being!" She always uses that excuse. But in my mind, I figured she's just trying to keep up with me. "Okay Carla. I appreciate your concern, but you know what I am doing, and last night I was at a club, so I couldn't hear my phone." At a club? Oh.. Who you were with? Your home girl? I mean your home boy, Fredo's sister?" "Here we go again." I said. "What do you mean? I just asked a simple question!" "I mean what difference does it make? You know what I do!" I said. I'm on the verge of telling Carla, "Yeah, I was with a bad young chic, in which I fucked all night, and made some big money with!" But I'm weighing my options up before I make such a bold statement. She is the reason, I was able to make money in prison and not to mention her nephew is my plug! Then two I've already accomplished my goal, through her. I don't think her nephew gives a fuck about our relationships. He's about the money I'm spending with him. "What difference does it make?!" "Okay Tory, that's okay.. You have a nice day, don't let me hold you up!" Said Carla. "Why the fuck are you begging this nigga!" Said Patricia in the background. She's probably boosting this whole ordeal up! "So what kind of games are y'all playing?" I asked, getting very agitated by the second now. ... "Tory?" Said Katina. Are you okay?" Katina had woken up, and snuck up behind me on the balcony! Stunned me so suddenly, I almost jumped out of my skin. I was caught up in my argument with Carla, that I hadn't noticed Katina sneaking up on me. "Yeah I'm all right?" I answered before I knew it. "Wow! Who the fuck was that? Asked Carla." "Look. I will call you back later!" I said. "Fuck you getting mad for? You're caught, not me!" said Carla and hung up the phone. That bitch Patricia probably loved this moment. I walked back in the room, as Katina followed me smiling. "Well Mr Goodbar, looks like you have a problem on your hands! That was your Mexican girlfriend wasn't it?" "Yeah, that was her." I said. You're going to make that Mexican chick stab you!" Laughed Katina. I stood there shaking my head." Oh baby it will be okay. Fuck her! Shit, we can get together and sho nuff be a real power couple!" Said Katina, as she circled me like she was about to go in for a kill! "I'm just saying bae, we are making money, and it's very obvious we are feeling each other! Said Katina, and she stopped in front of me and gave me a kiss. After the kiss, she stood back and looked me deep in my eyes, and resumed her seduction on me. "I mean baby.. For real.. You were just using that chick. Your situation caused you to finesse and survive! And so you use that senorita to your advantage to make your then position as comfortable as you could! And of course, you had a strong desire for some sex! And on top of all that you got a plug through her!" On everything I love, she was hitting the hammer on the nail! Because truly, there wasn't much genuine love between Carla and I. I was just infatuated because I was locked up at the moment. The survival tactic is always living with me, so yes she was right about me using Carla, to get paid. I'm an opportunist for real! And besides.. Katina was a young 30-year-old boss bitch! Walked right out of my dreams. The essence of my desire. "You are making it hard for me, baby chill out!" I said. Because I was truly weighing my options. "I know why you're hesitating. You think she's going to fuck it up for you with your plug! You think they're going to let some pussy fuck their money up? Shit nigga, I know you're shopping good with him, so you leaving her isn't going to fuck your relationship up!" "You got a point there." I said. "Dig this, I ain't trying to tell you what to do boo, but to make sure, why don't you holler at your people and tell him what's what, I bet you $100 against a bucket of shit, I am right!" Shooting her shot! And to be truthful about the matter, I was already making an exit plan in my mind, so I can be with this sexy ass young bossed up mentality, chic. "Okay.. I'm going to hit him up , and talk to him." Why wait? Weight broke the wagon my nigga!" Said Katina. "You've been around your brother and old school uncle too long! Popping like you from the '80s like me! And you are really persistent about the matter. What's up?!" I asked Katina. "What's up?! Look bae," said Katina as she pulled me back on her. "I'm tired of beating around the bush, let's go on and make this shit work. Bae I want you, and you know it ain't About the money! Yeah y'all help me, it boosted my already endeavors to the moon. So, I got my own! A six-figure bitch, with her own home, and whips! Then I want you to be my man! Fuck the bullshit!" "Okay, okay. Just give me a week or two, and I'll be ready!

Chapter 14

2 days later

I was back in San Antonio laying low, after leaving Birmingham Alabama. After the argument between Carla and I, she didn't text or call. I assumed she was mad as fuck, so I didn't bother to hit her up. But ironically, I did hear from Patricia. She had texted me shortly after

I hung up the phone that night in Birmingham with Carla. I'm like "what a bitch!" When I did look at her text. It was a devil face emoji! And the next was a long drawn-out text about me handling Carla, like she was dumb, but on the other hand, she wants to hook up with me.. without Carla! "Wow"! I was saying to myself as I reread the text and laughed. "Bitches like Patricia are sheisty!" I said out loud, as I was texting her back. [What kind of games are you playing? And where are you?] I'm about to get this hoe straight! I don't know if Carla is right beside her or what. But at this point, I kind of don't give a fuck! They shouldn't be playing childish games with me, if she is right there. Then in my mind I'm like," What the fuck! You shared me with your friend!" And then it hit me like a ton of bricks! "Fuck! This is the same type of shit I got caught up in last time!" I said out loud to myself in my living room. I was up, pacing the floor like hell now. When fucking two friends go wrong! I think it's time to split! Meaning get the fuck out of San-Antonio! I wasn't going to get myself caught up anymore, messing around with women that are friends. I almost got killed, and ended up back in prison because of some bad jealous stuff. If it wasn't for Maria, I would be gone! Speaking of Maria, I haven't really been touching bases with her much. She told me she had met a guy in Mobile and they are kind of tight, so I respected that. My phone started ringing, jolting me out of my thoughts. It was Patricia! "Hello?" Umm, Mr Tory? What kind of games am I supposed to be playing? I'm not playing any games with you! I'm just telling You what's real!" "And that is?" I asked, being sarcastic. "And that is, stop playing with my friend, and just let her know what it is!" Said Patricia. "What, what is?" I said, playing dumb. "That you're a hoe!" Said Patricia. I got quiet on that."Uh-Huh! The cat got your tongue?"Said Patricia. "I think you are in her ear a lot! Influencing this shit!" I said. No nigga! Your actions. And you know that the Mexican chics ain't really used to certain type of nigga! Tory, you're that certain type of nigga she ain't used to! Bottom line! "So. How does that have anything to do with you? Sounds like you are in our business, for some reason!" "She's my friend Mr!" "Yeah, so much your friend that you're ready to come over here and get on this dick!" I didn't offend her; she was used to this type of talk! Patricia is from the hood And she is an ex stripper. "You wish! But then too, I might as well, because Carla, through dealing with you! She may even try to block you and her nephew's business!" "That's a lie!" I said. I knew she was just bullshitting, because I've already talked to Carla's nephew about our business relationship and his aunt. His reply to that was "yo homes, I don't have anything to do with her romantic affairs and her punta!" "Wrong answer Patricia she can't block that!" "Oh really?" "Yeah.. really. Check this out You coming through or what?" I asked. Because I was tired of talking to her on the phone. Besides, I'm leaving here in a couple of days. Carla won't even know it. I might let Patricia know, so I can keep her taking that packing to the federal penitentiary to my partner Fredo. I know she's going to want to keep that money rolling. I pay her good and give her much needed fucks! "Yeah, I will come over there." "Okay.. Where is your friend?" I asked. I don't know, probably at home on the phone with her new friend! Oops!" said Patricia, like she revealed that information on an accident or something. "Friend.. I mean new friend huh?" "Don't act like you care or something Tory.. Because you know what you're doing. But anyway I'll be over there shortly." "Okay." I said with my phone already on Carla's number

Chapter 15

I don't know why I'm calling Carla, right after Patricia's Revelation! She could be lying, but truth be told, I want to see for myself. Because, honestly I'm feeling some kind of way now! That shit hit me by surprise. Why should I care when I'm about to run off with another woman? I don't know, I guess it's my ego right here. Now that she's not answering her phone, for me like normal, I'm really getting pissed!

double pissed off actually. Mad because she may have another dude, and mad at myself because I'm mad because she may have another man! "This shit crazy!" I said to myself as I called Carla again, for the third time. Voicemail! "What the fuck!" I said, as I looked at my phone and was bewildered. She playing the game wrong, but after a few minutes of just thinking and keeping it real with myself, I got it together. Well, I gotta keep it player. And respect the game. Besides I'm heading to Alabama, shortly I can't lie, at times, I'm just a typical nigga in a relationship! I want my cake and eat it too! I want to do what I want to do, but I don't want My main squeeze or old lady, do the same. And get mad if she does or if I think she is! matter of fact, even if I feel that she has potential to! My doorbell rang, and my dick got hard at the same time. Fuck Carla!.. Right now. I'm about to punish her friend for her neglect. Or get back! I opened the door for Patricia ,And she had me in awe! Her outfit that is. This dark chocolate mini stallion, had on a tight ass, powder blue, Adidas velour tracksuit! gripping every curve she has. "Why are you looking at me like that?" Asked Patricia. I must have been drooling or something, but I was slowly appraising her body. "Oh my bad! Come on in." I said, as I stood to the side to let her in. I was watching that ass all the way in. "This is going to be one lit session" I said, as I closed the door and followed Patricia to the couch. "What do you mean session?" Said Patricia. I started laughing. "Tell me Tory.. What is a lit session?" "It's going to be lit, when we clash!" I said. "When we clash?" Said Patricia. "Yeah, Clash! What do you want to drink?" I asked Patricia, as I headed to my bar. "Some Hennessy and coke." Said Patricia. "Okay coming right up!" I grabbed Patricia a cup and put a little ice in it. I was regularly looking up at Patricia , as she sat there rolling a blunt. Thinking about how I was going to fuck! Her! Patricia must have felt my vibes and eyes on her. She stopped rolling the blunt and looked up at me. "What?! Why are you looking at me like that?" "Thinking about the whole situation at hand,ya feel me?" I said. "Yeah I feel you." Said Patricia as she proceeded to roll the blunt. "So what are you going to do?" Asked Patricia. Shit, I'm playing it how it goes!" I said, as I walked over to Patricia and Handed over the Hennessy and Coke, I mixed up. "Playing how it goes? What does that mean?" "I mean.. If Carla doesn't want to continue being with me, I'm going to play the field. I will probably move to Alabama. I said. Patricia fired up that blunt, and was looking me in the eye the whole time! She wanted to say something. "What?" I asked. "I was wondering where that leaves me?" I thought about it for a second before answering. For dramatics! "Well Patricia, you know we still can do our thing?" "Meaning?" Asked "Patricia, meaning we are still going to get that money up out of that prison!" I said. "Oh yeah? How do you know Carla isn't going to block that?! But she will make it difficult"! "Shit, just don't let her know! You can't let the right hand know what the left hand is doing!" I said. "Huh?! She is Going to know! Hell me and my team need her, because she's going to know when they're going to have the dogs there, sniffing around our cars and us, as we come in! With you leaving and me still there taking doping that would be dangerous! She's going to know that it's coming from you, and she's not involved with you anymore. Shit she's going to get super jealous!" "Calm down woman and hit the blunt!" I said as I passed the weed back to her. I'm really kind of ready to Just get off this conversation from now. "You should be the ambassador for women's sweat suits." I said, as I was looking her up and down, slowly with unyielding eyes. In full LL Cool J effect. licking my lips, and by my bottom lip. She could tell I'm ready to fuck, so she stands up and response to what I said about the sweat suit. "What? I look good in it?" "Hell yeah!" I said as I grabbed my throbbing soldier. She was flexing on me. Turning that ass around to where I see them hips curved out. Then to the side where that ass is poking out! "OOOO Weee! A lit session is on the way!" I said, In a low sexy tone. "You keep saying that! A lit session! I want to know what that means! And what does it persist?" Patricia was feeling good by now. I know that Hen and good exotic weed is working on her! Making her more horny than she already is! She was taking off the jacket of the sweat suit, revealing that fine ass shape of hers, to the fullest! She was smiling moving to the music I had planned. throat baby ! That cores was strengthening the already thick sexual energy we already shared. "Come here!" I said As I leaned forward from the couch, and pulled Patricia between my legs. "Damn you fine!" She was doing a little sexy dance, as I caressed her hips and ass. No lie, Patricia , hands down, is a bad chick! The kind that will have you ready to fuck on site! She was turning around doing her dance, flexing that ass in my face. I bit her left butt cheeks through her sweatpants! "Getting kinky huh?" as she continued to slow grind. Now I'm gripping and rubbing her thighs, but slightly tugging on her sweats, in an effort to pull them down gently. All the time, I want to snatch them down! Thinking about the times, when I first started working in Carla's office at the prison, how she used to get smart with me! Nah, I will save the Savage mode till I get in that pussy! She was assisting me with her tight sweats, by wiggling and winding as I pulled them on down. "Damn!" I said, as I bit her right butt cheek. This time I sucked on it, and was placing my middle finger, in her tight twat. She had on a thong, which matched her sweat suit. I slowly peeled her thong off of her,and soon as she stepped out of them, I was spreading those chocolate cheeks. She put a sexy arch in her back, as I proceeded to eat that pink pussy from the back! "Oh! Oh! Shit!" Moaned Patricia . I was licking her from the back, middle finger working the front, and my thumb was working her clit! Bringing her massive pleasure! A few minutes of torturing Patricia with my hand and finger game, I slammed her down on my dick! "Ahh! Oh shit! Oh shit! Oh my God!" Said Patricia. We were rocking my couch, as she was backing that ass up on me! And I was meeting her a third of the way, with intense thrusts! Patricia kept up the mantras of "oh shit's" and "OOO I'm coming!" For about 10 minutes straight. I stood up, and made her bend over facing and grabbing the couch. And commenced to pound her from the back like I was upset with her! I kind of was thinking that She's possibly drawing a wedge between Carla and i. That thought made me grab her short hair, and started pounding her like a mad Russian! Oh shit, um cumming! oh fuck! Said Patricia. "Oh yeah?! Right now?" I asked. "Yea nigga!"Said Patricia, about out of breath. With that being said, I sped it up! "Weee!"She was squealing like a pig, as she was catching multiple orgasms, back to back! And I have been holding back my first nut for so long, and now I was growling! "Arggg! Shiit!" I kept on stroking though. "The bed! Take me to the bed." Said Patricia and I still was poking! "This is a lit session!" I said to Patricia .

Chapter 16

Karla

"A lit session huh?!" Said Carla as she sat in her room looking at Patricia and Tory betray her! Tory didn't know that Carla had taken his key and got a duplicate made. He had some business to go handle one day I was there. I had spent the night. Tory had an extra key to his place, laying on his dresser. I had become very suspicious, and jealous to a point of obsession! I went out, and got a key made very quickly and went to one of the I Spy stores and got a camera. It was designed to be an ornament or home fixture. Like a ceramic fruit. Fake banana, formed into a cartoon like character. With little eyes, in which the camera was watching, filming, and recording everything! I managed to put one in the living room, and one on his dresser, which was made like a fake plant. "This home needs a little more decoration about it!" I Said, when Tory asked about the little decorations. "Needs to be a little spiced up! Just a little." He wasn't too suspicious about my little decorations. Although he did move the plant out of his room. Good thing he did. Because I had cameras in his room, and at times, he would pull out drugs! Although I knew about them, it was a possibility that I would use that or anything against him, if I'm in that mindset. "So Patricia wants to play this game?" I Said to myself. And I watched her, bounced up and down on my man like that! She had totally disregarded their agreement. And that agreement was that Patricia was by no means, at any time, except if she was with me, to get with Tory, in no sexual capacity. "She violated the agreement like the slut that she truly is!". Also, she now knew that Patricia had told Tory about her having another guy on the side. "I'll fix you Patricia!" Said Carla, as she watched Tory banging Patricia from the back, like he was mad at her! Carla was sitting there, at her house downing Tequila shots. With tears streaming down her face, she was still watching, Tory and Patricia. "I want to bust all on you like the song says!" Said Tori is Patricia was giving him some sloppy head. Carla laid back, with her toy in her hand, as she watched the video. She has seen enough to make her horny as an inmate on ecstasy! Though she was very furious at the both of them, her pussy was like a volcano, ready to erupt! "Sisss!!Oh my God! Whispered Carla, and she placed her 9-in toy on her clit. She placed it inside of her, and stroked to the rhythm of Tory ejaculating in Patricia's mouth and face. "Aww!"Screamed Carla, as she was coming at the same time, so quickly! She was visualizing Tory cumming inside of her! "You son of a bitch!" Screamed Carla and she toyed herself into an orgasmic frenzy. "You're supposed to be mine! And you're freaking off with my slut!" Carla was discombobulated, to the first degree! She wanted her cake and eat it too! Carla was having a flame with Patricia first. It was only sexual, no emotions attached. For Tory, it was supposed to have been the same.. A fling, manifested from her unfulfilled desires! All Carla used to think about was, how it would be to have a secret sexual relationship with an inmate while she's working at a prison ! She used to see a lot of inmates, which were very attractive to her, and attracted to her! She used to close her office door sometimes and fantasize heavy, about fucking an inmate. Then Toriy came! One of her close cousins had told her that she had a girlfriend whose friend was incarcerated at the same prison she worked at. And asked her a favor of looking out for him, the best way she could. That was cool with her. She figured she would make him her runner/aid. And from there, maybe feed him a meal or two. Sneaking him a cigarette or a Black & Mild. Something small and petty. She had him come to her office, and once Tory walked into her office, she looked up at him And from that point on, her fantasies were coming to fruition! Talking about laws of attraction! Be careful what you think about and wish for a lot, because you might just get it! She got her desires fulfilled, but unfortunately things didn't turn out the way she planned. Things had taken a turn, in their relationship, for the worst! All she was thinking or trying to figure out, what had happened! And if she was to blame, she wanted to know, what did she do wrong? She shared Tory with Patricia! That's where she fucked up at. Because now, that sneaky slut, is backstabbing her! They're going to run off together! That's how Carla's mind is running, right now. Driving her to a point of revenge! Then to top it off. Tory's trip to Birmingham did raise suspicions. He said he was handling business, with Fredo's sister. But Carla's instincts are telling her otherwise. This is where he's running off to! To be with that slut! And Patricia's probably going with him! Carla had got up and cleaned herself up, and now She was thinking. She was devising a plan for revenge!

Chapter 17

2 days later

All set, to get ready to blow this place, I was tying up all loose ends I had in San Antonio! First off, I met with my plug, to make sure our business relationship is solidified. DudeHas the best cocaine and heroin in the Southwest! After fucking Patricia into a daze, I gave her a big package of Coke and heroin, to take up in the federal prison, to my partner Fredo. He was pumping dope good in there, and investing with his sister out here! I was scheduled to meet with Patricia or just send work through the mail, so we can keep things rolling at that Federal joint. I had two more things to wrap up, before I left. One is I need to holler at Carla. She hasn't been answering the phone in a while. So, I had already said, fuck it, but something in me wanted to get with Carla, in hopes that she would change my mind! Who the fuck was I fooling? I knew I was feeling Carla, a little At the beginning of the relationship. But that clingy And jealous shit, was a distraction for me! But now that she's playing hard to get, I realized I kind of want her! Maybe because I've heard that she was fucking with some lame-ass C.O! That's her flavor I guess. That competitive spirit in me, won't let me just let things be and go ahead and leave, as planned. I'm ready to hop in my ride, and head to Birmingham Alabama . But I'm about to call her, one last time! If she doesn't answer, I'm splitting this scene. But before I do, I want to hit this little spot I go to at times. It was close to downtown. A little hole in the wall club, so to speak. The name of the club was called Aunt Lynn's place. They had live bands in there most of the time. Mostly black people hung out there. Nice little duck off spot to just chill or low key be on a pussy hunt! As I was at the moment. It was this little chick, who sang with the local band, named Tammy. I used to call her Lil T .She was an up and coming singer. A sexy little woman! Stood about 5'2 or 5'3, with a body of a track runner or a gymnast. Just the way I like them! Nice little round ass, under mouth size titties, nice curves, and a little gap between her legs! So sexy that if you stare too long, I'll be picturing me getting my pound game on! She was on stage now, performing a rendition of Alicia Keys and Khalid's song, "So Done." Along with a male band member. I must admit, she can sing very well, but the whole time I was hypnotized by that gap! The thing she had on was making that gap highly noticeable! I was sitting there thinking about how I was going to let her ride my dick. Tammy and I were very familiar with each other. I had a job with her, for a brief moment at this plant. I used that job, just to get to know a lot of people. Particularly drug users and potential hustlers! Tammy and I had got cool, through those arrangements. She started buying exotic marijuana from me, her and a couple of coworkers. Then members of her band also smoked. I used to flirt with her on a regular basis. She would turn down my advances, on the strength of knowing I had an old lady. But once I told her, I was about to leave my old lady, she got kind of in gear. I've been telling her how I enjoyed hearing her sing, and perform! So she invited me to come out tonight and check her out, so here I am! And she was performing, we managed to lock eyes, as if she was already looking for me! She was in fact looking for me, because once we locked eyes, her smile brought it! I returned a smirk which kind of made her frown on top of her smile! It's getting interesting! Tammy and I have always shared this chemistry. Although she would deny the sexual part of it. I would make advances towards her and she would be like: "Oh no! You have a woman, and I respect people's relationships!" And I would be looking at her, like Arnold, on different strokes. When he says: "What you talkin bout Willis?!" And she would respond like: "I'm serious Tory!" And I would back off. But on the strength, I'm about to leave and she invited me here. It's a go tonight!

Chapter 18

Carla

Carla had seen, where Tory had been calling her repeatedly, within the last week. She wouldn't answer. She had made up her mind that it was over with, but She was going to get some revenge though! Starting with the slut Patricia! The last couple of days at work, Carla was being very quiet and strictly business! Patricia was trying to act her normal self, but it was in her spirit, and she didn't know how to keep it at bay much. That was causing her to do somewhat awkward things in the office. Like ask Carla some stupid questions, she see that Carla is being very quiet and professional. "Carla, have you.." "You mean Captain Mendes?" Interrupted Carla. Patricia looks bewildered at Carla's response, such formality." Excuse me!.. I meant, Captain Mendes, have you seen Tory?" Stupid move! Patricia was being messy now, due to her not liking Carla's change in attitude towards her? "Ah..Sergeant Coleman, It is against U.S. penal system policies, to discuss an ex-convict outside of penal or correctional business! So I'm going to have to write you up for..." "Write me up?!!" "Yes Sergeant Coleman, and if you keep being insubordinate.." "Insubordinate my pussy bitch!" Interrupted Patricia. And she stood up from her desk. The ghetto side of Patricia is clearly about to take over! "What the fuck you mean? You're the one who introduced me to the bullshit you had going on!" That statement just about done it with Carla! "I beg your pardon?" Said Carla trying to sound professional, yes standing up at the same time in defense. "I beg your pardon hell! You know just what I'm talking about"! Patricia was about to blow the whole scene! "Sergeant Coleman, this is a direct order for you to clock out! Now!" "Bitch miss me with all that fake ass formality! Don't be mad cause he doesn't want you any more!" said Patricia as she was stepping across the office to Carla and Carla was meeting her halfway! "Fuck you! You backstabbing slut!" By now, Carla and Patricia were rushing each other! They were fighting like cats and dogs which drew people out of their offices. A couple of C. O'z , Sergeants, captains, came to restrain the women. But both of them were ambitious about getting to each other's ass! It took the officers a couple of minutes to separate the two. The staff was in total shock after the fight. Rumors recirculating . The warden's secretary told one nosy / messy female stewardess. And she told a messy inmate, who in turn told a fucked up male officer and it went on and on. Carla was so mad, that she was spilling the beans on Patricia about why and which started to fight. Not exactly the way she planned to get revenge, but so be it! She's going to start now, even if it compromises her job!

Chapter 19

Tory and Tammy

While Carla and Patricia were at work fighting over me, I was at Tammy's crib about to get busy! After Tammy and her band were through performing, she came to my section and had a couple of drinks with me. We conversed and laughed and caught up a little bit. I'm being very cordial, but my eyes were roaming up and down her little fine body, anticipating the moment to get her in the bed! An hour later, here we are now, sitting in her living room, smoking on some exotic marijuana, and sipping on some Hennessy. Tammy was on the verge of choking off the exotic marijuana. "Here come and get this shit Tory!" Said Tammy and she began to cough. I quickly handed her a Corona. "Here drink this! It'll help clear you up!" She got up after she recuperated. "I got to put on something more comfortable. "That stuff is making me hot!" Said Tammy as she was fanning herself. I was smiling and looking at her as she was walking off. "What are you staring at Tory?!" Said Tammy and she looked back real quick, to catch me looking at that ass! "Shit, you!" I said, as I unconsciously grabbed my already hard dick! That made her stop in her tracks. "Alright now Tory! That's going to get you in some trouble! I'm warning you, I'm toxic!" Said Tammy, as she walked off still pointing back at me. It's obvious that Tammy was feeling herself right about now. And there was No doubt in my mind, that it was about to be some hot sex going down! Tammy came out of her room with some sexy ass Victoria's Secret luxury on! The color on the fit was royal blue. A lace, chemise and g-string hookup. She had on some 6 inch matching heels. "Do you like this lingerie?" Asked Tammy, as she strutted up to me and slowly turned around. "Hell yeah I like it!" I said, as I sat back and began to unbuckle my pants. She grabbed her phone and changed the music.

She had her Bluetooth sitting on the coffee table, in the living room. "Just me and you!" Tony, Tony, Tony old jam was playing through the speakers. "Hey!" Said Tammy And she began to groove! She was feeling herself, and I was feeling her too! Literally! I stood up and went to groovin with her. I was slowly touching on her little curvy hips, and pulling her up strategically on my throbbing dick! That she was grinding on my tool, all sensual and things. I was smoothly dropping my pants, boxers ,and stepping out of my shoes at the same time. Once she realized that I was butt naked, within the blink of an eye, she laughed. "Tory you are so crazy"! By now, I was sticking my tongue in her mouth letting her get a grip on this tool, as she was admiring it so hard. She was stroking me down, like a champion dick handler! Quickly, I turned her around, slid that thong to the side, and entered her from the back. "Oh Tory!" Moaned Tammy, with a tremor in her voice. "Yeah I know!" I said. "Shit baby! I ain't got nothing but the head in, and a little bit more!" "What! It feels like my whole pussy is filled up!" I laughed at that comment and applied the pressure! I was thinking there's no need in me playing with this little fine woman. I'm about to make her remember me! She was bent all the way over, hands on her coffee table, allowing me to give her much dick from the back."Ah,Ah,Ah!" Hollered Tammy, matching my strokes and pounds with a long moan. "Let's go to bed. Please!" Said Tammy. I imagine her legs were getting weak along with her back, because I was working on her! Once we got to the bed, she kicked those heels off and I laid back on the king size, with my big shiny dick, sticking up like a Telegram pole! She looked at it and shook her head smiling. "Baby, I don't know!" Said Tammy. "You got it. Come on and get up on this dick!" I said, as Tammy was straddling me. Once she was down on my helmet head, she began to gradually ride it! Her juices were flowing, something serious. She was cumming up on entry, as you could tell that she was a big cummer. I was wet all down my balls, and groins.

Cautiously, Tammy adjusted Her legs. Now she was riding this dick with some leverage. I was gripping her ass and snatching her down on the full length of my shaft! After fucking Tammy continuously for about an hour or so, we both fell asleep, instantly. The next morning, I woke up and she was still knocked out. I woke her up, to let her know I was on my way out. Now, I had to run back to my apartment one last time before I leave. As I was riding, I was thinking about how I just pained Tammy! That's a prison terminology or slang for when somebody gets beat down in a fight. I just used it in another arena of a beatdown! She told me I knocked her period on. As I was laughing to myself about that, I got a phone call. It was from Carla!

Carla

"Fuck it! I lost it and told the warden and I.A. everything!" "What the fuck! Everything?!!" "Blame that slutty, backstabbing bitch Patricia!" "What do you mean Carla?!!" I began to tell Tory about the fight and how it started. "Oh my god! What the fuck is wrong with y'all!?" "Don't raise your fucking voice at me! You dog!" "Okay Carla, calm down!" " Calm down! No, you calm down! You and that slut got together behind my back Tory! Both of you are very disloyal! You caused me to lose my fucking job!" "How in the fuck did I help you lose your job?! I didn't tell y'all to go to work and fight! You know what.. Fuck it I'm out of here!" "Out of here!?" I asked because he's not going anywhere, until he testified before the ethics board. "Yeah you heard me right! Out of here!" said Tory. "No mister, you're not going anywhere, until you testify before the.... "Testify?" Interrupted Tory. "I do not testify. You got me fucked up!" "Oh you're fucked up all right! And you're just going to leave me? You owe me Tory! And that's when the phone went blank. "Tory! Are you there?" That's when the phone hung up. I almost threw away my new iPhone! "He thinks he's leaving me for that slut in Birmingham, he got another thing coming!"

I jumped up and ran to my nightstand. Where I have my purse, my car keys, and my. 38 snub nose and out the door I went.

Tory

"This bitch has blown a head gasket!" I said to the interior of my car. I was pulling up to my apartment, when Carla called me with the crazy stuff. I know I'm about to leave this whole state ASAP! By the time I was walking into my building I got another phone call. It was Patricia! "Tory, I guess you know what your crazy girlfriend Done did!" " I already know! She called me and told me everything! Why did y'all do that stupid shit?!" I asked, as I was pacing my living room. "Tory that crazy bitch started with me! She was acting all formal and was talking about writing me up, for some shit She wouldn't have never written me up for!" Said Patricia . And I had to ask what she was getting written up for. "Oh, I asked her about you! Maybe I shouldn't have done that, but Tory she was making me mad with that robot/police ass shit!" " What the fuck man"! That's all I could say. "So where are you now Tory? At your apartment?" "Yeah. Getting the rest of my shit, and I'm about to get the fuck on!" "Oh yeah. Why Carla was spilling the beans, they went and searched your partners belongings, so we are all under investigation!" Said Patricia. I stopped pacing at once, when she said that! "Was my partner clean? He didn't have anything on him did he?" "No, but they still locked him up in solitary confinement. Investigation purposes. They're probably going to transfer him to another facility!" Said Patricia. "Damn!" That's all I could say. "He is solid isn't he?" Asked Patricia. "Oh yeah! real stand-up guy, who won't tell on anybody . "Well I hope so!" Said Patricia. "Well look.. Can I come and see you, before you leave?" I thought about it for a second. Something was telling me to say no and get the fuck on. But here I am thinking with my dick! As if I hadn't just had a wild and freaky night with Tammy! "Okay, you need to come on now then!" I said. "Okay! I'm on my way now, shouldn't take about 5 minutes!" I hung up the phone, and started packing some more things. That's when I got a message from Carla. It was a video message. "Now what could this crazy motherfucker be talking about now?!" I said. I open the text to a video. "Who the fuck is.. This?" I was watching Patricia dancing in front of me as I sat on the couch and watched with my dick in my hand. Where and how in the fuck did she get this?! I was standing there bewildered, as I watched the video. "It's a fucking camera in here!" I said, as I was spinning around in confusion, like where the fuck is the camera? "Aww man, these bitches done played!"I immediately called Patricia and my doorbell was ringing at the same time! My heart was racing and I was completely angry as fuck! "Who is it?!" I said as I approached the door I also heard a phone ring outside of my door, then it dawned on me that it was Patricia at the door. I snatched the door open, because I couldn't wait to confront this bitch, for this sleazy move! Planting a camera in my apartment. "Bring your ass on in!" I said to Patricia. She was hesitant for a moment. "Dude.. What the fuck is wrong with you first of all?" "You know what's wrong with me! Don't play dumb!" I said as I gave her my phone with the video playing. What the fuck?! Tory I don't know anything about that! Wait a minute.. Nigga this is your apartment ! I should be the one raising hell!" "Man you know I wouldn't fucking do no super childish shit like that!" I said getting on my defense. "Yeah right! How many niggas in that penitentiary you done sent that video to!?" Said Patricia almost getting hysterical. "Calm down! I wouldn't do no shit like that! We got to find the motherfucker! Ain't nobody been in my crib but yall! Then at that moment that's when it all hit the both of us at the same time, "Carla! We both said at the top of our lungs. And speaking of the devil, in comes Carla! "What the fuck!" I said when I saw her. "Yeah you two backstabbing perras! Carla was calling us backstabbing dogs.. With a big ass pistol pointed at both of us!

To be continued

About Author

Author Corey Bryant is 50 years old. Corey was born in Opelika, Alabama. As a child, Corey enjoyed reading all kinds of books and magazines. At the age of 19, Corey was incarcerated in the state of Alabama prison system. After serving about 3 yrs he started writing but did'nt get serious until he served 20yrs in prison. That's when he wrote and completed a couple of novels, including Yielding To Unfulfilled Desires vol 1 and part of vol 2 and R.i.C.O. vol 1 and Crossing the lines. Corey still enjoys reading, writing, and spending time with his family.